Praise for L.A. Witt's *The Closer You Get*

"*The Closer You Get* is funny, it's about family and how they screw up the lives of everyone around them, it's about living in fear that your deepest secret would be found out and the possible consequences, it's also about choices and most of all it's about the love of one person becoming as essential as breathing. I loved the prose and internal dialogue, and Kieran's first person POV showed his vulnerability despite the self confident image he projected as Alex shattered his defenses."

~ *Reviews by Jessewave*

"*The Closer You Get* is a gorgeous romance that I loved from beginning to end. Successive re-reads have not dimmed my pleasure in reading *The Closer You Get,* and I look forward to revisiting Alex and Kieran yet again in the near future."

~ *Romance Junkies*

"This is the first book by L.A. Witt that I have had the privilege of reading but it certainly will not be the last. Ms. Witt is a masterful storyteller and her characters are well developed."

~ *Guilty Pleasures Book Reviews*

Look for these titles by *L.A. Witt*

Now Available:

Nine-Tenths of the Law

The Distance Between Us

A.J.'s Angel

Out of Focus

Conduct Unbecoming

Tooth and Claw

The Given and the Taken

The Healing and the Dying

The Closer You Get

L.A. Witt

Samhain Publishing, Ltd.
11821 Mason Montgomery Road, 4B
Cincinnati, OH 45249
www.samhainpublishing.com

The Closer You Get

Print ISBN: 978-1-60928-791-7
Digital ISBN: 978-1-60928-552-4

Editing by Linda Ingmanson
Cover by Angela Waters

First Samhain Publishing, Ltd. electronic publication: November 2011
First Samhain Publishing, Ltd. print publication: October 2012

Dedication

To everyone who said
Kieran deserved his own story:
I agree.
This one's for you.

Chapter One

"Mom, I know it bugs you, but I can't *not* go."

On the other end of the line, my mother sighed. That heavy, sad sigh I'd heard so many times over the last few years. "I know, but..."

I stared at the sidewalk beneath my feet, slowing my gait and trying not to let any frustration slip into my voice. "I'll come see you while I'm in town. I promise I will. That's why I'm coming down for a few days, so I'll have time." I paused. "But, I have to go to the wedding. He *is* my dad."

She said nothing, and the silence lingered. We'd been on the phone since before I left my apartment, talking in circles just like we had two other times this week. She'd been inconsolably depressed in the three years since the divorce, and with my dad's wedding coming up, she'd gotten a lot worse.

Still holding the silent phone to my ear, I continued down the familiar ribbon of pavement that spanned the mile or so between my place and the house I'd lived in briefly when I'd first moved to Seattle two years ago. Up ahead, like a beacon of sex and relaxation, Rhett and Ethan's mailbox came into view. I walked a little faster.

To my mother, I said, "Listen, I need to let you go. Will you be okay tonight?"

"I'll be fine," she said. "Jackie's coming over in a bit anyway, so I should go."

I released a breath. At least she'd have someone to talk to. Chances were, she and my elder sister would spend half the evening commiserating about their troubles with men. There would probably be booze involved, if I knew the two of them, but neither would be alone or driving, which let me rest easier.

"Okay, well, tell her I said hello," I said. "I'd better let you go for now. And like I said, I promise I'll come see you when I'm in town. Take care of yourself, Mom. Please?"

"All right," she said. "Have a good night. Love you, Kieran."

"Love you too, Mom. I'll see you in a couple of weeks."

After I'd hung up, I looked at the call timer. Forty-five minutes. Exhaling sharply, I clipped my phone to my belt. I rolled my shoulders and took a deep breath, trying to force some of the tension out of my stiff muscles.

Tonight, I was *going* to have a good time. That was all there was to it. I sympathized with my mother, and I wanted her to be happy, but I could wallow only so much in the fact that she insisted on wallowing. That and I had my limits when it came to guilt. What did she expect me to do? Blow off my dad's wedding? I didn't want to go any more than she wanted me to go, but if a few hours of pretending to be happy for Dad and his new wife meant preventing some family drama, then so be it. Of course, doing that meant dealing with drama from my mother's end.

I sighed and rubbed some more stiffness out of the back of my neck. I couldn't win.

As I started down Rhett and Ethan's short driveway, all that tension melted out of my shoulders. I couldn't help grinning to myself. An evening with my former roommates—not to mention good friends and *hot* lovers—was exactly what I needed to get my mind off all the family insanity. Exactly what I needed and long overdue. Work and other commitments had kept the three of us from getting together for more than the occasional beer over the last couple of weeks, and it had been far too long since I'd seen the inside of their bedroom. Hopefully, that dry spell would end tonight.

On top of my dry spell with Ethan and Rhett, the last guy I'd been casually seeing had shipped out on a deployment last month. Since he'd left, I'd been on quite the unlucky streak when it came to finding even a one-night stand. A satisfying one, anyway. To say the least, I needed to get laid, and Ethan and Rhett were usually more than happy to oblige.

We wouldn't be jumping into bed the minute I walked in, though. Rhett's daughter would be there for a little while tonight before she went out with her friends to celebrate her twenty-first birthday. When Sabrina was around, everything between her dads and me was strictly platonic. No flirtatious glances, no suggestive looks, and certainly no touching.

Once she was gone, though? I shivered.

I went up the stone walkway to the front door and, as I'd done hundreds of times, let myself in. Familiar voices drew me to the kitchen, and when I walked in, Ethan and Rhett looked up from washing the dinner dishes.

"Oh, good," Ethan said. "Bartender's here. That means we can do Sabrina's birthday shots."

"Hey," I said as I took off my jacket. "I'm not on the clock."

"So?" Rhett dried his hands on a dish towel. "We're just doing one celebratory round with her before she goes out. Might as well have a bartender do the honors, don't you think?"

I released a dramatic sigh and hung my coat over the back of a chair beside the kitchen island. "Okay, fine. But only because it's her birthday."

"I knew you'd see it our way." Rhett reached under the counter. "Besides, you know we'll make it worth your while after she takes off." I bit my lip when he produced a bottle of Patrón from the cabinet. I glanced at Ethan, and his trademark smirk raised goose bumps down the length of my spine. Working as a bartender, I'd long ago learned there was a great deal of truth in the saying that tequila makes some people's clothes fall off. In this case, tequila in Ethan made *my* clothes fall off.

My mouth watered. This was going to be one long night.

"So, is Sabrina here yet?" I asked.

Ethan gestured toward the hall. "She and her friends are downstairs getting ready to go out."

Rhett put his hand on my waist. "Which means we have a minute or two." With that, he kissed me. Not just a quick kiss hello, either. Obviously we were on the same wavelength tonight, because as I wrapped my arms around him, his tongue teased my lips apart. His stubble was coarse beneath my fingertips, and when his tongue stud grazed my lip, I pulled in a breath through my nose.

I had no doubt Ethan kept an eye on the hallway in case Sabrina was on her way up from the lower floor. She only needed to know I was her fathers' friend and former roommate. There were some things a girl didn't need to know about her dad and stepdad, and the fact that I was their occasional lover fell very firmly into that category.

"Hey, quit hogging him," Ethan said, chuckling.

Rhett broke the kiss but held on to me as he looked past me at his boyfriend. "What are you going to do about it?"

Ethan didn't speak. Fingers slid up the back of my neck, and when they tightened in my hair, I closed my eyes and whimpered softly. Rhett let me go. As his arm left my waist, Ethan's replaced it.

"Oh, what do you know?" Ethan's lips touched just below my jaw. "Looks like I have his attention."

Rhett said something, but I was aware only of Ethan releasing my hair and turning me around so he too could give me a hint of what was in store for me tonight. Of the two of them, he was the more aggressive kisser, demanding access to my mouth with more force than Rhett. More force than usual, even for him. Not that I offered either of them any resistance. Had the three of us been alone in the house, I'd have already been on my knees right here in the kitchen, whether because Ethan would have ordered me to them or his kiss would have simply dropped them out from under me.

But we weren't alone in the house, so we separated, pausing to exchange a "just wait" look before he let me go completely.

Ethan cleared his throat and leaned against the kitchen island, the rapid tapping of his fingers on the granite countertop betraying the casual appearance he tried to convey. "Think Sabrina would be upset if we told them to hurry up and get out of here?"

Rhett laughed and kissed Ethan's cheek. "Patience." He combed his fingers through Ethan's gray-sprinkled dark hair. "We have all night." He winked at me, and I moistened my lips. We had all night, and knowing us, we'd use it. Someone must have forgotten to inform the two of them they were in their forties and had no business possessing that kind of stamina. I sure as hell wasn't going to tell them.

"When is she going out?" I asked.

"They're meeting some friends at a club at eight." Ethan looked at his watch, then went back to drumming his fingers. "So they're probably taking off in the next half hour or so."

"You know, Ethan," I said with a grin, "I get the feeling you're looking forward to this evening."

He glanced at the bottle of tequila, then at Rhett, then at me. "You think?"

Rhett rattled his tongue stud across his teeth, and Ethan and I both squirmed.

"You're not helping," Ethan growled.

"What?" Rhett put up his hands. "I didn't do anything."

"Right." Gesturing at Rhett, Ethan looked at me. "This one's been teasing me all damned day."

Rhett glared at Ethan. "Says the man who kept sending me suggestive e-mails at work."

"What?" Ethan batted his eyes. "I was just asking what you wanted to do tonight."

"Uh-huh. And very explicitly detailing a few suggestions."

"Hey, how come I wasn't copied on these e-mails?" I folded my arms across my chest and leaned against the kitchen island. "Don't I get a say in what we're doing tonight?"

"You'll get a say," Ethan said. "You'll be saying a lot of 'oh God, oh God' if we—"

"Tease," I muttered.

"And we'll have plenty of time for all of that." Rhett glanced toward the kitchen doorway. "But *after* Sabrina leaves."

Ethan's fingers drummed faster. I fidgeted.

Rhett cleared his throat. "Oh, Kieran, I meant to ask. We're getting tickets with Dale and a few other people for a Mariners game. You want to go?"

Thankful for the subject change, I said, "Sounds like fun. When?"

"I think Dale said it was..." He furrowed his brow and looked at Ethan. "Was it next weekend?"

"Weekend after," Ethan said.

"Right, right." Rhett raised his eyebrows. "You in?"

Scowling, I shook my head. "That's the weekend I have to go back to Sacramento. Dad's getting married."

"Damn, that's coming up already?" Ethan said.

I nodded. "Unfortunately. I can't wait for it to be done and over with, let me tell you."

"Your mom still harping on you about it?" Rhett asked.

"Yep. She doesn't want me to go. And I really don't want to go either, but..." I shrugged. "What can I do?"

"I suppose bailing on your dad's wedding isn't an option?" Ethan said.

"Unfortunately, no."

Ethan started to speak again, but footsteps and chattering female voices came up the stairs, and all three of us turned our heads in that general direction.

"That would be the birthday girl," Rhett said.

A second later, Sabrina stepped into the kitchen, flanked by a couple of her friends. She looked at me and smiled. "Hey, Kieran. Long time no see."

"Too long," I said as she hugged me. "Happy birthday."

"Thank you." She let me go and looked at her dads. "We're going to go ahead and take off; is that cool?"

Thank God. Ethan and I exchanged glances, and I didn't have to ask if we were on the same page.

"Not yet you're not," Rhett said. "I told you, you're not leaving this house until you've had a celebratory drink with us." To his daughter's friends, he said, "One round, then she's all yours." Rhett gestured at the three empty shot glasses and looked at me. "Make yourself useful, barkeep."

"Barkeep?" I folded my arms across my chest again. "I *beg* your pardon?"

"Oh, come on, Kieran," Sabrina said. "Just pour them so we can go party. Please?"

"Okay, but just for you." I picked up the bottle of tequila.

"It's about time you were old enough to come out with us," one of Sabrina's friends said as I poured the shots.

"No kidding," the other said, elbowing Sabrina playfully. "Damn near a senior, and you can finally go out with the big kids."

"Hey, not my fault my birthday landed at the end of the damned school year." Sabrina glared at Rhett. "You know, so I ended up being the baby in my class for my *entire* school career."

Rhett offered a sarcastically apologetic look. "Well, your mother and I could have—"

"La, la, la!" She put her hands over her ears and closed her eyes. "I'm not hearing this! La, la, la!"

Ethan laughed, then did a double take at her. He raised an eyebrow. "When the hell did you get your belly button pierced, young lady?"

She looked down at the barbell, which her shirt did nothing to hide. "Uh, a while ago." She raised her eyebrows, probably expecting him to say something more about it, but he and Rhett just looked at each other and shook their heads. There really wasn't much they could say about her piercings or her two tattoos. She was an adult, and besides, Rhett had several tattoos and a piercing of his own. Even Ethan had finally gotten some ink last year. Like fathers, like daughter.

"Just don't let your mother see it," Rhett muttered.

"Are you kidding?" Sabrina said. "She still hasn't forgiven me for getting my tongue pierced."

"Neither have I," he said.

"Hypocrite."

Rhett rubbed his eye with his middle finger.

"All right, all right," I said. "When you're all done playing the dysfunctional family, your drinks await." I slid the shots across the kitchen island. The guys had already sliced up some limes and had a salt shaker handy. Judging by the number of limes on the plate, they weren't planning on stopping after their daughter left. I wondered if I could talk them into doing body shots again tonight. Body shots off either of those two were—

Breathe, Kieran. The thought made me light-headed, and I casually leaned against the counter.

Oblivious to my distraction, Sabrina licked the back of her finger and picked up the salt shaker. Then she looked up, eyes darting back and forth between Rhett and Ethan. "What?"

Rhett cleared his throat. "You already know how to do tequila shots?"

"Um..." She looked at the salt on her finger, then back at her father. "I Googled it?"

Ethan snickered and gestured for her to give him the salt shaker. "Sure you did." He licked the back of his own finger and sprinkled some salt on it. "I believe her, don't you, Rhett?"

"Completely." Rhett took the shaker from Ethan. "One hundred percent."

Sabrina raised an eyebrow. "I'm detecting some sarcasm here."

"What?" Rhett scoffed, looking up from salting his finger. "No, no, *never.*"

"Yeah," Ethan said. "When have *we* ever been sarcastic?"

I snorted, and they both eyed me. I put up my hands. "What?"

"Come on," Sabrina said. "Tequila shots. Focus, old guys."

Rhett raised his shot glass. "To being old enough to drink, even though your dad already knows about that incident during your senior year."

Sabrina's eyes widened. "You...knew about that?"

Rhett grinned. "I do now."

We all laughed, though Sabrina's face still registered a hint of panic as she glanced at her father again.

Ethan raised his glass. "To Sabrina surviving twenty-one years of Rhett's parenting."

"And thirteen or so of *yours*," she added.

They clinked their glasses together, licked the salt off their fingers, and threw back the shots. Rhett swallowed it, grimaced and shook his head before reaching for a lime. Neither Ethan nor Sabrina even flinched at the tequila, but the limes made both of them squint.

Rhett set the lime rind down and gave his daughter a dirty look. "You know, most people find tequila a bit strong." He paused. "The *first* time they try it, anyway." One eyebrow rose.

Her cheeks colored and she batted her eyes. "I guess I just like it. I've never had tequila in my—"

Both of her friends tried and failed to muffle snorts of laughter.

Rhett gave Sabrina the most disapproving look he could muster, though the corner of his mouth threatened to give him away. Before he could say anything, though, Ethan clapped his shoulder.

"Girl's a chip off the old block, isn't she?"

"What?" Rhett scoffed. "I never drank before I was twenty-one."

"Only because the only thing available at the time was moonshine," I said, pretending I wasn't ready to shoo the girls out the door because...*come on, hurry up, all of you.*

"I *beg* your pardon," Rhett said.

Ethan shrugged. "You can't really argue with him, you know."

Rhett shot him a glare. "Says the man from the era before alcohol was even invented."

Sabrina looked at her friends. "See? Told you they were cool."

"Maybe they should come with us," Beth said.

"They're not *that* cool."

Rhett chuckled and put his arm around Sabrina's shoulders. "Happy birthday, kiddo."

"Thanks, Dad." She hugged him, then did the same with Ethan.

When she turned to me, I thought she was about to embrace me again, but instead, she put a hand on my arm.

"Can I borrow you for a minute?" she asked.

I blinked. "Uh, sure. What's up?"

She gestured for me to follow her, and we stepped out into the hallway. "Is there any way I can talk you into doing me a huge favor tonight?"

I raised an eyebrow. "That depends. What's the favor?"

"My girls and I are meeting some friends, and there's this guy who's going to be there. I really, really want you to meet him."

"Me? Why?" And why tonight of all nights?

"Because he's really super shy," she said. "And he wants to learn his way around the gay clubs and all of that on Capitol Hill, but he's just..." She paused, then exhaled. "The thing is, he only knows a couple of gay guys, and they don't get along at all."

"But you think he'd get along with me?"

"Trust me, you wouldn't get along with those two jerks either," she said. "Is there any way I could talk you into coming with us tonight and meeting him?"

My eyes darted toward the kitchen where my evening's plans waited with a bottle of tequila, then back to her. "Does it have to be tonight?"

"It took me two weeks to convince him to go out with us," she said. "Please? I know you and my dads were going out tonight, and I'm totally springing this on you at the last minute, but I really need your help with this."

I resisted the urge to fidget. "Why me?"

"Because you're the only guy I know who actually knows the gay scene on Capitol Hill but isn't a hardcore partier. The other guys I know, they just want to get hammered, and half the time don't even remember if they got laid, let alone who they were with. Alex...isn't that type. At all."

I shifted my weight. "What exactly is it you want me to do?"

"Just take him out," she said. "Show him the whole scene isn't as terrifying as he thinks it is."

I threw another glance toward the kitchen. "Can you give me his number? I can, you know, another night—"

"No, he'd never go for that." She shook her head and put up her hands. "It took me until yesterday to convince him to come tonight, and if I tried to hook you guys up one on one, he'd think I was, you know, trying to hook you guys up. I don't want to put him on the spot or make him feel like I'm sending him out on a blind date or something." She clasped her hands together beneath her chin and batted her eyes. "Please, Kieran? I'll owe you big time."

I blew out a breath. Much as I didn't want to be anywhere but here tonight, I also knew what it was like to be the new kid trying to figure out the gay scene. For that matter, enough college kids came through the bar where I worked, drinking themselves senseless and doing things that even I—unrepentant manwhore that I was—wouldn't do. It was way too easy to get roped into that, and it could get really dangerous, really fast.

It was only one evening. Ethan and Rhett weren't going anywhere. Chances were, they'd understand.

Releasing a breath, I nodded. "Okay, sure. I'll come meet him."

"Thank you, thank you, thank you," she said with a big smile. "I owe you big-time."

I made myself return the smile, then followed her back into the kitchen. Damn conscience.

"Okay, who's the designated driver?" Rhett asked Sabrina's friends as we walked back into the kitchen.

"Beth," Sabrina said, gesturing at her brunette friend.

Rhett pulled out his wallet. He handed Beth a twenty. "That's for gas, food, sodas, whatever."

"Awesome, thanks." Beth put the twenty in her purse. To Sabrina, she said, "Ready to go?"

"Yeah." Sabrina looped her arm around my elbow. "And we're taking Kieran with us."

Rhett and Ethan both looked at me with wide eyes.

Ethan cleared his throat. "You, what?"

"We're just borrowing him for a night," Sabrina said.

"You know, it's a good thing I'm gay," I said. "Or they would seriously get the wrong idea."

Sabrina blushed. Both of her dads laughed.

"All right, all right, get out of here." Rhett glared at me. "*All* of you."

"Sabrina, you'll be careful tonight, right?" Ethan asked.

In an exasperated voice, she said, "Yes, Dad. I won't drink until I drop, and I'll make sure to drink some water in between, and I'll eat something. Am I forgetting anything?"

"Don't forget to tip the bartender," I said.

"Right." Ethan nodded, pretending to be totally serious. "What he said."

"I will," Sabrina said. "Don't worry."

"Okay, have fun tonight," Ethan said. "Happy birthday."

"Thanks, Dad."

"Call us if you need anything," Rhett said.

"I will." She looked at me. "Ready to go?"

"Um, yeah, I'll be right there."

Sabrina and her friends filed out of the kitchen, and as soon as they were gone, I turned to her dads.

"You guys don't mind, do you?"

Ethan chuckled. "We'll make do, but what the hell are you going to do at a party full of college girls?"

My cheeks burned. "Uh, actually, Sabrina asked a favor." I explained the situation to them.

Rhett waved a hand. "Hey, we all know what it's like to be that kid."

"Yeah, I know," I said. "I'd just rather stay here tonight."

"I'd rather you stayed too," Ethan said. "But we'll make it up another night. And hey, if nothing else, say hello to this kid, get his number, then bail and come back here." He lowered his voice. "You know we'll be awake for a while."

"Of course you will." I chuckled. "*Matlock* isn't on until late, is it?"

"Hey, fuck you."

I laughed. "Okay, I should go. I'll call you guys later this week."

"Please do," Ethan said.

I kissed them each in turn. On my way out, I glanced back just in time to catch Ethan and Rhett exchanging the most mouthwatering look as Ethan picked up the bottle of Patrón. Rhett licked the back of his finger and reached for the salt shaker.

Suppressing a groan, I followed the girls out to the car.

So help me, Sabrina, this guy had better be worth it...

Chapter Two

My younger brother would've given his right arm to be in a car full of college girls headed to a party. Not me. Even if I was straight, I would never have laid a hand on my friends' daughter. As it was, being gay, I was more interested in getting my hands on her fathers anyway, which is what I was supposed to be doing now. But no, I was in a car full of college girls headed to a party.

I exhaled. My altruism was rapidly receding in favor of frustration. Still, I was here, on my way there, and I'd promised Sabrina I'd meet this kid. My plan was to meet him, break the ice, exchange phone numbers, then bow out and grab a cab. With any luck, I could get back to the house in time to catch some sizzling three-way sex with two tequila-buzzed older guys.

For now? Car. College girls. Party.

One man's heaven was another man's purgatory.

"I still think it's a travesty that Alex is gay." Beth's voice drew me out of my thoughts and into the conversation going on in the car. From the passenger seat, she glanced back at me. "No offense."

I waved a hand. "None taken."

Lisa, Sabrina's other friend, said, "I'm telling you, if that man was straight, I would date him in a heartbeat."

"I second that," Beth said. "I swear to Christ, every hot man at school is either gay, taken, or a complete asshole."

"Some are probably all three," I said.

"Bastards," Sabrina muttered.

I chuckled. "What do you care? Your dads won't let you date until you're thirty anyway, remember?"

Beth and Lisa laughed aloud, and Sabrina's cheeks darkened.

"So, this Alex guy," I said. "I assume he's single?"

"Oh, yeah," Beth said. "I don't think I've ever seen him date anyone."

"Is he cute?"

"Uh-huh," all three girls said in unison.

"Cute?" Sabrina clicked her tongue. "He's gorgeous."

Well, that was a plus. Good-looking. College. No one had ever seen him date. Probably meant any guy he'd "dated" was gone by sunrise. My kind of man.

"Don't you have a picture of him on your phone?" Lisa asked.

"Oh, you're right." Sabrina reached into her purse. "I'd forgotten all about that." She pulled out her phone and scrolled through a few pictures. "Ah, here it is."

I took the phone from her.

Oh, hello. Maybe I could be persuaded to stick around for a while tonight after all. The lighting and resolution didn't let me get a very good look at his eyes, but what I could see of him was certainly attractive. Clean cut, clean shaven, with dark hair that was just long enough to run fingers through. Or get a good grip on.

Settle down, Kieran. Meet the guy first.

I cleared my throat and handed the phone back. "Nice-looking guy."

"God, yes." She put her phone back into her purse. "Just wait 'til you see him in person."

"True that," Lisa said. "But then, all gay guys are cute."

I shook my head. "Oh, my dear, you only say that because you've never spent any time dating gay men. I assure you, there are plenty of unattractive men batting for my team."

"Not many," Lisa said. "You guys get way more hotties than we do. It isn't fair."

"Yeah," Beth said. "Even Sabrina's dad and stepdad are hot."

Sabrina wrinkled her nose. "Oh, eww, don't talk about my dads that way."

"What?" Beth said. "Face it, girly girl, for two old guys, they're—"

"Shut. Up."

I laughed to mask my sudden panic at Rhett and Ethan being brought into the conversation, as if someone might catch on to what we had going on. Sabrina didn't need that. Neither did I.

I quickly changed the subject back to Alex. "So, how did you meet this guy, anyway? He in some of your classes or something?"

Sabrina nodded. "He just transferred in at the beginning of the year from another state."

Mercifully, the conversation stayed safely in the realms of Alex and school for the rest of the drive. Rhett and Ethan weren't mentioned again, thank God.

"Here we are." Beth turned on her signal and slowed down.

I barely kept myself from groaning when she pulled into the parking lot of one of those places that was like a pub-sports bar hybrid. The type of place that probably had a house country band some nights, football other nights, and a jukebox that still played vinyl. My *favorite* kind of place.

On our way in, we passed a row of neon beer signs and walked in through a tinted glass door that had tarnished sleigh bells banging against the window. Seattle had banned indoor smoking years ago, but places like this still always managed to have a hazy atmosphere, like the air had never quite cleared after decades of cigarettes.

The bar was lined with customers whose belt buckles were probably at least six inches across. Some quietly drank, others made animated gestures with their beers as they yelled at an umpire on one of the grainy TVs above the bar. Frying grease crackled faintly in the background, and the thick smell of all things fried and salty hung as heavily in the air as the haze.

Through that haze, I made eye contact with one of the bartenders, and his eyes widened with both recognition and horror as the color slipped out of his cheeks. It only took a second or two for me to place him: he was a frequent patron at the gay bar where I worked. We'd flirted a few times, and I was pretty sure he and one of the bouncers had been sleeping together for the last few months.

If his expression was any indication, I was the only one in this establishment who knew about any of that, and he desperately wanted to keep it that way.

I pretended not to notice or recognize him, and followed the girls to the back of the room. Their friends—maybe a dozen or so guys and girls—greeted Sabrina with hugs and birthday wishes. They'd commandeered a few booths by the pool tables, and the beer was already flowing.

For a twenty-first birthday, though, they kept it pretty mellow. There were bottles, glasses, and pitchers of beer on tables, the odd mixed drink here and there, but the booze wasn't the center of attention. The group had obviously been here awhile, having settled into a couple of lively games of eight-ball, but no one was visibly drunk.

I could see why Ethan and Rhett weren't all that worried about Sabrina tonight. Her friends weren't a wild bunch, from what I could see. Besides, she was a smart kid, had her head screwed on straight—clearly nature over nurture, I often teased her dads—and she was the one who'd chosen this place for her birthday instead of one of the racier clubs downtown. A few beers in a place with neon Budweiser signs and pool tables instead of a potentially dangerous binge under flickering disco lights. She actually stood a chance of remembering her twenty-first birthday party.

"Where's Alex?" Sabrina asked the group. "Tell me he didn't bail on me."

Someone gestured with a pool cue. "He's playing cricket with Shane and Cory."

"Oh, good." She put her hand on my elbow. "Thank God, he actually showed up."

"Were you concerned he wouldn't?"

Her cheeks reddened. "A little."

I shot her a glare but then followed her.

"He's just really, really shy," she said as we crossed the mostly empty club. "Took me forever to even get his name out of him. He's—oh, there he is." She pointed at the dartboards, where one guy was getting ready to throw while two others watched.

I furrowed my brow, looking at each of the guys in turn. Two of their backs were to me, which kept me from matching anyone up with the face I'd seen on Sabrina's phone.

"Which one?" I asked.

"Gray T-shirt."

My gaze shifted to the one she'd indicated, and I suddenly had a feeling this evening would be worth the sacrifice of leaving Rhett and Ethan with a bed and a bottle of Patrón.

The gray T-shirt Sabrina had used to identify him rested over a set of broad shoulders, and his tight-but-not-too-tight jeans clung to deliciously narrow hips. From here, I guessed he was an inch or two taller than me, which was also a bonus. I wasn't a fan of having to crane my neck up or down to kiss someone. Nothing threw cold water on a kiss or a hot fuck like a damned neck cramp.

Of course, Sabrina had only brought me here to coax him into Seattle's gay lifestyle, but there wasn't a man alive I didn't automatically size up in terms of whether or not I'd sleep with him. Even when I *wasn't* dying to get laid. Some people said that made me a slut. Hey, if the shoe fits...

Sabrina nudged me toward him. "Come on, I'll introduce you."

Oh, yes, please do.

As we approached, the three dart players looked our way, and when we got close enough to see him clearly through the haze, Alex's eyes almost made me stumble. Maybe it was just the dim, neon-accented light of the bar, but I didn't think I'd ever seen eyes that dark. And for that matter, his mouth was enough to do a number on my ability to walk. He didn't have an ungodly bee-stung pout or a thin, iron-hard sneer, but his lips definitely held my attention. *Just* slightly fuller than those of so many guys I'd met, and having kissed my share of men, I'd learned that mouths like those were usually the source of spine-tingling kisses and spectacular blowjobs.

Alex gave me a wary look, and I could have sworn he shrank back from me a little. I didn't know if it was because he had no idea who I was, or if he knew exactly who I was. That, or he wondered why the hell I was so fascinated with him.

Sabrina gestured at me. "Alex, this is Kieran, the guy I was telling you about. Kieran, Alex."

A shy smile spread across his lips. He met my eyes for a second, then dropped his gaze and extended his hand. "Hi, nice to meet you."

"You too." I shook his hand, but he still avoided my eyes. So she was right, he was shy. If the attraction was mutual, this could be fun. It usually took some doing to crack through a shell like his, but in my experience, it was always worth it. Shy guys were, almost invariably, freaks in bed. The one who kept biting his lip and wringing his hands could nearly always be trusted to, once he was comfortable with someone, use those lips and hands to create a mind-blowing orgasm or two. The quiet one was always the one with a drawer full of handcuffs and a penchant for the kind of sex that left marks. The blushing one who couldn't quite maintain eye contact on a first date had no problem forcing me to my knees on his bedroom floor and making me beg to suck his cock.

A little time, a little patience, and I was willing to bet money I could find out what kinks hid behind Alex's timid exterior. One thing at a time, though. Introduce him to Seattle's very active gay lifestyle. Then, if he was game, introduce him to my bed.

I glanced at Sabrina, and the upward flick of her eyebrows asked if she could bow out or if I wanted her to stick around to help break the ice. I gave her an "I've got this" nod, and she gave me a thumbs-up just before disappearing into the crowd.

Turning to Alex, I said, "So, can I buy you a drink?"

His eyes widened. Dear Lord, from his expression, one would've thought I'd just asked him if we should get a bottle of lube and a hotel room.

I inclined my head. "You know, a beer? Something?"

Nodding, he said, "Uh...sure. If you want to."

I squinted toward the bar, trying to make out what they had on tap. "What's your poison?"

"I'm not picky," he said. "Whatever you're having."

I was thinking of ordering a shy college kid with a mouth made for blowjobs. I cleared my throat. "Local microbrew okay?"

"Yeah, sure. Sounds fine."

"Great. I'll be right back." I went to the bar.

The bartender quickly poured the drinks, refusing to make eye contact with me. He shoved the pint glasses toward me and muttered a price. Normally, I'd be livid, having minimal patience with bartenders who were rude or cold, but under the circumstances, I didn't hold it against him. It wasn't rudeness, I guessed, just the fear that I would out him.

Not a chance of that. I was completely discreet when it came to my customers, and wouldn't acknowledge them on the street unless they acknowledged me first. Discretion, discretion, discretion.

And tonight, I could add a little distraction to the mix. The terrified bartender could have insulted my mother, and the only thing on my mind would have been "give me my beer so I can get back over to the gorgeous kid who's waiting for me".

I slid a ten across the bar, told him to keep the change, and picked up the glasses without giving him a second look. Probably exactly what he hoped I would do.

I returned to the dartboards and handed Alex his beer. We drank in silence for a moment, and I racked my brain for another icebreaker.

Finally, I gestured at the dartboards. "Want to play?"

He shrugged. "Sure. You any good?"

"I'm not great, but I can hold my own."

"Ever played cricket?"

I cocked my head. "Cricket?"

"Yeah. It's pretty basic."

"Good, because I can't promise I'll even hit the board."

Alex laughed quietly. "We're probably evenly matched then." Our eyes met, and his widened slightly, probably at the realization of how his words could be misread. With a sharp gesture toward the board, he quickly said, "You want to throw first?"

"Yeah, sure." I set my drink on one of the chest-high tables and picked up three darts. "Okay, how does this work?"

"You have to hit each number between fifteen and twenty, three times apiece," he said. "Same deal with the bull's-eye and its outer ring."

"Sounds simple enough." I aimed a dart and let fly. It just barely missed the twenty and stuck to the board in the five section. "Damn it." The second dart clipped the metal between the four and eighteen, then toppled to the floor. At least the third made me look less like an idiot, landing squarely under the twenty.

"One point." Alex nodded toward the scoreboard. "Put a slash under the twenty. Second time you hit it, make the slash an 'X'. Third time, circle it, and the number's closed."

"Noted." I picked up the piece of chalk and made the slash as he'd said. Then I handed him the darts.

As he lined up his first throw, I said, "So, Sabrina tells me you're new to the area?"

"Yeah." He glanced over his shoulder before shifting his focus back to his throw. "Well, I mean, I got here at the beginning of the school year."

"Still learning your way around?"

He threw the dart, which landed under the nineteen. "Yep, still learning the area."

"I know the feeling. It took me a good year or so to get the hang of getting around this city."

"Really?" He looked at me again and this time didn't look away. "How long have you been here?"

"Little over two years."

"Where are you from?"

"Northern California. You?"

At that, he faced the dartboard again, this time with a quiet chuckle that almost sounded sarcastic. Maybe even a little bitter. "I'm from a tiny speck on the map in Montana."

"I'm guessing there isn't much of a gay scene there."

Alex laughed, the boldest, most assertive sound I'd heard from him yet. "No, not much of a gay scene." He threw the dart, and it hit the board *hard* under the seventeen spot. Then he gave a quieter laugh and shook his head, as if responding to an unspoken punch line. His third dart hit the eighteen.

After he'd marked his points on the scoreboard and retrieved the darts, he handed them to me. "You're up."

Curiosity had me itching to ask about his hometown, but I decided against it. Not until I had more of a feel for him. Could be a touchy nerve.

I aimed, threw the dart, and cursed when it bounced off the very bottom of the board and clattered to the floor. The second did the same. “Damn it.” I sighed theatrically. “Something tells me that last point was a lucky shot.”

“How are you holding it?” Alex asked.

“What?”

“The dart.” He nodded toward the one remaining in my hand. “How are you holding it before you throw it?”

I held it up, positioning it like I was about to throw, but didn’t move.

“There’s your problem,” he said. “Your finger’s over the top. That’ll screw you up.”

I furrowed my brow, looking at the dart in my hand. “So how am I supposed to do it?”

“Thumb and forefinger on each side.” He held up another dart, demonstrating how to hold it. “Your finger’s on top. Should be more like this.”

I furrowed my brow, looking at his hand, then mine, then his again.

Alex stepped a little closer and gestured at my hand. “May I?”

“What? Oh, sure, yeah.”

He reached for my hand but hesitated just before making contact. His fingers hovering over mine, he looked at me, eyebrows raised. Then he swallowed hard and grasped my hand. He rotated my hand a few degrees, and once he was apparently satisfied with the position, he quickly let go.

"There. Try it like that." He stepped back, and we both exhaled.

I focused on my throw, on keeping my hand steady, and turned the way he'd suggested and *steady, damn it.* I threw the dart, and just barely missed the fifteen spot. Still, it landed solidly instead of joining my last two attempts on the floor.

"You still have to aim it," Alex said, not even trying to hide his amusement.

"Very funny." I went to retrieve the darts. "I thought you said you weren't all that good."

"I know the principles," he said. "I'm just not great at applying them."

Holding the darts out for him, I said, "You're still winning."

"We'll see how long that lasts now that you know what you're doing." He took the darts from me, and both of us jumped when his fingertips brushed mine.

While he took my place and aimed his first throw, I went for my drink. Alex took his first shot, then lined up his second. Even with his need for concentration and my preoccupation with the beer on my tongue, the silence was awkward. Tense. Needed to be broken, like, *now*.

I swallowed my beer. "So, what are you studying?"

"Pre-med." He threw the dart and it landed firmly under the eighteen. Third dart poised in midair, he said, "What about you? What do you do?"

"I'm a bartender."

The dart flew through the air and connected with the board with a *thunk*. "A bartender? So, you don't mind giving money to the competition?" He gestured at the bar.

"Just don't tell my boss I'm here, all right?"

Alex laughed as we switched places. "Your secret's safe with me. I appreciate you coming too, by the way. I hope Sabrina didn't twist your arm as hard as she twisted mine."

I looked over my shoulder at him. "You had to have your arm twisted to meet me?"

"That's not what I meant," he said, sounding half-amused and half-unnerved.

"Just giving you shit," I said. "Anyway, you staying in town for the summer or going home?"

"Staying here." The words came out sharply, like he didn't even want to consider the latter option. "I'm, um, I'm working full-time right now. Figured I should make some money this summer instead of wasting it going home."

"And in between working, checking out the more fun things the city has to offer?"

Some color rushed into his cheeks, and he laughed shyly. "Yeah, that was the plan."

I finished the turn, and after we'd switched, I said, "So, what is it you want to check out? Clubs, that kind of thing?"

Alex shrugged. "Guess that would be a good place to start. Somewhere I can, you know"—he looked at me—"meet guys." We held eye contact for a moment before he turned back to the dartboard. It was a second or two, if that, but just long enough to create a tingle at the base of my spine.

I cleared my throat. "Not too many places like that where you come from?"

"Uh, no. I'm from a town that has three times as many bars as stoplights, and every one of those bars has dead animals on the walls." He looked over his shoulder at me. "I don't have the faintest clue where to go or what to do once I'm there."

"Well," I said. "I might be able to help you with that part."

Shyness and boldness battled for dominance in his eyes, and I thought he might say something. He didn't, though. Instead, he turned his attention back to throwing his dart.

Sipping my beer, I watched him. So he'd had a year at a university in a gay-friendly city. Probably dated a little, played the campus field a bit, and now he was ready to expand his horizons. Timid with the occasional break of matter-of-fact assertiveness. Oh, yes, this could be a lot of fun, especially if he wanted someone to help him explore some of the dirtier aspects of being a gay man in this town.

Someone threw their arms around my shoulders from behind, nearly making me drop my drink.

"Having fun over here?" Sabrina asked, more of a giggle in her voice than usual.

"Well, I am." I looked at Alex. "You?"

Just before bringing his beer to his lips, he said, "I'm having a good time, yes."

"Good," she said. In a stage whisper, she said to me, "You're being gentle with him, right, Kieran?"

I looked right at Alex. "Define 'gentle'."

He gulped. I grinned. Sabrina giggled.

"Okay, boys, don't have too much fun." She patted my shoulder, then wandered off to the rest of her friends.

Alex coughed into his fist. "So, how do you know Sabrina?" Still focused on me, he sipped his beer.

"I, uh, I lived with her dads when I first moved here." I paused. "They needed a roommate for a while, so..." I made a dismissive gesture with my glass. *And I've been fucking them on a regular basis ever since.*

"I have to say," he said, "it blew my mind when she told me her dads were gay. She doesn't bat an eye over it, and that's when I realized I was living in a very different world now." Amusement tugged at his lips, but there was something darker in his expression that made me curious what kind of world he'd come from.

"Well, get used to it," I said with a wink. "Seattle isn't one hundred percent gay-friendly, but you're not in Kansas anymore."

"So I've noticed." He laughed dryly. "By the way, it's your throw."

"Oh, right." I set my beer down and picked up the darts.

As I aimed, my phone vibrated. I groaned. *Fuck, please tell me Mom isn't calling again.* I unclipped it from my belt. The screen lit up with Rhett's name and a text message:

Having fun there, or coming back here tonight?

I chuckled. Had the message come from Ethan, it probably would have said "*Still want to get fucked tonight?*" Same meaning, different wording.

I looked at Alex. Then I wrote back:

Think I'm going to stay. Call you guys later this week. Have fun. :)

Then I clipped my phone back on my belt and resumed my game.

Alex eventually beat me at that round of cricket, but it was close. He only had me by three points, so that was as good an excuse as any for a rematch. Had to see who really was the better player, after all. Since I won that game, we decided to go two out of three. Then three out of five.

Seven games and three beers later, I pulled my phone off my belt to check the time. I blinked a few times, certain I was misreading the numbers. How the hell was it quarter to twelve already?

"Damn, it's almost midnight," I said.

"Is it?" Alex looked at his watch. "I'll be damned." He exhaled. "I should probably get out of here. I'm working an early shift tomorrow."

"Yeah, me too."

"It was nice meeting you." His smile was still shy but decidedly more confident than when we were introduced earlier. "Thanks for letting Sabrina twist your arm."

I grinned. "I think this was well worth having it twisted a little."

We held eye contact, and as the silence went on, the color in his cheeks deepened.

I cleared my throat. "So, um, listen, if you want the grand tour of Capitol Hill, I could certainly show you around. Take you to some of the places on Broadway." *And maybe show you the inside of an apartment a few blocks off Broadway.*

"Sure, that'd be great." He shifted his weight, obviously struggling to hold my gaze. "If you're, you know, if it's not too much trouble for you."

"Not at all. What are you doing tomorrow night?"

He hesitated, then shook his head. "Nothing that I know of."

"And you are twenty-one, right?"

"With a few months to spare, yes."

"Why don't you meet me at Wilde's, then?"

"Wilde's? That's that gay club on Broadway, isn't it?"

"Most of the clubs on Broadway are gay clubs," I said. "Wilde's just happens to be the best in my not so humble and *very* biased opinion as an employee. Have you been to any clubs?"

"Beside this?" He gestured at our surroundings.

"This is a sports bar. Big difference, trust me."

He laughed quietly. "I'll take your word for it. I have been to a strip club before, though."

"Have you, now?"

He nodded.

"Enjoy it?"

"I think I might've enjoyed it more had there been some guys on the stage." His smile was characteristically shy, but there was just enough of a devilish sparkle in his eyes to bring a grin to my lips.

Oh, yes, you do *have a wild side, don't you?*

"Well, if you want to meet me at the club tomorrow night," I said, "I'm off work at seven."

He gnawed his lower lip. I was certain he'd decide against it, find a reason to bow out, but then he gave a subtle nod.

"I'll be there."

Chapter Three

I often told people I worked at Wilde's because I liked people-watching. To a degree, that was true. The profession of bartending has a rather symbiotic relationship with the hobby of people watching. Bars attracted the depressed and the desperate, the lonely and the philandering, the mourning and the celebrating. All different, all interesting.

I took the job at this club when I moved to Seattle, figuring it would tide me over until I could land a more lucrative gig, maybe in a five-star restaurant or something. Two years and some change later, I was still behind this bar. The money was damned good, and the people-watching? Wilde's was a prime spot for that. This wasn't a typical drink-your-sorrows-away bar, though some people used it for that. Wilde's was unabashedly the place where the beautiful and the horny came to get laid.

My co-workers alone were worth showing up here every day: they were stunning. All of them. Tailored tuxedo shirts and pants showed off glorious shoulders and asses, and cummerbunds emphasized narrow hips. In fact, if I wasn't mistaken, at least six of the guys who worked here had modeling contracts. Not a day went by that I wasn't certain someone would pick me out as an imposter and boot me out of the place for not being up to the same aesthetic standards of the other bartenders. I made the best Kamikazes and Cock Chasers in Seattle, though; maybe that was why they let me stay.

When I wasn't ogling my co-workers, the clientele offered no shortage of eye candy, either. Wilde's had a well-deserved reputation for being a magnet for hot gay men. It wasn't unusual at all for an A-list celebrity to strut through, but even they had to work at it to stand out. Adonis himself would have been hard-pressed to turn heads here.

I fucking *loved* this place.

Tonight, the club was packed and the crowd was gorgeous. I was almost disappointed I wouldn't be working the closing shift; as the night wore on, the dancing would get more risqué and the clothing more optional. Pity I wouldn't be around to see it.

In between making drinks for all these beautiful men, I kept glancing at the door. The clock was closing in on seven, which meant Alex would be along soon. I'd already given the bouncer a heads up so he wouldn't make Alex pay the cover, and as soon as my replacement finished changing clothes, I'd be free to go. Then it was just a matter of waiting for Alex, hoping he didn't decide this was a bad idea after all, and—

There he was.

I was a little surprised that he'd caught my eye. By all rights, he should have blended into the background. From the way he dressed to the way he moved, he was...subdued. He wasn't unattractive by any means, but there was nothing flashy about him, and anything that didn't flash or glitter didn't stand out here.

Walking between guys who danced under the heavy shadows and bright, flickering disco lights, in a crowd of men who'd all dressed specifically to stand out and show off, Alex brought to mind a black cat prowling through a flock of peacocks. His surroundings nearly made him invisible, but he was still undeniably *there.*

Had he given off a bolder, more confident vibe, he would have turned every head in the room. Even without flash and glitter, it was his timid posture and nervous eyes that undoubtedly kept him off most radars. Oh well. Their loss. With any luck, this one was mine, all mine, at least for tonight.

He finally made it through the crowd and reached the bar.

I rested my hands on the edge of the bar and leaned toward him so he could hear me over the music. "Hey, you made it."

"Yeah, I did," he said, a mixture of relief and shyness in his expression. He cleared his throat and looked around with wide eyes. "This place is...busy." His gaze locked on a pair of nothing-on-top-leather-on-the-bottom guys competing for the crowd's attention on the dance floor. Poor kid was completely out of his element here. He must have thought he'd just teleported to a foreign country or something.

"Busy is good," I said. "More money in my pocket."

"I suppose it is." He turned back to me, and the quick down-up of his eyes made me shiver.

I shifted my weight. "The guy who's here to relieve me should be on in a few minutes; then I need to change clothes before we go."

He grinned, and damn if he didn't give me another not-so-subtle down-up. "Don't want to go out like that?"

Oh, it was so tempting to mention I had no problem going out dressed like this if my clothes were just going to end up on the floor anyway. Tempting. Very tempting.

I just returned the grin. "I like to play it a little more casual when I go out."

"Fine by me either way," he said.

"You want a drink or anything while you're here?"

He shook his head. "No, I'm fine, thanks."

Chad, my replacement, clocked on, so I slipped into the back to put on something a bit less formal. After I'd changed clothes, I stopped to take a quick look in the mirror in the back room before I returned to front of the bar. I wasn't excessively vain, but I did like to be somewhat presentable. Especially if I planned to get laid, and tonight, I did. Oh my God, I did.

"Preening?" Wes, another bartender, said. "You got a hot date or something tonight, Frost?"

"A date, yes." I nodded toward the door dividing this room from the rest of the club. "Kid in the black shirt sitting at the bar."

Wes leaned out the door to look around. Then he came back. "Not your type, is he?"

I shrugged. "Only one way to find out."

"Since when do you date church mice?"

I laughed. "Honestly, Wes. He's just a bit shy."

"A bit shy?" Wes snorted. "He looks scared out of his damned mind out there. God, don't hurt him, man."

"Oh, I fully intend to, believe me."

Wes shivered. "Damn you, Kieran. I swear, if I wasn't married…"

"Ah, but you are." I took one last look in the mirror, then started for the doorway. On my way out, I clapped Wes's shoulder. "But if you boys are ever down for that threesome, you know where to find me."

He shoved me playfully. "Tease."

We both laughed, and I headed out.

Alex and I stepped out of the club and into the comfortable evening air.

"Want to grab something to eat?" I asked.

"Yeah, sure. I'm assuming you know a good place?"

"I know plenty of places." I made a sweeping gesture to indicate the street and all its establishments. "Broadway has some of the best food in town. What are you in the mood for?"

Our eyes met. Fortunately for him, the sign above Wilde's glowed red and yellow, which kept me from knowing for certain if he was blushing. Just the same, he dropped his gaze and cleared his throat.

"Pretty much anything," he said.

I hope that applies to more than just dinner. I gestured down the road. "There's a café a few blocks this way."

"Sure, sounds good."

We started down Broadway. My feet ached as they often did after a shift, but I opted to have us walk instead of drive. Traffic could be a bitch on this street, and even if it wasn't, Broadway was one of those streets better appreciated on foot. Better for people-watching, better for catching the signs and slogans in shop windows. There was a gaudy boutique not far from here that always had a random, strategically-placed sex toy in their window displays. Printed flyers announced shows and political rallies. Those were things that simply wouldn't be noticed from a car window.

Just as I'd planned, the walk from Wilde's to the café gave Alex a sample of the area's culture. This was the heart of Capitol Hill, Seattle's predominantly gay neighborhood, and it flew those colors proudly. We passed a couple of bookstores with pro-gay slogans in the windows. Tattoo parlors. Eclectic coffee shops and eccentric clothing stores. I could always tell when a rainbow or a pink triangle caught his eye; the double-take was subtle, but it happened. Every time.

As we passed another tattoo shop, Alex paused to look at some of the art in the window. After a moment, we kept walking.

The café was a few blocks up from Wilde's and another block or so down a side street. It was one of those hole-in-the-wall places that had somehow stayed in business in spite of being nearly invisible and barely advertised. Word of mouth probably kept it alive more than anything, especially since there wasn't a soul on Capitol Hill that wouldn't swear this place's coffee was brewed from the tears of angels. That, or opium and a dash of crack. And for people in Seattle to say that about an establishment's coffee? That was something.

When we walked in, the waitress showed us to a table. She offered us menus and ice water, and when she spoke, Alex startled slightly. It took me a second to put two and two together, but then I realized her voice—feminine with just a touch of gravel—probably sounded unusual to him. The kid probably hadn't seen too many transgendered people in his hometown. And his reaction wasn't one of horror or disgust, just surprise. Curiosity.

Oh, you have a lot to learn, my friend.

"What can I get you to drink?" the waitress asked after we'd been seated.

Her voice still had Alex off balance, but he recovered quickly and looked at me.

"Recommend anything?"

"You *have* to try the coffee," I said. "It's like sex in a cup."

Without the glowing sign overhead for camouflage, he couldn't hide the blush this time. Clearing his throat, he nodded. "Sure. Coffee."

Laughing, the waitress wrote it down. Then she looked at me. "Anything else?"

"Just coffee for now," I said.

After she'd gone, Alex raised an eyebrow. "Sex in a cup?"

"Wait 'til you taste it." I winked. "It's good, trust me."

"Guess I'll find out, won't I?" He glanced in the direction our waitress had gone and sat up a little. Lowering his voice, he said, "Forgive my ignorance, but is she..." He bit his lip, eyebrows knitting together in a *help me say this without sounding stupid* expression.

"The term is transgendered," I said, keeping my voice discreet.

"Oh." He paused, glancing at her again. "Well, maybe you can answer this for me, then." He shifted, folding his hands on the table. "One of my classmates was...transgendered, you said?"

I nodded.

"So, how do I know whether to refer to someone as 'he' or 'she'? You know, without being offensive?"

"Ask."

"That's not considered rude?"

I shook my head. "It's more polite than being presumptuous. Usually, a person prefers to go by whichever gender they're presenting. If you're not sure, just ask."

"Oh." He gave a subtle nod. "Okay, I've been curious about that for a while. Good to know."

Our waitress appeared a moment later with our sex-in-a-cup. As she took our orders, Alex didn't even bat an eye. Having had his question answered, he wasn't so nervous now and made as much eye contact as a naturally shy person could be expected to.

That was certainly a point in his favor: curious about people he didn't understand, conscientious of their feelings. Even if I just wanted a piece of ass, I didn't put up with bigotry of any flavor. Just last summer, I'd thrown a guy out of my apartment when he'd made a slur about the race of an actor in the porno we'd been watching. I was easy, but I did have some standards.

Standards that Alex had so far met with flying colors.

While we ate, we shot the breeze and made small talk. We compared notes on the drudgery of working in customer-facing jobs. Though I loved being a bartender, it had its moments. Still, there wasn't enough money in the world to make me join him in the world of retail sales.

Alex was fascinated with my stories of the gay pride events that were held annually in this neighborhood, and he was jealous as hell when he found out I'd met two of his favorite musicians at Wilde's.

"I would have sold my soul to meet them," he said, shaking his head.

I chuckled. "They were pretty cool. Hot as hell in person."

"I can imagine. I mean, I saw them in concert a few years ago, and they were—" Alex stopped abruptly, staring at something outside. I followed his gaze, but there was nothing out of the ordinary.

"What?" I asked.

He shook his head. "This is definitely a different world for me."

Furrowing my brow, I said, "How so?"

He gestured out the window. "Let's just say two guys 'being gay' in public wouldn't go over well in my hometown."

I looked again, and this time figured out what had caught his eye: beside one of the newspaper dispensers, a couple looked intently at a piece of paper, alternately gesturing up and down the street like they were trying to figure out how to find something. If not for the guy on the left resting his hand on the small of the other's back, I wouldn't have guessed if they were gay or straight.

Evidently satisfied they knew where they were going, the couple walked on.

I turned my attention back to Alex. "You really are from a small town, aren't you?"

"When I said I was from a tiny little speck-on-the-map town, I wasn't kidding. It was one of those places where you aren't gay if you know what's good for you."

"Oh, *that* kind of small town," I said with a single nod.

"Yeah. That kind." He folded his arms on the edge of the table and let his gaze drift back to the vacant space where the couple had been standing. "Trust me, in Rayesville, you were better off with a visible swastika tattoo than giving anyone a reason to think you *might* be gay."

I thought he might have meant it as a figure of speech, an exaggeration, but a subtle shudder suggested there was more truth to it than not.

I cocked my head. "It was that bad?"

He nodded. "I think half the town was part of the local Neo-Nazi group." Meeting my eyes, he added, "Needless to say, the closet was the safest place to be."

I shivered, counting my blessings that my family and community had never made a big deal about me being gay. "Coming to Seattle must have been a switch. Plenty of openly gay guys, a chance to play the field without having to look over your shoulder."

"Play the field?" With a self-conscious laugh, he dropped his gaze and stared into his drink. "Can't say I've spent a lot of time doing that. Any time, for that matter."

Something in my gut tightened. "Wait, you haven't...since you moved here..."

"No."

"And you moved here last summer?"

"A few weeks before school started, yeah."

I chewed my lower lip. "Do you mind if I ask a personal question?"

He raised his eyebrows. "Go ahead."

"You don't have to answer if you don't want to, but..." I hesitated. "Have you...dated? At all?"

Alex swallowed. Then he shook his head. "No. Never."

"Not even casually?"

"No."

"So you're..."

"A virgin?"

I nodded.

So did he.

Chapter Four

Oh. My. God.

The V-word was usually my cue to run in the opposite direction. I didn't consider myself the right guy to guide a virgin to sexual enlightenment, and I didn't feel the need to be anyone's teacher.

Admittedly, my first instinct now was to find the quickest, politest escape. I didn't move, though. Walking away smacked of throwing him to the wolves. At twenty-one, stepping out of a back-ass-wards small town and into the big-city gay lifestyle, he was just asking for someone to take advantage of him. Or for someone to come along who assumed Alex knew more than he did or had more experience. Someone who assumed he had any experience at all.

Sighing, he ran a hand through his short hair. "I know, kind of ridiculous for someone my age."

"No, no, not ridiculous," I said. "If you're from a place like that, it sounds like it was just as well." I paused. "Have you ever done anything with a guy?"

"No." Color rushed into his face. "I've never even been kissed."

"Never?"

He shook his head.

"Wow." Good God, it was a *travesty* someone this gorgeous had never been touched. I rested my chin on my hand and absently ran my index finger along my lower lip, wishing I could do the same to his. A mouth like that, and he'd never been kissed? *Oh, we will have to remedy this, my boy.*

Before my mind had a chance to wander too far down Deflowering Alex Lane, I cleared my throat. "So, did you date girls in your hometown? Like when you were in school?"

"No." He reached up to scratch the back of his neck. "I knew I was gay, so..."

"Well, yeah," I said. "But you wouldn't have been the first to have a girlfriend to keep people from figuring out you were gay."

"True. It just seemed like, I don't know." He wrinkled his nose. "Seemed like I'd be using them, you know? Lying to them."

"Fair enough."

"That, and I was terrified that I'd be with a girl, try to get intimate with her and something would give me away."

"And no one ever caught on that something might be off since you weren't dating anyone?"

"Not when I told everyone I was busting my ass to make sure I got into a good medical school." He chuckled. "Dad's a surgeon, and whenever he raised an eyebrow about me not being interested in girls, I'd just remind him I wanted to follow in his footsteps and didn't want to be distracted by dating. Worked every time. I don't think he ever suspected a thing."

"Smart move," I said with a slow nod. Deep down, I couldn't shake this unsettled feeling. Being young and new to a big city was one thing. No experience at all? Not even an in-denial experience with a female? Holy fuck.

"Is, um, is that something guys balk at?" he asked. "Knowing I have zero experience?"

"Depends on the guy," I said quietly.

He chewed the inside of his cheek. "Is it something *you* balk at?"

I blinked, startled by the question and the semi-brazen subtext that may or may not have actually been there.

"Not really." Guilt twisted in my gut. Yes, of course it was something I balked at, but not for reasons I could quite articulate to him. Instead, I added, "It's nothing to be ashamed of or anything, if that's what you're wondering."

Alex relaxed a little.

I went on. "Honestly, it's probably something that should have you balking at men. I'd be more concerned about someone taking advantage of you."

I thought that sentiment might unsettle him more, reminding him he was at a disadvantage when it came to venturing out into the dating world, but my comment seemed to have the opposite effect. His shoulders relaxed a little more, and the breath he released was almost a sigh of relief.

I cocked my head. "What?"

"Nothing." He thumbed his chin and let something outside the window hold his attention for a moment. Then his eyes flicked toward me again. "I guess it was something I was worried about, and thought I might be concerned about nothing." With a humorless laugh, he added, "Good to know I wasn't just being crazy."

"Not at all," I said. "I mean, most guys probably wouldn't be like that, but you can never be too careful."

The conversation dwindled, and with empty plates and coffee cups in front of us, we finally decided to get out of there. I wasn't sure where to go after this, aside from resuming our walking tour of Broadway and its side streets. We'd think of something, though hauling him back to my apartment in a breathless tangle of clothes probably wasn't on the menu now.

The pause in conversation while we'd paid our checks and left the café had let the silence set in, and I struggled to find a way to get us talking again. I tucked my hands into my coat pockets, and a glance confirmed he'd done the same. Though a cool breeze blew in off Puget Sound, the evening was hardly cold, so I guessed he'd done it for the same reason: to occupy his hands.

As we wandered down a side street, it was Alex who finally spoke.

"You said you moved up here, what, three years ago?"

"Two."

"How long did it take you to learn your way around here?" he asked.

"Oh, I'm still learning some areas," I said. "Seattle can be confusing, but I got the hang of Capitol Hill pretty quickly."

"Dated much since you moved to the city?"

I shrugged. "Define 'dated'."

Alex furrowed his brow. "There's more than one interpretation of the word?"

"There are a few, yes." I smiled. "Some people don't think it counts as dating unless you exchange apartment keys and meet each other's parents. Others figure it counts if it goes beyond a one-night stand."

"Oh." He seemed to chew on that for a minute or so. Then, "How do *you* define it?"

I shrugged again. "I don't know. I'm probably not the most consistent person in the world when it comes to that."

"How so?"

"Well, I mean, I've had flings that have gone on for quite a while, but I wouldn't classify it as 'dating' in any kind of traditional sense," I said. "One guy and I were more or less exclusive for a few months because we just liked sex with each other too much to bother looking anywhere else."

"Really?"

I nodded.

"So, it was just sex?"

"Just sex. And we're still friends now. We just decided to move on and see other people, and even after we 'broke up', we still fooled around sometimes. Only reason we stopped doing that is he and his ex got back together."

"And you're still friends? Even now that he's back with his ex?"

"Oh, hell yeah. They're both great guys. Pity I wasn't involved with the ex beforehand. We could have had some incredible threesomes."

Alex's head snapped toward me, and his eyes widened. "You're joking, right?"

"About doing them together?" I asked. "Or threesomes in general?"

He cleared his throat. "Either, I guess."

"I've done both," I said. "Threesomes, and I've been a third for two guys who were in a committed relationship. In fact, I—" I caught myself before I let him know just how intimately acquainted I was with Sabrina's dads. "I've done that a few times."

"It didn't bother you? Sleeping with someone who's in love with someone else?"

"No. As long as he's not lying to his significant other about me and everything is on the up-and-up, I don't have a problem with it."

"You don't feel, like, used?"

"Of course not." I grinned. "I feel a lot of things with these guys, but used isn't one of them. Not in a bad way, anyway." That wasn't entirely true, I supposed. Things with Rhett and Ethan hadn't gone well for a short period in the beginning, and I *had* felt used at first. Once we'd ironed things out—once *they'd* ironed things out between them—everything had gone smoothly. It may not have been the ideal beginning to what we shared, but it worked now.

"Hmm." He went quiet again, staring ahead of us as we walked in silence. "I've always wondered about that."

"About what?"

"Separating sex and love. I guess..." He shook his head. "I guess I've been curious about...the physical side. I've wanted to experiment, but..."

"What?"

"This may sound kind of stupid, but..." He trailed off, and while I wasn't sure if it was a conscious move on his part, he slowed his gait. I dropped back to fall into step with him, and after a moment, he finally spoke again. "I guess I've kind of balked at the idea of figuring out sex and love at the same time. Like I wanted to sort one out, then the other. Both at the same time, it seemed a bit..."

"Intimidating?"

"Yeah, exactly."

"Well, contrary to popular belief, it is permissible to have one without the other." I pulled my hand out of my pocket and absently ran my hand through my hair, trying to keep the wind from blowing it into my face. "And quite frankly, sex is a hell of a lot easier to find. And maintain."

"That's good to know," he said quietly.

"Mind if I ask another personal question?"

He shrugged. "Go ahead."

I paused, trying to find the words. "When you say you're looking to get out and meet guys right now, what exactly..." I searched his eyes. "What exactly *are* you looking for?"

Alex stared at the pavement as we continued walking. "I'm not sure, to be honest."

"I mean, you said you're intimidated by trying to figure out sex and love at the same time. So, for now, are you after a relationship? Sex? Just friends who don't make a big deal out of you being gay?" *Because only two out of three of those options have any chance of happening between us.*

The streetlights were just bright enough to reveal the hint of extra color blooming in his cheeks. "I really don't know. I'm..." He was quiet for a moment, then sighed. "The thing is, I've spent my entire life making sure no one ever suspected I was gay. Now that I'm in a place where I don't have to do that..." Beside the brick wall of an apartment building, he halted, as did I, and he met my eyes. "It's like, I don't even know how to *be* gay."

A pang of sympathy burned in my gut. I couldn't imagine having to pretend I wasn't gay, having to keep my sexuality so far under lock and key that even I couldn't get to it. It was too significant a part of who and what I was.

I swallowed. "Well, I can help you figure it out. Just tell me where you want to start."

Sighing, he leaned against the brick wall, gnawing his lip and focusing on the ground between us. His shoulders dropped as he released a long breath. "Honestly, I want to try everything. I'm curious. I'm itching to figure out who the fuck I am. But, it's intimidating. All of it." He laughed bitterly. "It's like, everyone's supposed to go through that awkward, clueless phase when they're teenagers, but now that I'm not a teenager..." He made a frustrated gesture. "So, like I said, I'm not really sure where to start."

I swallowed. "I'm not really sure either."

Our eyes met. Then he dropped his gaze again.

"Alex," I said and waited until he looked at me before I went on. "I can take you to clubs. Introduce you to people. Show you where to meet guys your own age, or get a decent beer, or get a tattoo." I took a step closer, stopping when his posture stiffened. "My question is, is that *all* you want me to do?"

His Adam's apple bobbed. Somehow he held my gaze. Maybe he was afraid to look away; maybe he just couldn't move. Finally, he took a breath and said, "I...don't know what I want. From you or anyone else." With a halfhearted laugh, he looked away. "God, I sound so indecisive and clueless."

"No, you sound like someone who doesn't know how to be who he is. I think anyone in your position would feel that way."

He nodded, but kept his eyes down.

"Maybe I should rephrase my question." My voice threatened to shake, but somehow I kept it steady. "Since you don't know what you're looking for, are you opposed to me offering suggestions and you deciding whether or not to take them?"

He looked at me through his lashes. "What kind of suggestions did you have in mind?"

"I'm not sure yet. I guess I'm"—I took another step forward and rested my hand against the wall a few inches from his shoulder—"improvising."

He threw a wary glance toward my arm, then looked at me and swallowed hard. He fidgeted, like he couldn't decide if he wanted to stay there or move a more comfortable distance away from me.

"You said you want to try a lot of things," I said softly. "And I don't want to be presumptuous and assume you want to try them with me. But if you do..." I raised my eyebrows.

He gulped and broke eye contact, but he made no move to draw away from me. I'd crossed into his comfort zone, but I'd left plenty of room for him to restore a more bearable distance if he wanted it.

Once I was more or less sure he didn't want me to back off, I reached for his waist, and as soon as my hand made contact, Alex's spine straightened. Had it not been for the wall behind him, he might have backed away, and his eyes darted past me, scanning the deserted street and sidewalk.

"Relax," I whispered.

He swallowed. Shifted. Moistened his lips. "This is...we're out...in public..."

"I know," I said. "But you're not out in public in Rayesville."

He held my gaze, then closed his eyes. "I know, but..."

"Alex, this is Capitol Hill. There's no one around, and even if there was, the only one on this street who cares if you're gay or straight is me." I took a breath. "And that's only because I really want to kiss you."

His eyes flew open. "Out...here?"

"Out here. Unless you'd rather not." I raised my eyebrows again.

There's your exit, Alex. It's there if you want it.

I alternately looked at his eyes and his lips, hoping for something from the former to let me know I could have the latter. After a moment, I erred on the side of caution and drew back.

"Wait," he said.

I froze.

"I didn't—" He hesitated. "I didn't say I didn't want you to."

My heart beat faster. "You also didn't say you did."

He swallowed again. "Do I have to say it?"

"If you do," I whispered, "then I'll know."

The tip of his tongue swept across his lower lip. "I think you do know."

We locked eyes. Blood pounded in my ears. I moved in slowly, giving him every opportunity to change his mind. He put a hand on my shoulder, and I paused, waiting to see if he meant to stop me or encourage me. When his other arm slid around my waist, and the hand on my shoulder drew me closer instead of pushing me away, I crossed the sliver of space remaining between us. My body ached to be against his, to press him up against the wall and let him feel how aroused I was, to seek out proof he was equally aroused, but I was afraid to overwhelm him. One thing at a time. One thing at a time. *One thing at a time, Kieran.* Bracing myself with my forearm against the wall, I held back, and stopped myself before our chests or hips—*God,* I wanted to feel him—touched.

Tell me to stop, and I will.

My heart thundered. With every inch I gained, I expected the whisper of his breath on my lips, but it didn't come. Nor did my own breath ricochet off his lips to warm my skin.

Say the word, Alex.

Because he wasn't breathing.

I only want this if you do.

Neither was I.

Give me something.

His fingers tightened on my shoulder. I tilted my head, closed my eyes, and pressed my lips to his.

For a moment, we were both still.

With the release of a long breath across my cheek, he relaxed against the wall. With the release of my breath, I relaxed against him, though I somehow found the presence of mind—and the restraint—to keep our hips from touching.

Inhaling deeply through my nose, I parted my lips, gently encouraging him to do the same. He didn't resist. In fact, when I went to tease them farther apart with the tip of my tongue, he met my tongue with his. I deepened the kiss, seeking out every taste I could get. He whimpered and pulled me closer, pushing his hips against mine, and when his cock brushed mine through our clothes, a gasp apiece pulled our mouths apart.

I touched my forehead to his, and we panted against each other's lips. I couldn't remember moving my hand from the wall to the back of his neck and into his hair, but I had. I also couldn't remember when that hand had started shaking, but it was.

After a kiss like that, it was usually a foregone conclusion that in no time flat, I'd be bent over the guy's bed, drenched in sweat and begging for more, more, God, *more.* Or on my knees, right here on the pavement, sucking his cock until I was on the verge of coming myself.

Not tonight, though. Calling on every ounce of restraint I possessed, I held back. I wanted him. Holy fucking hell, I wanted him in more ways than he could probably imagine, but I still held back. I didn't want to be something he regretted.

My knees must have been trembling as badly as his, and my voice was unsteady as I whispered, "I guess you can't say you've never been kissed now."

"No, I guess I can't." He reached up and touched my face. "If there was ever a doubt in my mind, I can definitely say now that I am, without a doubt, gay." Our eyes met, and we both laughed softly.

"Well, just in case you're not sure..." I leaned in, stopping just short of his lips, and just as I'd hoped he would, he closed the remaining distance.

We skipped a slow, cautious intro this time and went straight to deep and passionate. I couldn't tell the hiss of his jacket over bricks from the whisper of hands over fabric, couldn't distinguish his sharp, uneven breathing from my own. All those sounds did was drown out anything else that might've tried to distract us, and nothing short of an earthquake or gunfire stood a chance of that. My senses were simply too wrapped up in Alex's shy-bold-shy embrace. One second, he explored my mouth with ravenous curiosity. The next, he drew back, his lips almost apologetic against mine. Then his fingers would tighten against the back of my neck and his kiss would border on violent.

One night with him. God, let me have one night in this man's bed. One long, hot, sweaty night...

I shivered and pressed my hard-on against him, moaning when he pushed back. Then I bent to kiss his neck. Just a taste of his skin, a touch, that was all I wanted, and oh God, it was a mistake if we were going to stop this any time soon. The heat of his body, the quickening of his pulse, the thrum of his voice, my lips didn't miss a thing. I was so hard now it was *just* this side of unbearable.

Alex's back arched off the wall and his fingers dug into my shoulders. Damn, I wanted to feel those fingers on bare skin. I wanted to feel his bare skin. All of it. I wanted to taste more than just his mouth and his neck. I wanted to drop to my knees, here and now, and suck his cock, and the very thought made me shudder so hard I gasped, and the breath I drew was made of his light cologne, and *fuck, fuck, fuck why are you so hard to resist?*

One. Fucking. Night. Any more than that would probably kill me anyway.

"Now I see why people like kissing so much," Alex whispered, gripping my hair as I trailed kisses up the side of his throat.

I raised my head and let my lips brush his. "Just wait until you find out why people like doing everything else."

Shivering, he bit his lip.

I ran my fingers through his hair. "And I'll be happy to show you, if you want, but not tonight."

He made a frustrated sound, but at the same time, judging by the way his shoulders relaxed and the trembling in his fingers eased, he was relieved. The pressure was off. One step at a time.

He licked his lips. "Would it be out of line for me to say tonight is very, very tempting?"

I sucked in a breath. "Out of line? No." I kissed him lightly. "Much as I don't want to, though, I should let you go." *Or we* will *go too far.*

Exhaling, he nodded. "Yeah, you're probably right."

"Don't you work tomorrow?"

"Unfortunately."

"I'm off tomorrow." I combed my fingers through his hair again. "I can pick you up if you want to go out."

Alex smiled. "Please do."

"Text me your address. I'll be there."

"Before we leave tonight, though..." He bit his lip again.

"Before we leave...?"

He swallowed hard and met my eyes. He didn't speak. He just pulled me to him and kissed me.

Chapter Five

I stopped inside my front door just long enough to turn the deadbolt. My keys landed on the counter, my shoes thumped against the couch, and my shirt was half-unbuttoned before I made it across my tiny studio apartment to my bed.

I pulled my shirt over my head and tossed it on the floor. With unsteady hands, I opened the nightstand drawer and grabbed the bottle of lube, then dropped onto the bed on my back. I fumbled with my belt and my zipper and the bottle, my hands shaking like I was the virgin, like I was all turned on and had no idea what to do with myself. Oh, I knew. I knew exactly what I needed to do if I was ever going to have a coherent thought again.

The bottle finally cooperated, and I poured some lube on my hand. I didn't bother warming it up. Too desperate for that. Too fucking hard. Couldn't wait.

The shock of cold lube on my cock made me jump, but all it took was one fast, slick stroke, and I forgot all about cold or warmth or anything other than how badly I needed to come. I gripped my cock tight and fucked my hand, grimacing and cursing, my eyes screwed shut and my toes curling and my back arching off the bed. It was mere seconds before I cried out and hot semen landed on my bare chest and abs.

I shuddered, exhaled, and relaxed. Eyes still closed, I just panted for a long moment. My entire body trembled. Aftershocks of my orgasm rippled through me. I never jerked off that fast. Never. Even if I just needed a quick release, I always drew it out for at least a minute or two. The wait was always worth it for a more intense orgasm.

Tonight? To hell with it. From the moment I'd kissed Alex, I'd been aroused out of my mind, and needed to do something about *now*. Another five minutes and I wouldn't have even bothered with the lube, which was a must for me when I was alone.

And even though my body was satisfied for the moment, my mind wasn't even close. I couldn't stop thinking about him. Had he been more experienced, more confident, I could only imagine the things we'd be doing right now. Right here in this bed.

Forget the bed. We probably wouldn't have made it this far. More than likely, I'd have dragged him into my apartment and shoved him up against the front door, and I'd have been on my knees so fast it would've made his head spin.

My mouth watered just thinking about it. He probably had no idea how badly I wanted to go down on him. I admittedly had a fetish for sucking cock. I loved it. Nothing in the world turned me on like using my mouth to turn a man inside out. God, I wondered what kinds of sounds Alex would make the first time someone—me, anyone—went down on him. I wondered if he'd be able to breathe. Just thinking about it, I could barely breathe myself.

After a few minutes, when the shaking had mostly stopped, I pulled a few tissues from the box on the nightstand and cleaned up. Then I went into the bathroom to grab a shower.

With a hand against the wall for balance, I closed my eyes and let the hot water rush over my neck and shoulders. My legs still shook, and even though my nerve endings still tingled from my orgasm, the lingering itch of desire remained. The ache was soothed for the time being, but it would take more than one round of quick-and-to-the-point jerking off to satisfy me.

I wondered if he'd done the same thing. He was turned on when we kissed, there was no denying that. Judging by the squeal of his tires when he pulled out of the Wilde's parking lot after dropping me off, he was in as much of a hurry to get home—or at least someplace more or less private—as I was.

It had been tempting to offer to take care of it right then and there in one of our cars. I'll stroke your cock, you stroke mine. Wasn't exactly a rare occurrence in the Wilde's parking lot. No one would have noticed.

But no, I didn't want to move that fast. With inexperience came skittishness. Even a handjob could be too much for someone as new to the game as Alex, and I didn't want to scare him off before I'd had a chance to show him everything he'd been missing.

Before I'd left to come back here, I'd briefly entertained the idea of going into Wilde's in search of a one night stand, or calling Rhett and Ethan. I already had someone for tonight, though, even if I *was* only fucking him in my mind.

Virgins weren't usually my thing, but Alex intrigued me. The thought of being the first to taste his skin was more of a turn-on than I thought it would be. Maybe because he was older than most guys were their first time. Naïve, yes, but mature.

And who was I kidding? Virgin or no, Alex turned me on. Where he lacked experience, he made up for it in spades with raw sex appeal. He had a mouth that was made for kissing, and he was aware enough of his own inexperience to let himself be guided.

It was impossible to know for sure just how much he was packing below the belt, but from what I'd felt earlier, he wouldn't disappoint when the clothes came off. And I hoped the clothes would come off. I had to know what he was like naked. I wanted to know what he sounded like when he came. Oh my God, I wanted to know what he tasted like when he came.

A shiver ran down my spine and…

Holy hell, I was already getting hard again.

I couldn't remember the last time a man had had this effect on me, arousing me to the point of insatiable distraction.

I wrapped my fingers around my cock. I pressed my other forearm against the wall. The surface was smooth instead of coarse but still reminded me of the cool brick wall on which I'd braced myself earlier tonight. The wall that had held us upright when a kiss tried to drive us to our knees.

Fuck, I wanted him. I wanted him bent over the nearest piece of furniture with my cock inside him. I wanted him standing over me while I tasted his cock. I wanted him out of his clothes, out of breath, out of his damned mind. I just fucking *wanted* him.

I had a million fantasies that I ached to live out with him, but only one parked itself in the forefront of my mind and kept my hand moving faster and faster on my painfully hard cock. Not the thought of grasping his hair while he went down on me. Not the thought of fucking him deep and hard and fast. Not even the thought of sucking him off.

Those fantasies were all there, and they all drove me insane, but it was his kiss that made my knees shake and my breath catch. Every thought took me right back to kissing him against that brick wall. I swore I could still taste his mouth, or feel his heartbeat against my lips, or smell the faint hints of coffee and that mouthwatering cologne that whispered his name to my senses.

I distantly heard myself groan. My knees buckled, and I slumped against the wall, still pumping my cock with my fist until my orgasm reached a point of painful intensity. I couldn't tell semen from water in my hand, and I didn't care because my senses were too busy pulsing with his name, his scent, his kiss, his touch.

Even as my orgasm peaked and fell, the room refused to stop spinning around me. I rested my shoulder against the wall, taking slow, deep breaths as my equilibrium took its sweet time coming back. A few times, I thought I might sink to my knees right there in the shower, but eventually my legs decided to hold me up.

I let my head fall forward so hot water rushed through my hair and over the back of my neck, and it was a wonder it didn't sizzle on my skin.

Twice in one night? Okay, that part wasn't unusual, but *that fast*? Damn, maybe it was just as well we hadn't jumped into bed yet. It would've been over too quickly, assuming either of us survived it.

The water started to cool, so I turned off the shower and got out. As I dried off, I caught my own reflection in the steamed up mirror. I wiped the condensation away, then leaned on the counter and met my own reflected eyes.

The cosmos is trusting you *with a virgin?*

I laughed to myself. Who would have thought? Someone like me? With someone who'd never even been kissed until an hour or two ago? Alex would probably pale at some of the stories I could tell. I was neither proud nor ashamed of being promiscuous. It was who I was, and I made no apologies for it. I liked sex, I'd had a lot of sex in my life, and I didn't bat an eye at things that would likely intimidate the hell out of Alex.

Yet I was the one the universe had seen fit to pin Alex against a wall and show him what another man's kiss tasted like.

The manwhore and the virgin.

Wow, this is crazy.

I thought of the way Alex had nearly recoiled when I'd put my arm on the wall beside him. *Wow.*

Not even touching him yet, just nearing him like no one had ever done. *This* is *crazy.*

My humor faded, and I held my own gaze again. *Really crazy.*

Releasing a long breath, I wondered if this was even a good idea. Hell if I knew the best way to guide someone into the world of physical intimacy. Of course I'd been a virgin at some point in my life, but that was a distant memory. Twelve years and a *lot* of men had come and gone since I was that nervously curious fifteen-year-old, and I'd never been afraid of what I was the way Alex's upbringing had forced him to be. How did I do this without scaring the kid half to death?

I exhaled again and turned away from the mirror to finish drying off.

How far this went and how fast had to be up to Alex. He was in control. Something told me he was as eager to shed his virginity as I was to help him do so, and I hoped that was more than just wishful thinking on my part. Hopefully it was also more than just wishful thinking that he wanted me to be the one to help him do this.

All I could do was see him again, let things happen how they would, and hope he trusted me enough to let me show him what he'd been missing.

You've gone twenty-one years without a man's touch, Alex. I promise you, it'll be worth the wait.

Chapter Six

I pulled up in front of the apartment building. With the engine idling, I double-checked the text message he sent me, making sure this was the correct place. It was, so I shifted into park.

I got out of the car and started across the parking lot, but since Alex was already on his way down the stairwell, I waited for him.

The sun was still up, so this was the first time I'd seen him in the daylight, and he wore it just as well as he wore the dimness of a club or the harshness of overhead streetlights. His dark hair contrasted sharply with his light skin, and those deep brown eyes—sparkling with everything from nerves to mischievousness as they met mine from across the parking lot—made my spine tingle. A smile fought its way onto his lips, like he was excited to see me but too shy to let it show.

Even more so than the day I met him, probably because I'd finally gotten to touch him, his body was absolutely mouthwatering. Broad in the shoulders, narrow in the waist, and wearing jeans and a white T-shirt like some men wore, well, nothing.

God. Alex. Want. *You don't even know.*

I cleared my throat as he crossed the last few feet between us. "Hey."

"Hey." His eyes lit up, but then his cheeks followed suit. He dropped his gaze, but made himself meet my eyes again. From excitement to nerves and back again in seconds.

He stopped a few feet from me, and we exchanged uncertain looks. With any other guy, a hello kiss would be in order. We'd already crossed that platonic line once. Then again, with any other guy, that first kiss would have segued into a night of fucking, so a kiss in the light of day would have been as tame and casual as a handshake.

With Alex? I just didn't know.

I nodded toward the car. "Shall we?"

"Yeah, sure." His shoulders dropped slightly as if he was thankful for the broken silence. Or at least thankful I'd broken it instead of waiting for him to do it.

Once we were in the car, I started the engine and glanced at Alex. "Hungry?"

"Very," he said as he buckled his seatbelt. "Got any place in mind?"

Yeah. Mine. I cleared my throat. "Um, not really. You in the mood for anything?"

We exchanged glances.

"Nothing in particular," he said quietly. "You?"

"I'm game for pretty much anything." *Any fucking thing, Alex. Just say the word.* It didn't help that he'd worn the same cologne, and now that we were in the car, the faint scent teased my senses with last night. One breath, and I could already taste his kiss. My nerve endings tingled with the same desperate need that had driven me to three orgasms before I could get to sleep last night. I gritted my teeth and tried not to white-knuckle the steering wheel as I pulled out of the parking lot. Restraint and I were *not* close friends.

"You like ethnic food?" he asked, and this time I was the one thankful for the broken silence.

"Some, yes."

"Indian?"

I wrinkled my nose. "Oh God, no."

He chuckled. "Not a curry fan?"

"No. Can't stand the stuff." I glanced at him. "What about Vietnamese?"

"Hmm, I like Vietnamese, but I'm pretty loyal to a place over in Fremont."

"No way in *hell* we're driving to Fremont at this time of night," I said. "There's a good one on Broadway, though."

"What about Thai?"

"Depends," I said. "You a one-star or a five-star man?"

Alex laughed. "Two-star. I like to actually taste my food, thank you."

"Yeah, me too. Just as long as you're not the five-star type."

"Don't like eating with someone who gets the hot stuff?"

"No, not if—" I cut myself off before I casually startled the hell out of him. Five minutes into this date or whatever it was, and I'd already almost mentioned my distaste for getting a blowjob from someone who'd eaten spicy food.

"Not if, what?" he asked.

"Not if," I paused, my mind racing for a slightly less explicit answer. "Not if he's sitting at the same table, no. That shit makes my eyes water even from a few feet away." *Good save, Frost. Good save.*

"Oh yeah, me too," he said. "So, you in the mood for Thai, then?"

I hesitated. Thai usually sounded great, but tonight? Meh. "Hmm, I don't know. Any other ideas?"

"You know the area better than I do."

I racked my brain for the list of restaurants I frequented. There were plenty on Broadway alone, which was where we were now, but I drew a blank.

The light up ahead turned red, and I slowed to a stop. "It's funny, I can usually think of half a dozen restaurants and just have to choose between them. Tonight?" I released a breath. "Can't think of anything."

"Maybe we..."

I glanced at Alex. "Hmm?"

He stared out the windshield. "We don't necessarily have to go *out*."

I looked at him again, and this time, our eyes met. He inclined his head. I raised my eyebrows. *Oh, you* do *mean what I think you mean.*

Glancing at the light, which was still red, I said, "My apartment's about six blocks that way." I gestured down the cross street.

"See?" He laughed shyly. "You thought of a place to go after all."

We looked at each other again. Alex swallowed hard. I couldn't be sure, but I thought he shrank back a bit in his seat. As he held my gaze, his eyebrows knitted together in an unmistakable look of "that's the most you're getting out of me, *please* do something with it."

I put on my right blinker.

Neither of us said a word between there and my apartment. I resisted the urge to tap my thumbs on the wheel or otherwise let him know I was so...what? Nervous? No. No way. I was Kieran Frost. I didn't get nervous, I got laid.

Still, I was jittery, struggling to subtly contain all this nervous energy—*no*, damn it, I was not nervous. If anyone was, it was my passenger.

I turned on my blinker again and started down another side street. Alex fidgeted, casually resting his elbow below the window and not-so-casually chewing his thumbnail. I felt for him. He probably had no idea what was going to happen, or even what he wanted to happen. Which meant he'd be following my lead as much as I needed to follow his.

No pressure or anything, Kieran.

Gulp.

I am not *nervous.*

I pulled into the parking lot and my usual space. My heart *wasn't* pounding like *I* was the one who'd never been with another man. Or like the man I'd masturbated to—repeatedly—last night was here, in my car, wearing that cologne and all but blatantly saying he wanted to go someplace private.

I played it as cool as I could. When I turned off the engine and he threw me a nervous glance, I returned a reassuring smile. After a second, his expression relaxed, though his shoulders were still tense and his forehead was still creased.

We got out of the car and walked in silence across the parking lot. On the way up the stairs, I surreptitiously checked out his ass in those snug jeans. What I wouldn't have given to have those jeans on my floor and those hips in my hands. Fishing my house key out of my pocket, I wondered if tonight was my lucky night, but I quickly reminded myself who I was dealing with.

Take it easy. Don't scare the poor kid.

I keyed us into my apartment and gestured for him to go in ahead of me. Once the door was closed behind me, habit had me reaching for the deadbolt, but I hesitated. I watched Alex looking around, taking in his surroundings, drawing and releasing a deep, nervous breath, and I decided against turning the deadbolt. There was nothing quite like the click of a lock to trigger some caged-animal fight-or-flight response. He was here because he wanted to be, and I didn't want to imply he couldn't also leave if he wanted to.

"You want something to drink?" I asked to break the ice.

He grinned, but his eyes hinted at the nerves he tried to hide. "You trying to get me drunk?"

I laughed. "I didn't say it had to be alcoholic."

Alex just smiled and put up a hand. "I'm okay, thanks."

"You sure?"

He nodded.

"If you change your mind, just say so." I set my wallet and keys on the end table.

"Will do." Alex looked around the room again, and his nerves once again showed themselves in the stiffness of his posture. He couldn't decide between folding his arms across his chest or hooking his thumbs in his pockets.

Because I lived in a shoebox-size studio apartment, we may as well have been in my bedroom even as we milled between the tiny kitchen and what passed for a living room. The bed was mere feet away, ready and waiting, and the occasional glances—which he probably didn't realize I noticed—made me wonder if the nearness of my bed unnerved or excited him.

"I guess we don't need to stand around, do we?" I forced a laugh. "Not many options in here, I'm afraid. Kitchen table, couch, or—" I hesitated.

"Your bed?" he asked, raising an eyebrow.

"It's an...option. Yes."

Amusement tugged at his lips, but then he dropped his gaze. "Jesus, I don't even know where to start with this. Whatever it is. I feel like such a stupid kid."

"No, you're just new to this game," I said. "No one expects you to know all the rules."

"That's encouraging," he said softly.

"You didn't know what was going on last night but seemed okay with where it went." *Right?*

"True. To be honest, the only thing I didn't like about last night—" He caught himself and bit his lip, still looking at the floor.

My heart jumped. "What didn't you like?"

Through his lashes, he met my eyes, and the corners of his mouth pulled up, turning his expression to something almost devilish. "Leaving."

I swallowed. "Yeah. Leaving." I managed to move enough air to chuckle. "That part sucked, didn't it?"

He nodded but didn't speak.

Pretending I was the cool and confident one, I said, "You know, we could always start where we left off last night."

He narrowed his eyes slightly in an unspoken request for clarification.

Holding his gaze, I started toward him. Just as I hoped he would, he took a step back. Then another. His back touched the wall, and his Adam's apple bobbed once, reminding me how badly I wanted to taste his neck again.

I put my hand on the wall, just above his shoulder. "Good place to start?"

His eyes flicked toward my arm, then back to my face, and some of the nervousness disappeared from his expression. "Very."

"That's what I thought." I slid my other arm around his waist, and—thank God for the wall holding us both up—kissed him.

His hands found my shoulders. Held on. Tighter. One arm went around me. Then the other. His fingers grasped the back of my shirt, and he pulled me closer to him. Between the wall and me, I had no idea how he could even breathe, but he did, every sharp release of warm air rushing across the side of my face.

I broke the kiss and looked at him. We were both out of breath, and for a fleeting second, the lust in his eyes matched the lust in me, but need surrendered to nerves. Fear. Maybe even a little embarrassment.

He broke eye contact and loosened, but didn't release, his grasp on my shirt. "Sorry, I'm just so..."

I ran my fingers through his hair. "You don't have to know what you're doing," I whispered. "I promise, you'll figure it out as you go." When he raised his eyes to meet mine, I added, "It's sex, not brain surgery."

More color bloomed in his cheeks. "I have the same amount of experience with both."

"Can't help you with the brain surgery part," I said. "But the rest? At the risk of sounding way too full of myself, you're in good hands."

Alex moistened his lips. "Somehow I don't doubt that." We both managed a soft, nervous laugh.

I stroked his hair. "Just tell me if I'm going too fast, okay?" I waited for him to nod, then leaned in a little closer. My lips almost touching his, I added, "*Am* I going too fast?"

"No." He shivered when his lip grazed mine.

"Am I going fast enough?" I kissed him lightly.

Against my lips, his curved into a grin. "Are you saying we can go faster than this?"

"Oh, Alex..." I bent and kissed his neck, pausing to inhale as much of that cologne as I could. "I've given a man an orgasm within twenty minutes of meeting him." The fingers on my back twitched, and his pulse quickened beneath my lips. "Another, I fucked within an hour." I dropped one last kiss on his neck, just above his collar, and raised my head so I could look him in the eye. "I assure you, we can go faster."

Alex gulped, his eyes widening and his brow knitting in true oh-shit fashion. "Maybe not *that* fast."

I kissed his mouth again. "Don't worry, we won't. I was just making a point." *Yeah, smart move. Made the point and scared the kid.* "We'll only go as fast as you're comfortable."

He nodded, relaxing a little.

"Come here." I took both his hands. Walking backward, I led him across the small room to my bed.

Alex balked, eyeing it warily.

I squeezed his hands. "Look at me," I whispered. When he did, I sat on the edge of the bed. "This isn't a point of no return. You're not committing to anything." I glanced at the vacant space beside me, then looked back at him and raised my eyebrows.

After a moment of weight-shifting hesitation, he joined me. I rested my hand on his leg, the other behind him on the mattress, and kissed his shoulder through his shirt. I inched closer to his collar. Alex fidgeted but didn't try to pull away, not even when I deliberately exhaled across his skin. Inhaling again, I paused, indulging in a dizzying moment with his intoxicating cologne.

I kissed the side of his neck and stopped again, giving us both a chance to savor the contact of lips on skin. His arm went around me, though there was a second of hesitation before he let his hand rest on my waist.

"You all right?" I whispered, my voice slurred with arousal.

"Mm-hmm." He shivered, tilting his head to the side and pressing his neck against me, inviting more kisses, more contact.

Following the curve of his neck, I kissed my way up to his jaw. He'd shaved recently, but there was just enough coarseness to abrade my lip and send a tremor through me.

I took my hand off his leg and reached for his face. With two fingertips on his chin, I turned his head toward me and leaned in like I was about to kiss him. I stopped, though, almost touching his lips but not, and we were both still. Breathing, touching, not moving.

Just as I'd hoped, he closed the distance and kissed me.

At first, his kiss was hungry and breathless, but then he backed off. Still deep, still passionate, but cautious. I combed my fingers through his hair, holding him closer and encouraging his tongue with the tip of mine. He didn't back off completely, though. A lack of confidence, not a lack of desire, so I didn't push him.

After a moment, Alex touched my face, and like a cat, I pressed against his fingertips. When he slid his hand from my cheek into my hair, I sucked in a breath through my nose. He closed his fingers around my hair, and though he didn't pull at all, it was enough to make me moan into his kiss.

It was also, apparently, enough of an advance to let his confidence creep back up. His kiss went from timid to curious, exploring my mouth with equal parts assertiveness and hesitation. I melted against him, pulling him closer to me.

Deeper and deeper, we kissed. Fingers combed through hair. Hands slid under clothing and met hot skin. Breath caught, goose bumps rose, and inhibitions fell. Only the occasional unsteadiness in his hands or hesitation in his kiss reminded me this was a nervous, inexperienced virgin. As far as my body was concerned, he was a deliciously unhurried lover, and I wanted him so bad it hurt.

I leaned back, tugging his shirt as I did. He took the hint and sank down to the bed beside me. Then, in a moment of boldness or maybe just an effort to get comfortable without realizing what he was doing, he got on top.

It had to be boldness, because as soon as he was over me, his kiss was hungrier, more aggressive. Not quite demanding, but not far from it.

All at once, he broke the kiss and sat up, sending a rush of panic through me.

“What’s wrong?” I asked.

“Nothing.” He pulled off his shirt and tossed it off the side of the bed, but before he could come back down, I stopped him with a hand on his chest.

“Wait.” I looked him up and down. We both sucked in sharp breaths as I ran my hands over his newly exposed skin.

He didn’t have a six-pack or anything like that, but his abs were beautifully flat, the muscles quivering beneath my fingertips. Starting just below his navel, a thin line of dark hair all but beckoned my fingers to follow it beneath his jeans to his cock. One look at the swell of his erection beneath his jeans made my mouth water.

All in due time.

I met his eyes. Arousal and nerves vied for dominance in his expression, from the way he slowly moistened his lips to the twin creases between his eyebrows. With a hand on the back of his neck, I drew him down to kiss me.

"Doing okay?" I whispered against his lips.

"Yeah, I'm—" He sucked in a ragged breath as my fingertips trailed up his back. "I like this."

"Good." I kissed him again, and we melted into each other. Somehow, one of us unbuttoned my shirt. We shifted again, and when his back landed softly on the comforter, I was on top. I sat up and shrugged off my shirt, but before I came down again, I whispered, "This all right?"

"Yeah," he breathed, tugging my shoulder to bring me back down.

"If you want to stop," I murmured, kissing his neck, "just say so."

"Please *don't* stop."

I laughed, biting my lip when my breath raised goose bumps on his skin.

I kissed my way down to his chest. Alex wriggled beneath me, startling and shivering every time my lips or breath met his skin. He'd never even known what it was like to have someone breathe on him. No one had ever breathed him in.

Closing my eyes, I drew in a deep breath of heat and cologne, and shivered. It took every bit of restraint I had—and I didn't have much—to remember he was new to this. No matter how much I desperately wanted him to put on a condom and fuck me, or let me put one on and fuck him, there was no way he was ready for that. *But when you are ready for that, Alex, Jesus Christ...*

For the sake of my own sanity, I pushed those thoughts to the back of my mind and focused on what I was doing now.

I held his nipple between my teeth and teased it with the tip of his tongue. He squirmed beneath me, grasping my hair and releasing sharp, uneven breaths.

I flicked my tongue across his nipple once more, then, one kiss at a time, started down the center of his chest. Every time my lips met the warmth of his skin, he gasped, and I barely kept from shivering again. I still couldn't believe *no one* had ever tasted or touched him this way. I was the only one in the world, the only man who'd ever felt his abs contract beneath a light kiss, or heard his helpless moan, or tasted the faint saltiness of his skin. I couldn't get enough of him. His kiss, his hands, his mouth, his skin. I wanted more.

Alex gasped as I trailed my fingers along his zipper, and I hesitated, remembering his lack of experience.

"This okay?" I asked.

He nodded.

"You sure?"

Another nod. He squirmed as I unbuttoned the top button of his jeans. I searched his face for signs of resistance, but he gave me none. I drew his zipper down as slowly as I could, half teasing, half giving him a chance to stop me.

He didn't stop me, though. Instead, he reached for his belt with trembling fingers. Once his zipper was down and his belt unbuckled, I hooked my fingers under his waistband, and he lifted his hips so I could pull his jeans and briefs out of the way. I tossed his clothes aside and leaned down to kiss him while I let my hand drift down his chest and abs. He trembled at my touch, but didn't try to pull back or push me away.

When I closed my fingers around his cock, he whimpered, and a low growl emerged from my throat. *Oh, the gods were kind to you, weren't they, Alex?*

My mouth watered as I stroked him slowly. Raising my head and meeting his eyes, I whispered, "Can I just say, it is a *crime* that no one has ever sucked this cock."

Alex moaned and squirmed, pushing his cock against my hand.

"And you should know," I whispered, kissing beneath his ear, "that's one of my favorite things in the world to do. Just say the word, Alex, and I will."

"Yes," he breathed. "Please, yes."

I didn't hesitate.

As soon as my lips made contact with him, his back arched off the bed, but the moan of delirious ecstasy was mine. If he hadn't believed me when I'd said this was my favorite thing in the world, I was sure he did now. I explored every inch of his cock, from base to head, licking, teasing, stroking, sucking. *Fuck,* there was nothing in the world hotter than going down on a man, except, I discovered just then, maybe going down on one who'd never experienced it before.

His gasps and whimpers weren't just of arousal, but wonder, the sounds of a man who'd never felt a tongue tease the head of his cock, or lips slide almost all the way down to the base and back up. He'd have sounded like that and trembled like that with whatever man had been the first, and just my luck, that man was me. For now, maybe only for tonight, I was the only one in the world ever to taste him like this.

And I couldn't get enough of him. I rested my weight on one arm and stroked him with my free hand, moving my mouth in time with my strokes, faster and faster, and the more he came unglued, the more I thought I would come myself. The first hint of salty pre-come drove me insane, and I gave him everything I had, stroking and sucking him, teasing him with my hand and my tongue.

"Holy shit, Kieran..." He gasped. "Oh God...oh my God..." A tremor shook him from head to toe and lifted his back off the bed again. A heartbeat later, semen rushed over my tongue, and the helpless, breathless, disbelieving cry he released drove a whimper out of me.

I sat back, wiping the corner of my mouth with the back of my hand. His arm was draped over his eyes, hands shaking and lips parted as he took deep, rapid breaths.

"You okay?" I asked with a grin.

"Yeah." He lifted his arm off his eyes and exhaled. "I think so."

I cocked my head. "You think so?"

"Yeah, I'm good." Alex swallowed. He met my eyes but quickly shifted his gaze to the ceiling. He licked his lips. Then he gulped, and I barely heard the added whisper of, "I think."

Chapter Seven

I stepped off the treadmill and picked up my towel. Wiping sweat from my face and neck, I was only distantly aware of the fatigue in my legs. Lifting the towel and, subsequently, my water bottle, took a little extra effort. My upper body workout had been a brutal one, and my muscles felt like chewing gum held together with twine. Didn't really feel that either, though.

My body was here, finishing up one of my usual routines, but my mind was a million miles away. A mile or so away, anyway. In my apartment. Last night. The only ache I was acutely aware of was that knot of guilt just below my ribcage.

Cursing under my breath, I took my towel and water bottle, and went downstairs to take a shower in the bathroom between the bedrooms that, two years ago, had been mine and Rhett's.

He and Ethan let me use their workout equipment, which saved me from having to pay for a gym membership. I suspected it was also because they liked it when I was conveniently getting out of the shower right about the time one or both of them got home from work. That timing was, of course, deliberate on my part. Probably theirs too.

Tonight, I was too distracted to pay attention to the clock. I was lucky I could keep track of my workout, and I was pretty sure by the end that I'd done a few extra reps here and missed a set or two there.

All I could think about was last night, last night, last night.

The very thought of sucking Alex's cock raised goose bumps beneath the water that rushed down my shoulders and back. What we'd done was hot, but was it a mistake?

I exhaled and absently tried to rub the soreness out of my arms. Caught up in the heat of the moment last night, I'd gone down on him like I'd have gone down on any other man when we were too turned on to slow down. Desperate, hungry, hellbent on making him come, instead of making sure he not only enjoyed every minute but *experienced* every minute. I dove right in—well, down—instead of easing him into it.

It wasn't like I'd forced him, or he'd reluctantly let me do it against his will. He consented, and he liked it. Afterward, though, as the dust had settled and we'd come back to somewhat more rational states of mind, the uncertainty had crept in. Lying in bed together, we'd talked, but it was just small talk. Something to pass the time until someone could come up with a way to draw the night to a close. Eventually we had, and I'd taken him back to his apartment. There, we'd parted with a kiss and a murmured goodbye, but not much eye contact.

Now I worried I'd rushed him into and through something he may not have been ready for. He'd enjoyed it in the moment, but did he regret it in hindsight?

Did I have any business thinking I could guide him into this without doing more harm than good? I admittedly lacked restraint, and he had neither the experience nor confidence to know where boundaries were, let alone how to enforce them.

I sighed and turned off the water. We needed to talk, and soon, but I'd be damned if I knew how to start that conversation. Or get through it. Or finish it.

When I got out, the house was still empty and quiet, the halls echoing with the creak of the hardwood floor beneath my feet. About the time I'd gone in to refill my water bottle, though, Rhett came home. He walked into the kitchen and kissed me lightly.

"Good workout?" he asked.

"As always," I said. "That new triceps thing you showed me is kicking my ass, though."

"Good. That's what it's supposed to do."

"Yeah, but damn." I stretched my arms gingerly. "It's a good thing I'm not working tonight, or I'd probably drop a bottle."

"Assuming you could lift it to begin with," he said, snickering.

"Ass."

He laughed. "You'll get used to it."

"So you say," I said into my water bottle. "By the way, sorry I bailed on you guys the other night."

"Oh, it's okay. Ethan had some tequila, and you know what that means."

"Ugh, I'm jealous."

He pulled a bottle of water out of the refrigerator. "Don't tell me you didn't have a good time."

"I did, but...Ethan? Tequila?" I whimpered. "Want!"

"Believe me, I know." He sighed wistfully as he unscrewed the cap on his drink. "And he was in *rare* form, so—"

"Fuck you."

Rhett hoisted himself onto the counter and took a drink. "So, how was the party, anyway? I assume you didn't have too much difficulty being around a bunch of twenty-somethings?"

I forced a laugh. “No, definitely not.” I stared at the tiles beneath my feet. “It was fun.”

“It was fun, but…?”

“That kid Sabrina wanted me to meet?” I sighed. “He’s hot. Oh my God, Rhett, he’s gorgeous. And…he’s a virgin.”

Rhett chuckled into his water bottle. “Not for long, with you around.”

I laughed again, this time with even less feeling. “Yeah, about that…”

His humor faded. “What’s wrong?”

“We, um, clicked. So we’ve done some fooling around.” I exhaled, rubbing my forehead with two fingers. “The thing is, I think I might’ve gone too fast for him.”

Rhett’s eyes widened. “How far did it go?”

I shifted my weight. “I sucked him off,” I said with a shrug. “That’s it. And that’s not a big deal for me, but I mean, up until the other night? He’d never even been kissed. By a male *or* female. I haven’t been with someone this inexperienced in my life, and I…” Shaking my head, I leaned against the kitchen island and exhaled. “I don’t know how to do this without overwhelming him.”

Rhett blew out a breath. “Yeah, I can understand that.”

“I think he wants to try everything, but how do I keep from going too fast?”

“Let him set the pace, I guess.”

“Yeah, the problem with that is I think he’s deferring to me.” I watched my fingers spin my bottle cap on the granite counter. “He has zero experience, no idea where to start, and I don’t know how far is too far. To be honest, I’m afraid I’ll get carried away and say ‘grab a condom and let’s go’ while he’s still getting used to the idea of being naked with another man.”

"Sounds like restraint's the name of the game here," Rhett said. "On your part more than his."

"I know. And you know me and restraint."

"Yes, I do," he said quietly. "By the way, if you're with this kid, do you want to back off with us?"

I shook my head. "He's not after a relationship, and neither am I." *Which is another thing I need to talk to him about, damn it.*

"Good." Rhett smiled. "I don't know if we're ready to give you up yet."

I managed to laugh and actually feel it. "You're not going to get territorial, are you?"

"Maybe..."

"Great. Just what I need. You, Ethan and Alex fighting over me."

"You could always see if he's up for a foursome or—"

"Rhett!" I stared at him. "Jesus, here I am worried about moving too fast with him, and you're talking group sex?"

He laughed. "Well, the poor kid's made it to twenty-one without doing anything. Needs to make up for lost time."

I raised an eyebrow. "I think you've been around Ethan too long."

"You're probably right." He winked, sending a tingle up my spine.

"Jesus, between the three of you," I said, "I'm probably going to end up hospitalized before long."

"Oh, come on." Rhett gestured with his water bottle. "Well, you and I haven't crippled Ethan yet. A young, strapping lad like you can handle three guys, don't you think?"

I pursed my lips. "You know, I wouldn't be opposed to trying three guys."

"At the same time?"

"Why not?"

He shook his head. "Somehow that doesn't surprise me."

"I don't think Alex would be game for that, though."

"Not yet, anyway."

"Let me try getting him into bed with one guy before I broach the subject of an orgy, if you don't mind." The knot of guilt below my ribs pulled tighter, and with decidedly less humor, I added, "Assuming that much isn't too much for him."

Before Rhett could comment, the rumble of the garage-door opener turned both our heads. A moment later, Ethan appeared.

"Oh, hey, Kieran." He kissed me quickly, then took off his jacket.

"Hey, what about me?" Rhett said.

"I'm getting there." Ethan draped his jacket over the back of a chair, then hooked a finger under his tie to loosen it. "Just wanted to get comfortable first." With that taken care of, he went to where his man sat on the counter. He put his hands on Rhett's hips and kissed him. "Better?"

"Hmm," Rhett said, "maybe one more. To be sure."

Ethan said something I couldn't hear and kissed him again. Looking at them now, no one would ever guess there was a time they couldn't stand the sight of each other. Then again, I doubted many people would look at the three of us and guess just how intimately acquainted we all were.

Once they'd finished saying hello, Ethan turned around and leaned against the counter between Rhett's knees. Rhett wrapped his arms around Ethan, and Ethan put his hands over Rhett's.

Nuzzling Ethan's neck, Rhett said, "Did you hear Kieran's got a virgin on his hands?"

Ethan released a sharp bark of laughter. "You're kidding."

I shook my head. "Nope. One of Sabrina's friends."

Ethan eyed me. "He *is* legal, right?"

"Yes, yes, he's legal. He's twenty-one."

"And he's a virgin?"

I nodded.

"Wow. Our delightfully shameless little slut, being trusted with a virgin?" Ethan snickered. "Oh Lord, what is this world coming to?"

"Ha, ha, very funny," I said.

"Can't imagine that'll last long, though," Ethan said. "I'd think just being in the same room with you would negate his virginity."

"He's got a point," Rhett said.

"Yeah. I mean, look at us." Ethan gestured at Rhett and himself. "Before you came along, we'd never done any of—"

"Bullshit," I coughed into my fist.

They both shot me a glare.

Then Ethan shrugged. "It could certainly be an experience for you. After all, you might get to boldly go where no man has—"

Rhett and I cut him off with a simultaneous groan.

I shook my head. "Let's not jump the gun here. I...don't even know if I should do this."

More serious now, Ethan said, "Well, does he want to?"

"I think so." I chewed my lip. "I just don't know if he even knows what he wants or what he's ready for."

"What does he say he wants?" he asked. "To get laid? A steady lover? A boyfriend?"

"Not a boyfriend," I said. "I don't think so, anyway. And I don't think he's all sentimental about it or anything. Doesn't need the first time to be 'special' and romantic or whatever. But I don't want it to be a *bad* experience."

Rhett eyed me. "I don't think it's possible for you and 'bad experience' to exist in the same bed."

"Seconded," Ethan said. "To be serious, I think he's lucky because you know what you're doing. My first time, Jesus Christ, we—"

"Ethan, do you even remember your first time?" Rhett asked.

Ethan glared at him over his shoulder. "Of course I do. Hard to forget losing your virginity in the back of a covered wagon." He elbowed Rhett playfully and muttered something profane under his breath. Rhett kissed his cheek, and they both laughed before Ethan continued. "Anyway, neither of us knew what we were doing. It was just as well it didn't last very long, because we were both too clueless to know it wouldn't hurt as much if we took our time and used more lube."

"Mine wasn't much better," Rhett said. "My very first time was with a girl, and we were both so clueless, we actually had to read the instructions on the condom wrapper. Twice." He paused. "First time with a guy, though, he had *way* more experience than me, and he had neither the time nor inclination to hold my hand and ease me through it all." He rolled his eyes, and added with a hint of bitterness, "It was every man for himself, and only one knew what he was doing."

"The thing is," Ethan said. "You're not a selfish lover, Kieran. You never have been. Err on the side of moving too slow, listen to his cues, and do everything you can to make sure he's enjoying all the things you do anyway."

"And if he regrets it afterward?" I asked.

"Then he regrets it," Ethan said. "And he might. If he thinks he's ready but figures out after the fact that he wasn't, there isn't much you can do."

Rhett nodded. "But if he is going to regret it, it's better that he doesn't also have a painful, awkward memory."

"Exactly," Ethan said. "Just guide him the best you can, make it the best experience you can make it, and let him decide how he feels about it. Trust his cues and your instincts."

"That's about all you can do," Rhett said. "The rest is up to him. Inexperienced or not, he *is* an adult. You can't be expected to be one hundred percent responsible for how he feels, or if he's absolutely certain if he's ready for something."

"Good point." Ethan put his hand on Rhett's knee as he went on. "And all joking aside, he could do a lot worse than being with you, Kieran. You've got an opportunity to keep Alex from going through what we all went through."

"Exactly," Rhett said. "It's not like it's a rite of passage to lose your virginity in a painful, awkward way."

"And if it is," Ethan said, "it shouldn't be. If Alex can avoid what we've all experienced...great."

"*If* he can avoid it," I muttered.

"He's with someone who knows his way around the bedroom *and* gives a shit about him," Rhett said. "I don't think an awkward, disappointing experience is in his future with you involved."

I laughed softly. "Glad you guys have so much faith in me."

"We know you," Ethan said. "You can't control how he'll feel about it afterward, but you can make sure he doesn't feel used. Make it about him. Like it actually matters to you how he feels."

"That goes a long way," Rhett said. "That was the worst part about my first time with a guy. He didn't care. Afterward, I didn't regret having sex, but I did regret doing it with him. I felt like I was half sex toy, half annoyance for him, and it wasn't a pleasant feeling. Honestly, if I hadn't already been with a girl, the experience might've put me off sex with either gender for a long time."

Normally, a comment like that would have been Ethan's cue to make a joke about "that'll be the day" or "not in this lifetime", but he just squeezed Rhett's hand. He must have known just how much that experience bothered Rhett, and that gave me chills. Having had a similar experience, I could relate, and my stomach turned at the thought of Alex feeling that way about me down the line.

Or, I realized, the thought of him feeling that way about me *right now*. After last night.

Ethan's voice drew me back to the present. "And, one other thing to keep in mind, I think the first time is bound to be overwhelming for anyone, even if you're taking it slow."

"He's got a point," Rhett said.

"I understand what you're saying," I said. "But there's being overwhelmed because it's a new experience, and there's being overwhelmed because you're not ready for it, you know? Or because the person you're with doesn't have an ounce of restraint and gets carried away."

"Kieran," Ethan said, "for all we tease you about being a slut, you're hardly the type who's going to take advantage of someone or push him into something he doesn't want to do.

Even if you did push him out of his comfort zone, wouldn't you retreat at the first sign it was too much?"

"Of course," I said. "In theory."

They both eyed me, silently asking for clarification.

I sighed. "Last night, he was fine with it. Totally into it. It wasn't until afterward that he had *what the fuck did I just do* written all over him."

"Okay," Ethan said. "So you take a step back and work back up to that point."

"It might be two steps forward and three back for a while," Rhett said. "But this isn't something you can't get him past."

"Exactly." Ethan leaned back against Rhett, putting his hand over Rhett's again. "Okay, things went too far last night. It's not the end of the world."

Rhett nodded. "The very fact that you're concerned about it says a lot."

"True," I said. "And I am concerned about it. Really concerned. I don't want to screw this up for him. I haven't been someone's first in a long, long time."

Ethan shrugged, absently running his hand back and forth along Rhett's wrist. "Just take it slow with him. I mean, he's already got an advantage over most guys in his position, simply because you have experience. Way better than having him fumble through it with someone else who's equally clueless."

"When in doubt," Rhett said, "talk to him." He glanced at Ethan and hugged him a little tighter. "I don't think we need to tell you how much it sucks to learn the hard way that you're not communicating enough with someone."

"No, you definitely don't," I said.

"You seeing him tonight?" Ethan asked.

I shook my head. "He's working a late shift. Probably tomorrow, though."

"Talk to him, then," Rhett said. "Get on the same page and go from there. The sooner the better."

"Good idea." I played with the cap on my water bottle. "I'll call him later on, see what he wants to do tomorrow."

"Well, if he has a brain his head," Ethan said with a smirk, "I think I know what he'll want to do tomorrow."

I laughed, my cheeks burning. "Yeah, we'll see about that. One thing at a time so I don't scare him off."

"Oh, I don't think you'll scare him off." Ethan's voice dipped to that sexy growl that drove me so fucking crazy. "Kill him, maybe. But not scare him off."

"Or raise the bar impossibly high for every guy after you," Rhett said.

"Well," I said with a grin, "if he's going to have standards, they may as well be high ones."

"Very true." Ethan eyed me, then exchanged glances with Rhett. "So, is this thing with Alex"—Ethan raised an eyebrow—"exclusive?"

"No, no, God, no." I snorted. "Since when have I ever bowed to the gods of monogamy?"

Rhett laughed. "Heaven help any one man who has to keep *you* satisfied on his own."

"Yeah, really," Ethan said.

"So, if you're not exclusive," Rhett said, "and you're not seeing him tonight…" He let the slight tilt of his head finish the thought.

"What are you doing tonight?" Ethan asked.

"I don't know." I sipped my water. "You tell me."

"You know," Ethan said. "All this talk of sex and virginity is making me thirsty." His eyes narrowed just enough to give me goose bumps. "I think I could go for some tequila."

I shivered.

Chapter Eight

The next night, I met Alex at the music store where he worked. On the phone, we'd agreed to go to a coffee shop on Broadway, not far from the place we'd had coffee the first night, and since he'd walked to work, I offered to pick him up.

We made eye contact as he slid into the passenger seat but exchanged little more than halfhearted hellos.

I gestured at the music store. "How do you like working here?" It was conversation, at least.

"Eh, it's retail." He buckled his seat belt. "Could be worse."

"There isn't much worse than retail, is there?"

"Well, no," he said. "But music sales aren't too bad. Though I would rather work in a bookstore."

"Would you?"

He nodded. "Employee discount would be so much more useful."

"So you're a reader, then?"

"Oh, yeah. I always have my nose in a book when I'm alone." He gestured at the store. "But this isn't bad. At least working here, I can get music at a discount, which is nice, since I need it while I study."

"Ugh, I could never listen to anything while I studied. Annoyed the fuck out of me."

"I can't concentrate without it." He paused. "And with as much studying as I have to do, I get bored with the music I have."

"So the employee discount at the music store is pretty convenient after all."

"It is," he said. "But you haven't seen how many books I can buy in a single go."

I glanced at him, and we both forced laughs, which gave away the tension we'd managed to ignore for a minute or so. It didn't want to be ignored now. The rest of the way to the coffee shop, we made small talk. Stilted, pause-riddled small talk, and the whole way, there was an undeniable undercurrent of something unsaid.

Come on, Kieran. Just say it. Clear the air and be done with it.

Right. Because I was so good at any conversation that didn't include asking someone's preferred drink or position.

At least the walk from the car to the coffee shop gave us other things to hang our small talk on. Some political slogans on a sign. A display of some exotic foods in a window. A dog on a leash that was somehow...not right. Neither of us could put our finger on it, but there was something weird about that dog.

Something weird that kept our conversation going until we were ready to order our drinks, had our drinks, and were sitting at a corner table with our drinks.

I sipped my coffee and grimaced. "Damn, this shit's bitter."

"What did you expect?" he said, chuckling. "It's espresso."

"Yes, I know," I said. "I'm just not used to it being quite so bitter *and* weak at the same time."

He rolled his eyes and laughed without enthusiasm. "Is everyone in Seattle a coffee snob?"

"I prefer 'connoisseur', and yes, it's a requirement for living here." I leaned closer and lowered my voice. "Helps me blend in with the locals."

Another halfhearted laugh with half-second eye contact.

I looked into my coffee cup. I wasn't great at conversations like this, but the only thing more awkward than the conversation we needed to have was the awkwardness preceding it. Might as well just bite the bullet.

I took a breath. "Listen, about the other night. I..." I paused, trying and failing to ignore the way my heart pounded. "I got carried away. I didn't mean for things to go that fast, it was just..."

"It's okay," Alex said. "It's not like I was telling you to stop. And"—he paused, and I couldn't be sure, but I swore he blushed as he added—"I liked it."

"I know you did, but..." I held his gaze. "Was it too much, too fast?"

He avoided my eyes.

I leaned forward and folded my arms on the edge of the table. "I'm new to this too, you know. I'm used to guys who are experienced, which is not at all a slam on you. Being inexperienced isn't a bad thing, I'm just..." I hesitated. "I'm not a hundred percent sure how to do this without it being too much for you. So, I need to know." When he looked up, the uncertainty in his eyes made me add, "Tell me honestly, Alex. You won't hurt my feelings. Was the other night too much?"

He swallowed hard. After a moment, he released a breath and nodded. "A little, yeah."

Though his admission justified my guilty conscience, the honesty let me relax.

"I'm sorry about that," I said. "I never meant to push you."

Alex made a dismissive gesture. "You didn't push me. Really, it's okay. I'm not upset or anything."

"Do you want to keep doing this?"

"Yeah," he said. "I mean, I think I do."

"You think so?"

"I'm..." Alex rubbed the bridge of his nose with his thumb and forefinger. "In theory, I want to do everything and I want to do it all now. In practice, I still want it. In hindsight, it feels like too much, too fast, and I...just don't know what I should do."

"Do you want to stop?"

"No, not at all. Just not sure how fast I should go."

"Then let's slow down." I put my hand over his. "I'm not in this to rush you or overwhelm you. You're calling the shots here."

He sighed. "That's the thing. Like I said that first night, I don't...I don't even know where to start. When I say I'm a virgin, I mean it in every sense of the word. I've never even seen another guy naked." He paused. "Well, not completely naked, at least, after the other night. In the showers at school, I got really good at staring at my own feet, never even looked at anyone else, because I was afraid the second I laid eyes on a guy, even accidentally, everyone would know I was gay."

"Let me ask you this," I said. "What do you *want* to try?"

"The short answer is everything." He shifted a little. "But I'm more nervous about some things than others."

I tilted my head slightly. "Such as?"

His cheeks colored a little, and he struggled to hold my gaze as he whispered, "Anal, for one."

"Most people are a little nervous about that at first," I said. "You don't have to do it, though. It's not a requirement."

"It isn't?"

I shook my head. "Of course not. You don't have to do anything. And besides, depending who you ask, the real rite of passage for a gay man is giving his first blowjob."

"Maybe so," he said. "But that's not the part that makes me nervous. Not *as* nervous."

"So, anal makes you nervous, but you want to try it?"

"Um, eventually. Yeah." He swallowed hard. "It doesn't...does it hurt?"

"If it does, someone's doing something wrong. Or going too fast."

"Really?"

I nodded. "Just requires some patience. You go slow. Don't just put on a condom, throw down some lube, and go for it."

He cocked his head. "What exactly do you do, then?"

"Some swear by the five-step program." I held up my hand and wiggled my fingers.

His eyes widened. "Seriously?"

"Yep. Start small, work your way up." I grinned. "Or find a guy with a really small dick."

"I'm guessing you're not that guy?"

"Afraid not."

He clicked his tongue and shook his head. "Damn the luck."

We both laughed.

Then, more seriously, I said, "You know, maybe there's a different approach we can take. Instead of putting you on the spot and having you call the shots when you're still learning the game."

"What do you mean?"

"I'm thinking the way we did it the other night, before I kissed you," I said. "Let me make the moves and the suggestions. If you don't like something, or you're just not ready for it, say so." I squeezed his hand. "You're never going to upset or insult me by saying something isn't for you."

"And if I want to suggest something?"

"By all means, suggest it," I said. "It's a safe bet that whatever you come up with, unless it involves flamethrowers or holy ground, I've done it."

He laughed. "Really?"

Chuckling, I nodded. "There honestly isn't much I haven't done. I think the socially acceptable phrase is I've been around the block a few times." I scratched the back of my neck and casually added, "Most people just say I'm a slut."

"And that doesn't bother you?"

"People can call me whatever they want." I picked up my coffee cup. "I'm not ashamed of it."

Alex sighed. "I envy you."

"For being a slut or for not being ashamed of it?"

He blushed, looking into his own mostly empty coffee cup. "Both. Trust me, my lack of experience isn't because of any lack of desire."

"I can only imagine. But it was a smart move to keep things quiet until you were in a safer environment. Sexual frustration sucks, but it's not worth some of the hell you might have caught."

"Oh, you have no idea. I consider myself very fortunate to have made it to adulthood with nothing worse than some serious sexual frustration and a bad case of tennis elbow."

"Well, now we get to make up for lost time," I said. "And you've come to the right place for that."

"Seattle?" He inclined his head. "Or you?"

"Both." I smiled. "And, you know, with some things, if you're not totally comfortable experimenting with another person, you can always try a few things on your own. With toys, that sort of thing."

"Toys?"

"Yeah, you know. Toys. Dildos. Things like that."

Blushing, he glanced around the coffee shop, then dropped his voice to a self-conscious whisper. "I guess I always thought…um…toys were more for women."

"Depending on who you ask, the same could be said for cocks," I said. "But as far as I'm concerned, what's good for the goose…"

Alex laughed. "Hadn't thought of it that way."

"Welcome to Kieran's dirty, dirty world." I paused. "In fact, I want to take you somewhere."

His spine straightened. "Where?"

"Do you trust me?"

"I…yes."

"Then come on. I think you'll find this educational."

We finished our coffee and left the shop. On the way up Broadway, after a few blocks, the red-and-yellow sign for Wilde's came into view.

"You taking me in here to teach me how to pick up guys?" Alex asked.

I put my hand on the small of his back. "No. We're not going into the club. Where we're going is for you and you *alone*." My emphasis on the last word furrowed his brow, but he didn't ask.

Two blocks later, I stopped.

"Ah, this is the place." I gestured at the bright pink neon sign above the Oh Zone.

Alex's lips parted. "We're going in…here?"

"Well, yeah." I shrugged. "They don't exactly sell this stuff at Walmart."

Swallowing hard, he looked at the display window. "Stuff?"

"Yep. I'll show you." I started toward the door, but Alex planted his feet.

"Kieran…"

I stepped back and took his hand. "Ten minutes. If you want to leave after that, we will. But give it a chance."

His eyes darted from the store to me and back again. Finally, he sighed. "Okay. Ten minutes."

"Ten minutes." I set my watch. "There. When that beeps, we're out of here if you want to go."

Alex nodded but didn't say anything. I led him into the store. When we stopped again, I gave Alex a moment to look around.

For me, this place was as natural and benign an environment as a grocery store. Totally comfortable, totally normal, and I was probably as familiar with the merchandise and its placement as the staff. Quite possibly more so. Put me in this or any sex shop in Seattle and I was like a bloodhound. I could find anything in minutes. Ethan had even tested the theory, coming in here with a stopwatch and a list of twelve items. Nipple clamps, a porn DVD featuring a particular actor, watermelon-flavored condoms, a bunch of other crap. I found everything in seven minutes flat.

Alex, however, was another story. His eyes were as big as the cock rings on the display beside him. He slowly scanned the store—all the way to the left, all the way to the right, back again—and gulped as he took in his surroundings. I followed the same trajectory, trying to imagine how it all appeared to someone as uncorrupted as Alex. By the time I'd set foot in a place like this for the first time, I'd had several lovers and watched plenty of porn. Alex…hadn't.

It didn't help that the sales staff either got really bored at times or were just insanely creative about displaying merchandise. Blowup dolls were arranged along the tops of shelves or suspended from the ceiling, most in hilariously compromising positions. One male doll had toys crammed into every available orifice, plus cock rings around his limbs, probably to emphasize the appearance of muscles. On his head, someone had fastened a bright pink strap-on. Not far from him, an O-mouthed female doll with a set of plastic Yoda ears on her head stood opposite another doll wearing a Darth Vader mask, and they were frozen in a duel with a pair of three-foot dildos.

All around the store were numerous flyers announcing specials, sales, visits from porn stars, things like that. I wondered if Alex noticed the papers were all held in place by stainless steel nipple clamps.

I couldn't be sure, but I thought he muttered something about not being in Kansas anymore.

Of course, it didn't help that the place also had its sections devoted to ridiculous novelties for bachelor parties and such. Last Christmas, I'd bought a giant penis-shaped Jell-O mold for Rhett and Ethan. For my birthday, they'd given me a cock-and-balls ice cube tray.

That was me, though. This all fit my sense of humor perfectly. What a way to put an inexperienced guy at ease: shelves full of plastic penises and weird stuff that was obviously intended for practical jokes instead of practical use. Not to mention plenty of practical stuff that looked like it should have been for novelty use.

Forget Kansas, Alex. You're not even in Oz anymore.

"So, what do you think?" I asked.

Alex he dropped his gaze like he was mortified I'd even acknowledged him in here. He cleared his throat. "Well, I can see how this is different than Walmart."

"Very much so."

He muffled a cough. "So, you wanted to show me something?" He looked at me with a *help me* expression on his face.

I grinned. "Yes, I want to show you everything."

His jaw fell open. "What?"

"Come on." I gestured for him to come with me. I was afraid he'd dig his heels in again, but after only a second's hesitation, he followed.

We wandered past a couple of racks of novelty crap, then the infamous Wall of Dildos, which we'd get to later. One thing at a time. For starters, I wanted to show him—

Alex's shoe squeaked on the floor as he stopped in his tracks. "What the fuck is *that*?"

"That is..." I stared at the thing, boggling at the thought of how many laws of physics would need to be bent in order to get it where it was supposed to go, never mind getting it there *comfortably*. "That is the biggest butt plug I've ever seen in my life."

"Wait." Alex looked at it, then at me. "That thing is meant to go in someone's *ass*?"

Still staring at it, I nodded. "In theory, yes. I'm going to tell myself it's only meant to be a conversation piece, though."

"I assume you've never used one?"

"Not that big, no." I gave it one last look, then shuddered and kept walking. "You watch much porn?"

"I've never watched any."

I looked at him. "You're kidding."

He shook his head.

"You're telling me you've *never* watched porn?" I said. "Never?"

He raised an eyebrow. "Kieran, I told you what my hometown was like. You think I wanted to take the chance of someone finding out I'd ever looked at gay porn?"

"Hmm. Good point." I nodded toward the rack. "Well, you're in luck. There's plenty to choose from here. You can find pretty much anything."

"You don't say," he murmured, regarding the rows of magazines and DVDs like they might bite him.

"Have a look," I said.

Alex glanced over his shoulder, then swept a look around the store again, eyeing the whole place warily as if an angry mob lurked around the corner, waiting to break out the torches and pitchforks the second he touched a copy of *Cocks and Rubbers.* I couldn't be sure, but I thought his face lost some color.

I put a hand on his arm, and he jumped.

"Don't be so nervous," I said. "No one's going to stare at you or even notice you."

He chewed his lip.

"Alex, anyone in this store is here for the same reason we are, and if they're going to stare at anything, it'll be"—I pointed at the gargantuan butt plug—"that."

"Can't imagine why," he said, throwing a wide-eyed glance in the same direction.

I laughed. "See? So, you have nothing to worry about."

He swallowed hard, then exhaled and relaxed. A little. Turning his attention back to the DVDs in front of him, he said, "I never thought there'd be quite so much...variety."

"If you can imagine it, it's here," I said.

He picked up a DVD and flipped it over to look at the back. Sucking in a breath, he cringed. "Okay, that just looks painful."

"What?"

He handed me the DVD.

I glanced at it and shrugged. "If he's a porn star, he's probably taken bigger cocks than that." *Hell, I've taken—*

"No, I didn't mean that," Alex said. "I mean unless his hips are double-jointed..."

I looked again, closer this time, and winced. "Oh, yeah, you're right. That doesn't look comfortable."

"Neither does this." He held up another.

I grinned. "You wouldn't think so, but believe it or not, having someone pull your hair like that? It's *awesome*."

He raised an eyebrow. "What?"

"Trust me."

He looked at the DVD again, then shook his head and put it back. "Next you're going to tell me people get off on being smacked around."

I picked up another video and cleared my throat.

Alex looked at it. His jaw fell open.

I chuckled. "You'd be amazed at the things that get some people off."

"Yeah," he said, still staring at the DVD. "So I'm gathering." Shaking his head, he looked at the rack again. "I think I'll stick to the less violent stuff for now."

"Sounds like a plan."

As we looked through the broad selection, my phone vibrated. I wasn't at all surprised to see my mother's name on the caller ID, since it had been a couple of days since we'd had one of our lengthy discussions. I let this call go to voice mail. I wasn't in the mood for a guilt trip. That, and I wasn't going to leave Alex alone in this place while I stepped out to take the call, and even as casual and laidback as I was, even I couldn't talk to my mom while browsing dildos and porn.

Alex and I migrated from the videos to the shelves of books and magazines.

"Well," I said. "You did say you like books."

"So, erotica, that sort of thing, I take it?"

"Yep."

He turned around, glancing at another shelf. "Wait, they have non-fiction too?"

"Yeah. How-to books, stuff like that. You want to get off?" I nodded toward the rack of porn. "Shop over there. Want to learn something?" Another nod, this time toward the bookshelves. "Over there."

"Self-help sex books," he said. "Huh. Interesting."

"Basically, it's 'Kieran in a book'."

Alex laughed. "Guess I don't need to peruse that section, then, do I?'

"You're welcome to if you want to."

"No, I'm okay." A devilish grin spread across his lips. "Why would I need Kieran in a book when I have Kieran in my bed?"

I winked. "You're a fast learner. Now let's go check out some of the other fun stuff."

"Such as?"

"Well, anything catch your eye?"

Alex looked up at the dildo-saber dueling blowup dolls, then gave me a pointed look. "No. Nothing in this place catches my eye. Just the same boring everyday stuff I see at Walmart."

"Smartass," I muttered. "Now follow me."

A moment later, Alex was face-to-face with the infamous Wall of Dildos. Before today, he'd probably never even seen a sex toy, and I could only imagine what went through his mind as he looked at a wall covered, from floor to ceiling, end to end, with vibrators, dildos, butt plugs, "massagers", and strange self-love devices that baffled even me. Tapered, textured, flared, ribbed, cock-shaped, bullet-shaped; there was something for everyone. And every orifice.

He shifted his weight, eyes still focused on the Wall. "So, that's one way to figure out if you, you know..."

"If you like anal?"

"Yeah. That." He blinked a few times, shaking his head as if in disbelief that yes, all those plastic, silicone, metal, gel, and God-only-knew-what-material phallic toys were still there. "So, um, do you shop in this section?"

"From time to time." I glanced at him. "I prefer the real thing these days."

"Not surprised," he said quietly. "How do you even know which one to get?"

"Try one. If you want something bigger, smaller, straighter, more curved, whatever, then get another. They're pricey, but they're worth it."

He gulped. "Any recommendations?"

"In terms of shape, the closer to—" A beep cut me off. I looked at my watch, then back at him. "That's ten minutes. Stay or go?"

He smiled. “Oh, I think I can handle staying.”

Chuckling, I turned off the stopwatch. “I knew you’d see things my way. Anyway, as I was saying, when it comes to shape, the closer to an actual cock, the better.” I gestured at some of the bizarre creations lining the wall. “Unless you’re turned on by the thought of putting a molded plastic cartoon character up your ass.”

Alex’s eyes widened again. “Pardon?”

“I suppose I should have warned you about one side effect of this shop.” I pulled a particular toy off the rack and held it up. “You may never look at the cartoon characters from your childhood in the same light again.”

“What…in the name of…”

“Crazy, isn’t it?” I shook my head. “I actually know a guy who owns one of these. Don’t ask me why.” I put it back on the rack.

Alex blinked. “Uh. I’ll pass.” He cleared his throat. “Okay, so we’ve narrowed down shape. What about”—he scanned the various implements—“size?”

“I’d start out with something smaller than an actual cock,” I said. “Probably don’t want to jump right to something like that.” I pointed at a dildo that couldn’t possibly have been intended for actual use. Not without subsequent medical attention, anyway.

“No, I think I’ll skip the battering-ram-sized toys, thanks.”

“Good plan.” I looked over the Wall myself, trying to think if there was anything else I should point out to him. “Oh, and vibrators? That’s more for women. Some guys might use them, I don’t know, but…” I shrugged. “I’m after the shape and size, not feeling like I have an angry bee in—”

Alex snorted with laughter. "You really have a way with words, Kieran."

"I'm just saying."

"Uh-huh." He pulled one off the rack and looked at the price. His lips parted. "Damn, these things are expensive."

"Yeah, but they're worth it. Trust me."

He swallowed. "So, what happens if I get a sort of small one, but then decide I want something a bit closer to...um...life-sized?"

I lowered my voice. "Well, by that point, you might be ready for something that isn't just cock-*sized*."

Our eyes met. Fear flickered across his expression.

"When you're ready, Alex," I said. "And not a moment sooner. If and when we get to that point, it'll be your decision, not mine."

He nodded, and some tension in his shoulders eased.

"Honestly, though, it's not nearly as big of a deal as you might think." I put a reassuring hand on his arm. "Start small, go slow, lots of lube, you'll be fine." I moved my hand to his back and leaned in so I was almost whispering in his ear. "The first time you come while you're playing with one of those, you'll wonder why you ever thought twice about using one."

"It makes that much of a difference?"

"Oh, yeah." I whistled. "I suppose you're not familiar with the male G-spot?"

"The what?"

"Well, 'prostate' just doesn't sound as sexy."

Alex blinked. "You're...kidding."

"Not in the least. The most intense orgasms I've ever had have been while another guy was fucking me, and it's all because of that."

Alex looked at the toy in his hand again, and as he hung it back on the rack, muttered, "The things you don't learn in Anatomy and Physiology."

"I think they save that one for Gross Anatomy."

Our eyes met again, and we both collapsed into laughter.

After we'd regained some semblance of maturity, I took his hand and led him to another section. "Let's have a look at one of the essentials."

"I'm almost afraid to ask," he said, but he let me lead him anyway.

"Lube. You can never have too much lube." I made a sweeping gesture at the enormous rack of bottles and tubes. They were mostly clear, though some were brightly colored, and had names like Liquid Orgasm and Slidey-Glidey.

"Okay, finally, something that makes sense." He picked up a bright red bottle. "Wait. *Flavored* lube?"

I grinned. "Oh, yeah, that stuff is fun."

"Seems like you wouldn't need lube with oral."

"You don't *need* a lot of things," I said. "Doesn't mean they aren't fun to play with."

"So, what's the point of it?"

"Well, if you want to go from a handjob to a blowjob"—I nodded at the bottle in his hand—"cough syrup cherry is a bit more pleasing to the palate than something that tastes like axle grease."

He grimaced. "That bad?"

"Dude, normal lube is awful." I picked up a tube of Slick 'N Strawberry. "This stuff isn't exactly Grandma's home cooking, but it beats the hell out of the alternative."

"Not sure I'd want to be licking Grandma's home cooking off your cock, thank you."

I laughed but shivered at the same time. Leaning closer, I said, "You can lick anything you want off my cock. Just name the time and place."

"I'll keep that in mind."

"Good," I said. "So, anyway, almost everything in this store is just for fun, but the condoms and lube? Those are essentials."

He bit his lip. "I was going to ask about that, actually."

"What?"

"Condoms." He cleared his throat. "I mean, I kind of assumed most people used them, but..."

"If you're worried about putting me or anyone else on the spot when it comes to condoms, don't be." I laced his fingers between mine, pretending not to notice the dampness of his palm. "Anyone who gets pissy or defensive about it isn't someone you want to be sleeping with anyway." I led him to the nearby rack of condoms. "And yes, I use them. Every time, every guy."

"Duly noted," he said quietly.

"And don't ever let a guy talk you out of using one," I said. "Not unless you're strictly monogamous and you've both been tested within an inch of your lives for everything under the sun."

We looked at each other, and the eye contact lingered for one, two, three seconds before he dropped his gaze and I muffled a cough.

He nodded toward the condom display. "So, must everything sexual have four billion options and varieties?"

"It's pretty easy to narrow these down, don't worry." I put an arm around his waist, just because I damn well felt like touching him. "Some are just gag gifts and stuff, I think. Like the glow-in-the-dark ones."

"I could think of a few practical purposes for those," he said, snickering as he absently put his hand over mine on his side. "In case you drop one or something."

"Well, okay, if you're the type to have sex in the dark."

He raised an eyebrow. "I suppose I don't even need to ask if you prefer to have the lights on."

"Absolutely." I kissed his cheek, then whispered, "If I'm going to work that hard to give someone an orgasm, I want to see the results of my handiwork, you know?"

Alex shivered. Shifting his weight, he gestured at the condoms again. "So, which ones are useful?"

"Normal, run-of-the-mill condoms," I said. "Ribbed are more for women, I think. They never did a damned thing for me or any guy I know. Flavored only applies if we're using them for oral, which we're not. And these"—I indicated a row of French ticklers or whatever the fuck they were called—"are just latex sea anemones."

"Oh, what a turn-on."

"Yeah, no kidding. If I wanted to fuck a jellyfish, I'd go to the beach."

Laughter from the next aisle over turned our heads. Alex's cheeks colored, and even mine burned a little. I looked at him with a sheepish expression, shrugged and tried not to laugh out loud myself. Apparently other people did still exist in the universe. Who knew?

"Anyway," I said. "Basic condoms. Nothing fancy. Can't go wrong."

He blew out a breath. "You know, I just can't get over how matter-of-fact you are about all of this."

"I'm comfortable with it all," I said. "You'll get there. The thing is, like I said earlier, anyone who's in this store is here for the same reason we are, so they aren't going to judge us. And if someone's got the time or energy to give a rat's ass about what toys or condoms or porn we buy, well, they have no life."

"True." He fidgeted, scanning the various brands of condoms. "What do other guys think of this stuff? I mean, do other guys get upset if you have porn, or toys, whatever?"

"If they do, they don't spend much time in my bed."

Alex pursed his lips but said nothing.

I moved my hand to the small of his back. "Alex, if someone gives you hell about any aspect of your sexuality, never mind how you explore it, they don't belong in your bed. If he criticizes you, makes fun of you, whatever, he has no business laying a hand on you." I reached up and gently turned his face so we made eye contact, then kissed him. "Listen, I've had enough bad experiences. I have no patience for anyone who's willing to make me feel bad about my good experiences, whether I had them alone, with someone else, or with a piece of plastic and a magazine."

Alex nodded slowly. "Makes sense." Then he looked around the store. "So, anyway, I definitely didn't realize there were so many, um, options."

"That's the beauty of sex." I moved my hand back to his waist so my arm was around him again. "The options are endless."

"So I'm learning. I could see how someone could unload a small fortune in this place."

"You have no idea." I chuckled. "With the amount of money I've dropped here, the owner's probably gotten himself a private jet."

He laughed. "Frequent buyer?"

"Very much so. I mean, it's not like toys and stuff are just for beginners or even one-on-one."

"Really?"

"Absolutely. One guy and I used to use toys all the time."

"Together?"

"Oh, yeah. Sometimes he'd use one on me, talk dirty to me, get me all wound up, and then after I came, I'd go down on him." I shivered at the memory. Sebastian, a toy and a bottle of lube was always a recipe for one long, incredible night. "*God*, it was hot."

Alex regarded me silently for a moment. "You really do like oral, don't you?"

"Very much so."

"I never thought...giving...would be that much of a turn-on."

"It is. I mean, when you can have a guy that spun up, damn near crying because of what you're doing to him? What could possibly be more arousing?"

Alex shivered this time.

"Trust me," I said. "It's one of those things that doesn't sound fun, but after you actually try it, you may very well like it."

"That seems to be a bit of a common theme here."

"Oh, it is. Sex is like food: try it, you might like it."

He laughed. "I'll remember that."

"So, anyway." I gestured at our surroundings. "That's the store. You want to get anything?"

I thought he might shake his head and start inching toward the door. Apparently Alex was pretty hell-bent on coming out of his shell, more so than I thought, so it shouldn't have surprised me when he cast another sweeping look around the store, or that that look was decidedly more at ease than when he'd first come through the door.

After a moment, he said, "That flavored lube could be fun."

Oh, you have no idea, lad…

"Flavored lube it is." We went back to that section and found one I'd tried before. I was all for experimenting but for the time being went with one whose taste I could vouch for. After all, the only thing worse than unflavored lube was *badly* flavored lube.

On the way to the register, I reached for my wallet, but he got his out first.

"I can get this," he said.

"You sure?"

"Yeah," he said. "I've got it."

"Okay," I said with a shrug. "I'll get the next one."

Our eyes met.

His said, *The next one?*

I narrowed mine slightly, hoping he heard, loud and clear, the unspoken, *Oh, yes. The next one.*

Swallowing hard, he looked at the bottle in his hand, then me.

"Shall we?" I asked.

He nodded but didn't say anything as we started toward the checkout line.

He was a little nervous with the cashier, blushing and avoiding eye contact, but he didn't hesitate or seem to have second thoughts. Maybe he just wanted to get over some fear of buying something in a place like this. A lot of people got jittery the first time they put something sexual on the counter. Buying condoms at the pharmacy was one thing. Buying flavored lube in a sex shop admitted to a willingness to get marginally more kinky than just having sex.

After money was exchanged, the cashier slipped the bottle into a plain paper bag. At least this place didn't use those unmarked black plastic bags that *screamed* "I just bought something naughty!" I wasn't sure Alex could stomach that. I just didn't tell him the Oh Zone was the only store within a six-block radius that used plain brown bags.

Nondescript bag in hand, we went outside.

"So, with that out of the way," I said, "what do you want to do now?"

Alex pursed his lips. He looked at the bag in his hand, then at me through his lashes. "We could always go back to my place."

I reached for his other hand. "I think I like that idea."

Chapter Nine

As much as our conversation had emphasized slowing down, Alex's trip through the Oh Zone had left him too wound up and horny to go *too* slow.

For that matter, watching him take that trip through that place had had the same effect on me. I couldn't help myself. Imagining myself licking that flavor of lube off his cock? Or picturing the look on his face the first time he found out just how good a toy could feel? A hard-on was a foregone conclusion. A hard-on, a stumbling-kissing-stumbling climb up the stairs, and a hell of a lot of whispered, breathless swearing on both our parts because his front door insisted on being *much* too far from the car.

The plain brown paper bag landed on the bed. Our shirts landed at our feet. Standing beside the bed, we kissed hungrily, running hands over bare skin and through hair.

He reached for my belt, and I jumped.

"I thought you wanted to slow down," I said, panting against his lips.

"I do," he said. "But this is ground we've already covered, so..."

"How much further do you want to go?" I sucked in a breath as my belt went slack.

"I'll let you know," he murmured against my lips, "when we get there."

"I just don't want"—I closed my eyes as his hand followed my loosened belt around to my back—"I don't want to push you."

"You're not."

"Would it be going too far to suggest getting out of these clothes, then?"

Alex swallowed. "No. Not at all. The sooner the better, I think."

We separated to strip out of our clothes, and I surreptitiously watched his body language, searching for shaking hands or any other sign that his boldness was just an attempt to cover a lack of confidence. Nothing. Not a thing. Maybe the home field advantage helped; we were in his territory tonight. One less unfamiliar thing to throw him off.

With clothes out of the way, Alex stopped. He gave me the slowest down-up look, and while it might have made even me self-conscious under normal circumstances, he'd never seen another man undressed before. I'd stripped to the waist in bed the other night, but that was as far as I'd gone. So, if he wanted to take a moment just to look, I wasn't going to stop him.

The upward slide of his gaze eventually reached my eyes, and we stared at each other for a moment. Then he reached for me. I reached for him. Skin to skin, we kissed, running hands up and down uncovered flesh.

Breathless and lost in each other, we somehow—hell if I knew how—went from standing to lying in bed together. He rolled onto his back, and when I got on top, the heat of his skin touching mine made me dizzy. There wasn't a stitch of clothing between us, and I sank against him to close what little distance remained. When my cock brushed his, we both moaned.

In a heartbeat, though, Alex's kiss went from bold to timid. His hands weren't as assertive. He shrank away from me as much as he could with the mattress beneath him.

Shit. I pushed myself up to give him some breathing room, but his uncertainty held fast.

Maybe having me on top was too much. Putting him on top also had the potential to overwhelm him; instead of being pinned down and implicitly at my mercy, the pressure would be on him to wield more control than he was probably comfortable with.

I rolled onto my side and encouraged him to do the same. Lying like this, on more or less level ground, he inched back out of his shell. Kisses deepened at his whim. His tongue explored my mouth and his hands made more firm contact with my skin.

Our hands gradually ventured farther down. I teased his nipple with my thumb. His fingertips drifted down my arm. My palm traced his waist to his hip. He put his hand on my hip, but stopped there.

We'd covered this ground up to this point but had gone no farther.

Grasping his wrist, I guided his hand between us. My heart pounded. When the backs of his fingers brushed the underside of my cock, we both gasped.

"This okay?" I whispered, barely breathing.

Nodding, Alex sought my mouth. I let go of his wrist and draped my arm over him while he parted my lips with his tongue. Just as I'd hoped, his hand stayed put. He might have been distracted by the deepening, breathtaking kiss—God knew I was—and may have forgotten his hand was there at all. I didn't know.

All I did know was his kiss. It occupied all of my senses, distracted me from anything and everything until, after only a moment's hesitation, he wrapped his fingers around my cock. My breath caught. So did his.

He stroked slowly, letting that warm, featherlight contact drift all the way up, down, up again. I resisted the urge to tell him how to do it, instead letting him get a feel for it on his own. It wasn't like he'd do something painful or anything. He'd touched at least one cock in his life and had probably done enough trial and error to know a few things that didn't work.

And, my God, he'd obviously learned a few things that *did* work. He tried stroking a little faster. A little slower. Gripping tighter. Loosening. Maybe I was just aroused to the point of delirium, maybe he had a fucking magic touch, but every stroke made my head spin.

He tightened his grip and stroked faster, and though the friction wasn't enough to be unpleasant, it could get that way very quickly. I put a hand on his wrist, and he stopped.

"Here." I reached for the plain brown paper bag beside us. "Something for you to try." I pulled the bottle out and unscrewed the cap.

Alex shot me an amused look. "This something you learned from those how-to books?"

"No, I didn't read any of those." I chuckled as I peeled back the safety seal. "I went to the school of hard cocks."

Alex groaned and rolled his eyes.

Laughing, I said, "Seriously, I just learned by trial and error." With the safety seal out of the way, I screwed the cap back on. "Give me your hand."

He held out his hand, palm flat, and I poured some of the lube into it.

While I did, he said, "So you just, try things? See what happens?"

"Mm-hmm." I closed the bottle top and put it aside.

"And if someone doesn't like it?"

I shrugged. "Try something else." I leaned forward and kissed him, guiding his hand back down. "Experiment. Do what you know you like—" I sucked in a hiss of breath as cool lube touched my skin and Alex's warm fingers closed around my cock. "Do what you think I'll like, and see what happens." I paused for another kiss. "Oh, and when it comes to blowjobs? Don't use your teeth. Otherwise, pretty much anything goes."

Alex laughed shyly. "I'll remember that when, um, we get to that point. For now..." He tightened his grasp. Stroking slowly, he brought a groan to my lips.

"Is this...am I doing this right?" he asked.

I nodded. "Fuck, yeah. And remember what I said. Experiment a little. Try different—" I shivered when he loosened, tightened, loosened his grasp. "Different things." I closed my eyes. "Ooh, yeah, just... God, yes...."

"Makes that much of a difference?" he asked. "The lube, I mean?"

"You tell me." I picked up the bottle again, and this time poured some into my own hand.

His strokes faltered as he watched me reach between us. My touch, and probably the coolness of the lube, made him tense, but the moan came the first time my hand slid easily up and down his cock.

His lips parted. "Oh...Jesus..."

For a while, he followed my lead. I went a little faster. So did he. I slowed down, he slowed down. My grasp loosened, his—

His *tightened*, sending a surge of electricity straight up my spine.

"Like that?" he asked with just enough of a lilt to tell me he knew damn well I fucking loved it.

"Yes, I do," I breathed.

Alex moved his hand faster, his slick, rapid strokes making my toes curl, so I quickened my own strokes.

He stopped for more lube. I slowed my hand so he could concentrate on getting the bottle open. After he'd poured some more in his hand, he put the bottle aside, and when he reached for my cock, both my hand and heart sped up.

"Oh, my God..." I tightened my grasp on his cock, and his low groan drowned out any sound I might have made.

"Just like that," he breathed. He screwed his eyes shut, and whether it was a conscious thing or not, his hips moved in time with my strokes, forcing his lubricated cock into my fist. "Jesus, Kieran, don't stop..."

"I won't." My lips grazed his as I spoke. "Not until you come."

He whimpered softly, and what was left of his hand's rhythm fell apart. "Fuck..."

"You want me to make you come?" I murmured. "Just like this?"

Another whimper, this time an obvious, desperate affirmative. His hand left my cock and grabbed my shoulder, slippery fingers searching for some sort of hold before finally settling on the back my neck.

"Come for me," I whispered, touching my forehead to his. "Don't hold back."

"I'm not, I'm...oh God..." A sharp, cool breath rushed across my lips and his curling fingers slipped across my skin. "Don't stop, please, please don't..." His voice fell to the most spine-tingling moan. A violent shudder went through him. His fingers dug into my neck, his hips thrust against my hand, and with a breathless moan, he surrendered.

Then he was still. I stopped my hand and slowly, carefully, released him. His grip on the back of my neck kept me from drawing back, so I too was still, letting him come down from his orgasm.

Finally, his fingers eased their hold on my neck, and he lifted his hand off so I could reach for the tissues on the nightstand.

Alex eyed his hand, then looked at me with an apologetic expression. "Sorry, didn't mean to get lube all over you." He glanced at the tissue in my hand as I wiped semen off my abs. His cheeks colored.

"Don't worry about it," I said. "We'll just take a shower later." I winked. "When we're done."

He glanced down at my cock, which was still quite hard, and bit his lip. I was about to suggest he didn't have to do any more than he already had, that he was welcome to keep doing what he'd already been doing and nothing more.

Then he met my eyes again, and the fierce determination in his silenced me.

"Could you..." He nodded toward the pillow. "On your back?"

"Um, yeah, sure." I finished cleaning myself off, then did as he asked, silently wondering just what he had in mind.

He leaned over me and kissed me lightly. "We did get flavored lube for a reason, didn't we?"

Oh God, yes. I swallowed hard. "Yes, we did."

"Then, maybe we should use it?" He grinned, but there was uncertainty in his eyes and in the creases between his eyebrows. Still, he bent to kiss my neck, and with each kiss, inched lower. My cock ached with anticipation, but Alex had to want this. Really want this.

"Alex, you don't have to do this," I whispered in spite of my body screaming at me to shut the fuck up.

"I want to." He kissed just above my navel.

I swallowed. "Are you sure?"

"I'll find out in a minute, won't I?" The playfulness in his voice didn't quite cover up the uncertainty.

"If you aren't into it," I whispered, "you can stop. It's okay."

"Noted," he murmured against my skin and continued moving down.

Down.

Oh God.

Down.

His lips made a soft, warm path over my hipbone, and my fingers curled around the comforter as he inched closer and closer to my cock.

Oh God.

He pushed himself up on one arm. With his other hand, he stroked me slowly, and I sucked in a breath as his palm and fingers slid deliciously over my skin.

Then...oh, Jesus Christ, then he went down on me.

His mouth was timid but curious, and his lips and tongue explored every inch of my cock. I wanted to guide him, but I let my responses speak for themselves, and God bless him, he hung on my every moan. When a flick of his tongue lifted my spine off the bed, he did it again. Again. Again. Then he moved on to something else before coming back and doing it again.

I was so turned on, I probably could have come just *thinking* about him sucking me off, but his uncertain, adventurous lips definitely held their own, and I had to grit my teeth to hold myself back.

Supporting himself on one arm, he held my cock in his other hand and slowly took me deeper in his mouth. Then he'd rise, pause, and come down again, a little deeper each time. I held my breath, willing myself to stay perfectly still. Wouldn't do either of us any good if I moved suddenly and accidentally choked him.

He took me even deeper and backed off suddenly. He hesitated, then tried again.

"Don't push yourself," I said before he'd gone too far down.

"Hmm?" He looked up at me.

"What you're doing, it's perfect," I said. "You don't have to force your gag reflex." I licked my lips. "That thing you were doing before, it was—fuck, yeah, *that*..." I moaned and squirmed under him. "Use your...use your hand."

He wrapped his fingers around my cock.

"Like that, yeah. Hand and mouth...together..."

I couldn't articulate it any better than that, but he got the message. He stopped to put more lube on his hand, then went down on me again. His hand slid down my cock, and his lips followed. Up, down, up. Up, down, up. Holy fuck, he was good. He was really good. Holy fucking...up, down, up.

"Just like that," I breathed. Tears stung my eyes. My back arched off the bed, and my hands flew up to grab the headboard. Again and again, he stroked my cock, both hand and mouth sliding down and up until I was on the brink of the total oblivion. Somehow, God only knew how, I found the presence of mind to remember he'd never done this before and might not be prepared for me to come in his mouth.

"Alex, I'm..."

His tongue. Sweet Jesus, he knew how to use his tongue.

"Fuck...oh, fuck, that's perfect," I moaned. "If you keep...if you keep doing that, I'm..."

He didn't back off at all. His hand gripped tighter and moved faster. His tongue circled and fluttered and flicked with more insistence.

"Alex, I'm..." My back arched. "I'm gonna fucking come, oh, fuck..."

If he wanted to stop, now was the time, but he didn't stop and I couldn't hold back and my fingers tightened around the headboard slats and with a breathless moan, I surrendered. He kept going for a few strokes but then stopped. He sat back, coughing, and when my vision cleared, I looked at him.

Panting, I asked, "You okay?"

He nodded and cleared his throat, his eyes watering a little. "Yeah, I'm fine. Didn't quite know what to expect."

"You could have asked."

Alex licked his lips and leaned toward me. "That would have been a bit of a mood killer, don't you think?"

"Killing the mood beats the hell out of choking, doesn't it?"

"Didn't kill my mood, and I didn't choke to death. I'm not bitching." He kissed me. His mouth was salty with semen and vaguely sweet from the cherry-flavored lube. I still couldn't believe he'd actually gone that far, taken that step. Tasting was believing, though, and I grasped his hair and sought every hint of my own orgasm on his tongue.

Finally I broke the kiss. Still breathing hard, I said, "Your mouth is...amazing."

He laughed shyly. "Beginner's luck?"

"Something like that," I said, chuckling. "Whatever it was, it was awesome."

"Glad you enjoyed it." He kissed me again. "So did I."

Eventually, we pried ourselves out of each other's arms and out of bed, grabbed a quick shower, and collapsed right back into bed. He rested his head on my chest and I lazily draped my arm around him, running my fingers through his damp hair. Finally, I could relax, with the need for an orgasm sated and my guilty conscience appeased. Yeah, maybe I went a little fast for him the first night, but tonight, he was all adventure and assertiveness, and I couldn't *wait* until he was ready to take things even further.

For now, though, I was content the way we were. Just lying together in bed, our hair still wet and my elbow still aching. We'd long since caught our breath and come down from the stratosphere. Now, we were just comfortable.

And...intimate.

A chill wandered through my veins. This was just the kind of comfortable intimacy that could tip the scales in favor of taking this too far in a different direction than the one we'd discussed awkwardly over coffee. A direction I had absolutely no desire to take.

I'd had relationships before, but aside from Chris, my last serious boyfriend, I'd never expected much out of them. Sebastian and I had been exclusive, but it wasn't out of any need to be territorial. We just liked fucking each other so much that we didn't have time to go looking for anyone else anyway. Sex was one thing, but love and relationships weren't for me.

Alex had told me the other night he was intimidated by the idea of figuring out sex and love at the same time. He'd said that, but intimidating or not, it was easy for the line between sex and love to blur. Before we went any further, I needed him to know that line could not blur. Not with me.

"Kieran?"

I jumped at the sound of my name. "Sorry, what?"

He laughed softly. "You were spacing out."

"Just thinking." I shifted onto my side so I could face him. Combing my fingers through his hair, I said, "Listen, before we take this any further, I want to make sure we're on the same page about...what we're doing."

A mix of curiosity and alarm widened his eyes slightly. "Okay..."

"I just want to make sure we have the same expectations." I took a breath. "I am *not* relationship material. I'm just, I'm not. So, whatever we're doing beyond being friends, I just need to make sure you know up front that it's purely physical." I paused. "You're free to date or sleep with anyone you want, and so am I."

For a moment, he said nothing, but then he nodded. "I can live with that."

"Are you sure? I mean, we can take this as far you want, physically," I said. "But the emotional stuff, I can't."

Alex shrugged. "I'm not looking for any of that right now anyway."

"Not right now, no," I said. "But when you do..." I gestured at myself. "I'm not the place to look."

He laughed. "Point taken. Somehow I don't think that'll be an issue." He paused, then quickly added, "Not that I wouldn't be attracted to you that way, I'm just not...not in that state of mind either."

I smiled. "Sounds like we're on the same wavelength."

"Yeah, sounds like we are." He watched his fingers trail along my arm. "So, tell me about some of the things you've done. You're obviously more experienced than I am, so..."

"Are you accusing me of being a slut?"

He straightened a little, eyes widening and cheeks darkening. "Um..."

I laughed. "Just kidding. I wear that title proudly."

"You would," he said, rolling his eyes. "I'm just curious. Call it living vicariously through you."

My face burned. Not embarrassment over anything I'd done—I was far too shameless for that—I was just a little on the spot. "I'm not really sure where to start."

"Well, you said you've had a threesome or two before, haven't you?"

I nodded. "A few, yes."

"So, are they as great as everyone says?" he asked. "I hear guys at school making it sound like two girls at once is the holy grail of all things sexual. Is the same true with two other guys?"

"*Oh* yeah," I said. "There's just something incredibly hot about fucking one guy while another is fucking you."

"Wow." His eyes took on a distant look, and I guessed he was trying to imagine the dynamics of three-way sex.

"It's hot, trust me."

"How does something like that even get started? I mean, how do you..."

"How do you get from being three clothed guys to three naked guys?"

"Yeah. That."

"Depends on the situation, I guess. First time I ever had one, my boyfriend and I both had a crush on a mutual friend. He and I talked it over, and then we approached our friend to see if he was game. Next thing you knew, clothes off, condoms on."

Alex laughed. "Wow. I can't even imagine."

"Honestly, I had no idea what to expect." I absently trailed my fingers down his arm. "It was completely foreign territory for me." I blew out a breath. "Probably should've stayed that way too."

"Why's that?"

"My boyfriend and I weren't in a great place at that point," I said. "The fact that we were both attracted to this guy to the point of distraction should have been a red flag, but we thought it would be fun. Maybe bring us closer together or some stupid shit like that."

"I'm guessing it didn't work that way?"

I shook my head. "Chris and I broke up for other reasons a few months later." Through my teeth, I added, "And they moved in together about six months after that."

"Sounds like three-ways and that sort of thing aren't a great idea, then."

"Oh, they can be," I said. "As long as everyone is open and honest from the get-go and don't act like possessive assholes or cheaters." There was more bitterness in my voice than I'd intended. I cleared my throat. "I've actually had a long-running thing with a couple that's worked out just fine."

"Define a 'thing'."

"We started when they were separated. They..." I paused, unsure how to explain it without tipping my hand about who my fuck buddies were. "Well, let's just say I had a casual thing going with each of them. And they both knew about it, so it was all cool. One thing led to another, we all ended up in bed together, and it just went from there."

"And you guys are still doing this?"

"Off and on. Things got a little rough in the beginning because of some jealousy issues, with them being split up and all. We admittedly all made some mistakes getting started, but once the two of them ironed their problems out, and we figured out what we all wanted out of it, everything was fine. They're back together, happy as can be, and sometimes, for fun..." I shrugged with one shoulder.

Alex furrowed his brow. "Wait, you're not talking about Sabrina's dad and stepdad, are you?"

My blood turned cold, and I stared at him with wide eyes. "What?"

"You said you lived with them when you moved up here," he said. "And she told me you were their roommate when they were split up." He raised his eyebrow.

I laughed. "Can't get anything past you, can I?"

"So, you really were—*are*—with them?"

"Casually, yes." I chewed my lip. "But please, don't say anything to Sabrina. It's not that we're trying to hide it from her out of shame or anything, but—"

"But what girl needs or wants to know about her parents' sex life?"

"Precisely."

Alex shook his head. "I wouldn't tell her. It's not my place to say anything about it, and, yeah, if I were in her shoes, I wouldn't want to know either." Then he shot me a mischievous look. "Suddenly I don't feel so bad about developing a penchant for older men."

"Older men?" I scoffed. "I've only got, what, six years on you?"

"Well, you *are* older than me."

"Not by that much." Under my breath, I muttered, "Older men. Hmph."

Alex snickered. “I guess that means all the girls aren’t blowing smoke when they say Sabrina’s dads are hot. I thought they were just doing it to fuck with her.”

“Oh, *no,*” I said. “Rhett and Ethan are smoking hot. Both of them.”

“Is that right?”

“Yes. In fact…” I reached for my jeans on the floor. I pulled my phone off my belt and sat up, thumbing through a few photos. Finally, I found the one I wanted. I’d snapped it at a baseball game while the two of them were focused on the game below, and it was a decent shot of both of them in profile. I handed him the phone. “See for yourself.”

“Oh, wow. And you’ve been with both of them?”

“Yep.”

“At the same time?”

“At the same time.”

“Damn.” He whistled and shook his head. “Seems like every gay man’s fantasy.”

“You have *no* idea.”

“No, no, I certainly don’t.” He chuckled and looked at the picture again. “Sabrina’s biological father is the one on the right?”

I nodded.

“I can definitely see the resemblance.” He handed the phone back. “So, they’re back together, but you guys still sleep together?”

“Sometimes.”

“Interesting.” He paused. “What else have you done? I hope I’m not prying; I’m just curious about what I’ve been missing.”

"It's fine, don't worry about it." I smiled. "So, what have I done? What haven't I done?" Ticking points off on my fingers, I said, "Sex on the beach, Mile High Club, ex sex, S & M. Never been with a woman, though."

"Ever wanted to?"

I shook my head. "Not really. I'm a 'try anything once' kind of guy, but I really don't see myself ever being intimate with a woman."

"Ever had any bad experiences?"

"Plenty," I said. "Hilarious, clueless, awkward, painful, embarrassing, you name it." I hesitated, wondering if I should tell him about some of the experiences that still had left my skin crawling. No, I decided, that could wait. Not here, not now. "I think the most embarrassing ever was getting caught by my dad."

Alex's jaw dropped. "Your dad caught you?"

I nodded. "I was seventeen, and my boyfriend and I lost track of time." I turned on my side and propped myself up on my elbow. "We'd been dumb enough to fool around in the living room, and Dad came home." I chuckled at the memory, shaking my head. "I mean, we covered up by the time he walked in. He didn't see anything, but he didn't have to be a rocket scientist to figure out what we'd been doing."

He rolled onto his back and laced his fingers behind his head. "So, what happened?"

"A very long, awkward silence. Then he left the room, we got dressed, and my boyfriend got the hell out of there." I idly ran my fingers up and down Alex's chest. "After a few hours, Dad and I sat down and sort of talked. He was obviously weirded out. I mean, who wants to catch their kid in the act, right? So we stumbled through the 'tell me you're being careful, please don't do it in my house, and don't let your mother catch you' discussion, and never spoke of it again."

"He wasn't angry?"

"Nah. He knew I had a boyfriend; he just didn't expect to see us like that."

"You and your dad have a pretty good relationship, then?" he asked. "I mean, aside from the awkward moment?"

"We used to." My chest tightened. Dad and I were on speaking terms, but the distance and strain had never gone away, and it probably never would. I could forgive, to an extent, but I couldn't forget.

"What happened?"

I gestured dismissively. "Long story. Had nothing to do with me being gay, though. He was pretty cool about that."

Alex exhaled. "I can't even imagine. If my dad, or anyone else in that town, knew I was gay, or if they'd ever caught me with a guy..." He shuddered.

I stroked his hair. "Those days are over, Alex. There will always be people who have a problem with what we are, but you're safer here."

"I know." He pushed himself up and kissed me. "By the way, I noticed your tattoo earlier but didn't get a chance to really look at it. May I?"

"Sure." I rolled over onto my stomach so he could take a look. Across my shoulders, I had an intricate tiger. It was a custom design by my ex, and as always, he'd done an amazing job. Every stripe, every tooth, was detailed to as close to photo-realism as a tattoo could get. I'd had it for over a year, and it still made me do a double take when I caught it in the mirror. There was no denying Sebastian was one talented artist, and I'd have paid him through the nose for this tattoo if he hadn't insisted on doing it for free.

Alex ran his fingertip along the outline. "That is really cool."

"Thanks."

"Painful?"

"Not as bad as I thought it would be." I looked at him over my shoulder. "Didn't you say you'd thought about getting some ink?"

"Been thinking about it for a while, yeah," he said quietly.

I rolled onto my back. "Any idea what you want to get?"

"Not really," he said with a shrug. "I figure I'll know it when I see it."

"Well, I mentioned the other night my ex is a tattoo artist," I said. "He did mine. Maybe the next stop on the Kieran Frost tour of Seattle should be his tattoo shop."

Alex smiled. "That could be fun." He ran a finger down the center of my chest. "The whole tour has been fun so far."

Trailing my fingers up the inside of his forearm, I said, "Enjoying it, are you?"

"Very much so."

"Anything else you want to do tonight?"

He came down to kiss me. "I kind of like this whole flavored lube thing."

"So I noticed."

"I might like to try that again."

"Would you?"

Alex said nothing. He just reached for the bottle.

Chapter Ten

The next day, Alex's shift didn't start until two, and mine didn't start until three, so I drove him to my ex's tattoo shop across town. When we walked into the shop, Sebastian's business partner Jason was in the middle of tattooing a client.

"Hey, Kieran," he said, glancing up from the wincing woman's shoulder. "Back for more?"

"Not today," I said. "Is Seb here?"

"Yeah, he's in the back." He craned his neck toward the back room and called out, "Seb! Get out here."

A voice came from the back. I recognized Seb's voice, but couldn't hear exactly what he'd said. A moment later, my ex-sort-of-boyfriend appeared in the doorway, and his eyes lit up. "Hey, long time no see."

"Much too long," I said. We exchanged grins, and in another time, he probably would have taken me into the back room to "go over that design on the computer". Ah, memories.

I put a hand on the small of Alex's back and gestured at Sebastian. "Alex, this is Seb. Seb, Alex."

They shook hands over the counter.

Alex gestured at Seb's arm, which was inked to the wrist. "Not only the president but also a client?"

"Pretty much." Never one to pass up a chance to show off the beautiful tattoos on his arms, Seb rolled up his shirt sleeve.

"Wow, those are gorgeous," Alex said.

"Thanks." Seb smiled. Gorgeous was an understatement. Both of Sebastian's arms were covered from wrist to shoulder with colorful, intricate designs, and he had plenty more beneath his clothes. To this day, I got goose bumps just thinking about the dragon on the left side of his abdomen, and the way it moved when he—

"Did you ever finish the right sleeve?" I asked, cutting off my own train of thought.

"A few months ago, yeah." Seb rolled his eyes, the light catching his eyebrow ring. "I swear, that thing took forever."

"I can see why," Alex said. "The details are incredible."

"He put it on too." I gestured at Seb. "This crazy fuck actually tattoos *himself*."

Alex's eyes widened. "You do?"

Seb laughed. "It's not as bad as you might think."

"I'll take your word for it."

"Well, there are some who say I'm insane, so..." Seb shrugged. "Anyway, what can I do for you?"

"I'm thinking about getting a tattoo," Alex said. "But then, isn't everyone who comes in here?"

"Oh, sometimes people come in to try to sell us crap," Seb said. "But in general, yes. What did you have in mind?"

"Not sure yet, to be honest. Kind of figured I'd know it when I saw it."

Seb nodded. "Okay, well, have a look at what's on the walls and what's in the books. If you see something that's close, or you get an idea, I can always do a custom."

"Mine is one of his custom designs," I said. "Trust me, he's a god."

Seb blushed. "Jesus, Kieran, I'm not that—"

"Oh, can it, Queen Modesty," Jason said without looking up from his client's shoulder. "Don't listen to him, kid. He's one of the best in the city."

Seb's cheeks turned a little redder. He cleared his throat. "Anyway, have a look. Let me know what you find." He gestured at the stack of portfolios on the weathered footlocker that passed for a table in the waiting area.

Alex took a seat and started looking through the books while I hung back with Seb.

I leaned on the counter, and Seb rested his elbow on the other side of it.

Keeping his voice hushed so even I could barely hear him, he nodded toward Alex. "He's cute. Doesn't seem like your type, though."

"Why not?" I raised an eyebrow. "Not enough ink or piercings?"

Seb shrugged with one shoulder. "I don't know, just...timid, I guess?"

I responded with a single, slow nod. "A little shy, yeah."

"Can't imagine you met him at Wilde's, then. That place would eat him alive."

"Friend of a friend."

The light caught Seb's eyebrow ring again. "A blind date?"

"Something like that."

"Think this'll end up being something"—he glanced at Alex, then at me—"more than your usual casual, lust-only thing?"

I shook my head. "No, I don't. Absolutely not."

Another glance toward Alex. Another look at me. "Okay."

"You sound skeptical."

"Maybe a little." He clapped my shoulder. "Only because I know you."

"So you *know* I don't do that."

"Exactly my point."

Furrowing my brow, I said, "What does that mean?"

"Nothing at all."

Before I could press the issue, jingling sleigh bells and a change in air pressure turned our heads in time to see a well-dressed brunette came through the door.

"Here's my twelve o'clock." Seb pushed himself off the counter. "You guys let me know if you see anything you like."

I eyed him, and he just grinned. Then he went to take care of his client, and I crossed the waiting area to sit beside Alex. I picked up one of the portfolios.

"I didn't realize he'd have so many books to go through," Alex said without looking up from the one across his lap. "And his work is incredible."

"He really is one of the best." I glanced at my watch. "We have plenty of time. Look all you want."

As I thumbed through one of Seb's books, my cell phone rang. I looked at the caller ID and groaned. "I'll be right back," I said, pushing myself to my feet.

"Take your time," Alex murmured without glancing up.

As I headed out the door, I flipped my phone open. "Hey, Mom."

"Hi, baby," she said. "Listen, about next weekend..."

I forced back a groan. The shop door thudded shut behind me, muffling the jingle of the bells on the inside. I leaned against a newspaper dispenser and tried to keep my frustration out of my voice.

"What about next weekend?" I asked.

"Well, Aunt Rose is coming for dinner on Friday night, and she'd love to see you."

Sighing, I pressed my thumb and forefinger into the bridge of my nose. "We've been over this," I said as gently as I could while still being firm. "I have to be somewhere on Friday. Sunday, I'm all yours, but there's nothing I can do about Friday or Saturday." Not that I wanted to be at the rehearsal or wedding, but two days of unpleasantness was worth it to avoid the drama my absence would cause.

My mother exhaled heavily. "Rose won't be able to come by on Sunday."

"It's okay," I said. "I'll see her next time I'm in town."

"Are you sure?" she asked. "She'd really like to see you."

I gritted my teeth. Thank God my folks hadn't divorced until I was an adult. It sucked having that foundation crumble when I was in my twenties, but this constant lesser-of-two-evils, who-do-I-piss-off-or-disappoint guilt would have been even less bearable as a kid.

"Sunday's the best I can do for this trip," I said. "Tell Rose I said hello, and I'll try to give her a call soon. Okay?"

"All right. Well, I'll see you on Sunday, then."

"I'll see you Sunday. Love you, Mom."

"Love you too."

After we'd hung up, I blew out a breath and rolled my shoulders. At least the calls were getting shorter as the wedding got closer. She had to know by now that I wouldn't or couldn't blow off the wedding. She still tried but seemed to be slowly accepting the reality of the situation. God, I felt bad for her, but I didn't know what else to do.

Clipping my phone back on my belt, I went back inside.

Alex glanced up as I walked in but didn't say a word as I joined him on the aged couch. He finished the portfolio in his lap, set it aside, and picked up another. With each book, he flipped through the pages faster and with progressively less interest. He barely gave each design more than a passing glance. I couldn't tell if he was bored or irritated. Or both.

"Anything catching your eye?" I asked to test the water.

He closed the book and set it on the stack. "Not really," he said flatly.

"You don't have to pick one out today," I said.

"That's good," he said with a forced laugh. "Because I don't think I can narrow it down anytime soon." He looked at me. "Ready to get out of here?"

"If you are."

"Please."

We said goodbye to Seb and Jason and left the shop. On the way down the sidewalk, I said, "You okay? You're awfully quiet."

"Yeah, I'm fine." He looked straight ahead. "Just didn't realize how many...options there were."

"The options are endless."

"So I noticed," he said, almost under his breath.

I watched him out of the corner of my eye as we walked, trying to gauge the sudden shift in his mood. It occurred to me then that, booty call or not, maybe throwing him in the same room as my ex wasn't a good idea. He had enough to take in. Or maybe he'd heard us and thought Seb was poking fun at him, not at me. Alex didn't know either of us well enough to know that was a constant thing between us.

Damn it. Should've taken him to a different tattoo shop, but ex or not, Seb really *was* the best.

Maybe that was the problem. Alex was all too aware of his own inexperience with men, and I wondered if he thought I was mentally comparing the two of them.

There are plenty of options, he might have thought he'd heard me thinking, *and look at me, Alex, I'm introducing you to one of* my *other options*. Damn it, way to think it through before taking him into my ex's presence.

"So, do you want to go look at some other shops?" I asked. "Plenty of other artists in town."

He shook his head. "No, I like his work. Just couldn't find one that jumped out at me." He paused. "So, he's your ex?"

"Sort of," I said quietly, trying not to cringe with guilt. "Ex-lover, if I had to give him a label. We never really had anything serious."

"He's cute." He smiled without much enthusiasm. "I can see the attraction."

"Yeah, his boyfriend's a lucky man." I slipped my hand into Alex's. A bit affectionate for our arrangement, but I wanted to see if he'd pull away. That, and subtly remind him he was my lover now, not Seb. When he didn't pull away, I said, "It didn't...bother you, did it? Meeting him?"

"What? Oh, no. Not at all." He ran his thumb along mine. "No, I was just thinking about all the designs. You know, trying to figure out what the hell I want to get."

"Well, there's no rush," I said. "Not like you have to get inked before you turn twenty-five or anything."

He laughed. "Glad to hear there's no deadline."

"No, definitely not." I glanced down at our hands. He hadn't pulled away. Hadn't pushed me away. Whatever occupied his mind had to be more than just the enormous variety of potential designs, but he wasn't hostile toward me as far as I could tell. Testing the water a little further, I looked at my watch again. "You know, we still have some time before either of us has to be at work."

"We do. Have anything in mind?"

I grinned, hoping he didn't notice me searching his eyes. "Oh, I could think of a few things."

"A few things?" He returned the grin, and his eyes narrowed mischievously. "Like, things that require us going back to one of our apartments?"

"Or at least someplace relatively private, yes."

He let go of my hand and put his arm around my waist. Whatever was on his mind, it must not have involved me, at least not in a negative sense, because he growled, "We'd better get going, then, hadn't we?"

Chapter Eleven

A few nights later, my shift ended at eleven, and since I'd walked to work, Alex came by to pick me up.

I slid into the passenger side and leaned across the console to kiss him. "Hey, you."

"Hey, yourself." He kissed me once more.

I sat back in my own seat. "Man, I'm glad to be out of there today."

"Long day?"

I nodded. "God, yes."

"Me too. If it had been a double shift, I think I'd have collapsed."

"I hear that. I love my job, but sometimes it can be brutal." I put my hand on his knee. "And I don't think I could survive a double shift now that you're around."

"Likewise," he said. "Still up for anything tonight?"

"Absolutely," I said. "You want to get something to eat first?"

"*Yes.*" He shifted into drive. "How about that café up the road? The one we went to the first time we went out?"

"Sounds good to me." I gestured toward Broadway. "Pull out of the lot and hang a left."

Broadway and the side streets were deserted. In mere minutes, Alex had parallel-parked in front of the café. Inside, the waitress showed us to a table, poured us some much-needed coffee and left us to look over the menus.

After we'd eaten, neither of us was in much of a hurry to leave, so we lingered, sipping fresh cups of better-than-sex coffee.

In spite of the caffeine, fatigue still wanted to close in on me. I set my cup down and rubbed my eyes.

"You sure you're all right?" he asked. "You look exhausted."

"I'm fine. I just need a damned day off." I sighed. "But I'm working all week because I have to go out of town this weekend."

"Really?" He sipped his coffee. "Where are you going?"

"Sacramento." Through gritted teeth, I added, "My dad's getting married on Saturday."

Alex cocked his head. "I get the feeling you're not too pleased about this?"

"No. Definitely not."

"But you're still going?"

Scowling, I nodded. "I really don't want to, but if I don't, I won't hear the end of it from anyone. That, and my mother's having a hard time with it, so I'm going to stop in and see her. Hopefully that'll cheer her up a bit." *And maybe I can stop getting guilt trips by phone every other day.*

"If you don't mind my asking," he said. "What exactly happened with your dad? I mean, what did he do?"

"It's not so much what he did," I said. "It's *who.*"

Alex's posture straightened. "Oh."

"My mom busted him cheating a few years ago," I said. "With at least three different women. He admitted it had been going on for a while, but he's never given us a straight answer about how long that is."

"Wow," Alex said. "That must have been horrible for your mom and you kids."

I nodded. "It was pretty ugly. She's never really gotten over it, and my brother and sister and I haven't ever been able to look at our dad the same again." I sipped my coffee, but barely tasted it. "So, yeah, I can't say I'm very enthusiastic about this wedding."

"I don't think I would be, either."

"But, blood is thicker than water, family's family, family comes first, blah, blah, blah." I rolled my eyes and set my coffee cup down. "Speaking of family bullshit, I'm curious about yours."

Alex swallowed. "What about them?"

"I'm just wondering, and if you don't want to discuss it, just say so," I said. "In the environment you grew up in, with everyone being so anti-gay, when and how did you figure out you were gay?"

With a quiet laugh that bordered on bitter, he dropped his gaze. "It's kind of ironic, actually."

"How so?"

Thumbing his chin, looking at the table between us with unfocused eyes, he said, "My dad was worried as hell about me or my brother being gay. I mean, I swear, the man probably laid awake at night worrying one of his boys would turn out queer." Alex rolled his eyes. "Spent my whole life being browbeaten with how good little heterosexual boys were to behave. Confusing as hell, believe me. So by the time I'm eleven, all I know is that gays are bad and disgusting, but I realize I'm not that clear on what exactly they are. I ask my mom, and she tells me they're men who have relationships with men instead of with women, like they're supposed to." He chewed his lip for a moment, his eyes distant.

"What happened after that?"

Alex sighed. "I was totally disgusted and horrified like I was expected to be, and it just got worse as I got older and started second-guessing every thought that crossed my mind. I noticed another kid's existence. Oh my God, I might be gay. I'm not into football. Oh, shit, what if I'm gay?" He paused. "I realize the kid sitting in front of me in math is so damned hot I can't think. Yeah, I'm *definitely* gay."

"First crush usually drives the point home," I said.

"Yeah, it did." He whistled and shook his head. "And he was gorgeous, let me tell you."

"So, did you accept it right away?" I asked. "Or was there some denial?"

"It took a little time, but I think I knew. There really wasn't any getting around it. I'd been so vigilant about anything that could possibly imply that I was gay, I ended up being hyperaware of it. When there was finally some writing on the wall, I couldn't exactly ignore it."

"That must have been rough, though. Given your situation."

He sighed, nodding slowly. "It was hell. It really was." He met my eyes. "You know how kids say 'my old man will kill me if he finds out' about something?"

A chill ran down my spine. "Yeah..."

"I sometimes wonder, even now, if mine would have. Quite literally." He swallowed. "Or at least beaten me within an inch of my life. He rarely laid a hand on us kids when we were growing up, but if he'd ever found out about this..." He trailed off.

"How old were you?" I asked quietly. "When you figured it out?"

"Thirteen," he whispered. "Fourteen when I really came to terms with it, and that's when I devised my little plan to throw myself into studying and make sure *no one* figured out I was gay. I knew exactly how not to be gay because it had been drilled into my head for so long, and I figured out I just needed to keep that up until I got out. And...here I am."

"You've spent a third of your life doing this?"

He was quiet for a few seconds. "Yeah. I guess I have." He exhaled hard. "Wow, when you put it like that..." For a long moment, he said nothing. Then he made a sharp gesture with one hand. "It's in the past, though. No sense spending the next seven years dwelling on it, right?"

"Well, no, but I don't think anyone would expect you to get over it overnight."

"No." He shrugged. "But I'm making progress." We exchanged smiles. He picked up his coffee cup. "What about you? When did you figure out you were gay?"

"Around the same age as you," I said. "Thirteen or so, and came out when I was fourteen."

"Your parents took it well?"

"Very," I said. "I was worried about it, but they were fine. I never thought they'd react like yours would have or anything, I just didn't know what to expect. Wasn't like they'd ever told people they desperately hoped for a gay son, you know?"

He laughed softly. "I don't imagine they did, no."

I sipped my coffee and set the cup back on the saucer. "They were surprised, and it was certainly an awkward conversation, but any concerns I had about being thrown out of the house or something were gone pretty quickly."

"You're lucky," he said softly. "I'd have given anything to have had that conversation with my parents."

I reached across the table and put my hand over his. "Honestly? It's their loss. No one wants to be rejected by their own parents, but it says a lot more about them than it does you."

"I know." He turned his hand over and beneath mine and closed his fingers around my wrist. "I learned a long time ago that they'll never accept me, and it took a few years, but I figured out that was on them, not me. There's nothing wrong with me."

"No." I ran my thumb back and forth on the side of his wrist. "There's definitely nothing wrong with you. And at least you're out from under their roof now."

He exhaled and nodded. "I'm thankful for that every day, believe me."

"Think you'll ever tell them?"

"Don't know." He absently watched his middle finger trace slow arcs along my arm. "Maybe. Someday. Probably when I'm in a committed relationship or something, since one of their biggest issues with gays is the idea that we're all promiscuous."

My cheeks burned, and I offered a cautious grin. "To be fair, some of us are."

He laughed. "Yeah, maybe, but ironically, you're also exactly what I needed to get all their bullshit out of my head. Some people might disagree, but I think this is the healthiest thing for me."

Chuckling, I dropped my gaze. "I don't know if healthy is the word I'd use, but—"

"I would," he said. "Totally."

"Seriously?"

"Think about it. You've taken it slow with me, every step of the way. You don't give me crap if I'm nervous or uncertain. We're using your experience at my pace." He leaned forward, clasping my hand in his and bringing it up to his lips. He kissed the backs of my fingers and met my eyes. "I don't see how this is anything but healthy."

"Maybe you're right," I said. "Interesting way to look at it."

"Beats the hell out of learning through trial and error with someone who knows as little as I do."

"Yeah, you've got a point."

"What was it like for you?" he asked. "I assume you were a novice at some point?"

I laughed. "Oh God, yes. There was definitely a time when I didn't know what the hell I was doing."

"I find that hard to believe." He winked.

I smiled, but it faded. "Believe it or not, I've had my share of awkward experiences. And some that were...unpleasant."

"Have you?"

I nodded. Shifting a little, I rested my elbow beside my coffee cup. "I haven't told many people about this, but my first time? Not an experience I'd like to repeat. And not one I intend to let you experience if and when we get that far."

"You don't have to tell me," he said. "I'm curious, but if you don't want to..."

"No, it's okay," I said. "I think you deserve to know what I'm trying to keep you from." I shivered, pretending my skin didn't crawl at the memory. Then I took a breath. "The first time I had sex, I was the bottom. And I had no idea what we were doing. None."

"What about him?"

"Well, let's put it this way," I said. "It wasn't his first time. He knew enough to know how to make it good for him. But for me?" I shook my head. "Not so much."

"So, what happened? If you don't mind my asking."

I took a breath. Avoiding his eyes, I said, "Most virgins don't last long their first time. Being on top, anyway. That initial excitement, I guess. Well, he...wasn't. So he went on for a while." I swallowed. "Quite a while."

Alex shifted a little, cocking his head. "I'm guessing it wasn't pleasant for you?"

"Not in the least." I shuddered at the memory. "Remember how I told you it's better to work up to it?"

"Right. The five-finger plan, wasn't that what you called it?"

"The five-step method, but close enough." I sighed. "Whatever you want to call it, he didn't do it."

Alex's eyebrows jumped. "He just went straight from...from zero to fucking you?"

I nodded. "He figured as long as we used enough lube, it'd be fine." I laughed bitterly. "Not that he used nearly enough, and quite honestly, I don't think he cared if it was fine or not, as long as it was good for him."

Grimacing, Alex squirmed. "God, I can't even imagine."

"After that, I was still interested in sex, but there was no way I was going to be on the bottom again."

His eyes got a little wider. "So...you only—"

"I go both ways now. Don't worry."

He relaxed. "What changed your mind?"

"A guy I dated in college who convinced me to try it one more time. He assured me if I gave him a chance, maybe I'd like it. All I had to do was tell him to stop, and he wouldn't bring it up again." I shrugged. "So, I figured I'd humor him. Didn't think it would last more than five minutes, and then he'd leave me alone about it."

"So...did it last more than five minutes?"

I shook my head. "Only took him about three minutes and two fingers, and he made me come."

Alex blinked. "Seriously?"

"Yeah. By the second time he did that, I was begging him to fuck me."

"And when he did, you liked it?"

"Oh my God, yes. After that, I couldn't get enough."

Alex chewed his lip. "I'm still a little skeptical, I have to admit."

"A lot of people are." I ran my finger along the edge of the saucer below my coffee cup. "It's daunting, especially when you have so many guys who've had experiences like mine and talk about how much it hurt."

"Not that I've heard many of the stories," he said. "But now that you mention it, it's just another reason I'm glad I have you to guide me through this."

"At your service." I picked up my coffee, which was cold and almost gone. Swallowing the last of it, I set the cup on the edge of the table and looked at Alex. "You know, to be serious, I have to say, it's amazing you came out of your environment without being completely fucked up in the head."

"I have my moments," he said. "I don't know, I guess since I knew it wouldn't last forever, I figured if I could hold out and keep it quiet for a few years, I could go someplace better."

"How did you even know Seattle was a gay-friendly city? If you were so worried about someone catching on, how did you research it or whatever?"

He laughed. "Another case of my dad inadvertently helping me. He always talked about 'places like San Francisco and Seattle' and how they were overrun with queers. I figured San Francisco might be a bit obvious, since he *really* loathed that place, but Seattle seemed like a more subtle move." He paused, looking into his coffee. "It's funny, if he hadn't been so vocal about everything that screamed queer to him, I probably would have shown a lot more of my cards earlier. As it was, he tipped his hand early on, so I kept mine close to my chest, and as far as I know, he's never suspected a thing."

"Smart move."

He shrugged. "Just survival."

I sighed and squeezed his hand. "It shouldn't be that way with your own family."

"Yeah, but what can you do? You can't pick your family."

"Isn't that the truth?" My dad was still pretty high on my shit list, and I'd never forgive him for the way he'd treated my mother. I wanted nothing to do with his wedding or marriage. But he certainly could have been worse.

The waitress appeared with a pot of coffee. "Refill?"

"No, thanks," Alex said.

I considered it for a moment, but then said, "None for me, either."

"Okay, well, you guys can stay as long as you want," she said. "I'm going to start closing up, but I'm not kicking you out."

"Closing up?" I pulled back my sleeve. "What time is— Good God, it's after midnight."

"No rush," she said.

Alex blew out a breath. "No, but I shouldn't stay out too much later. Boss doesn't like me falling asleep on the job."

"Yeah, same here," I said. "Could you bring us the check, and we'll get out of your hair?"

"Of course." She pulled a notepad out of her pocket, tore off the check and set it on the table.

We split the check, then left the waitress to finish closing up.

In the car, Alex started the engine, but when he reached for the gearshift, he hesitated.

"What's wrong?" I asked.

Blowing out a breath, he looked at me, "Even after all that coffee, I'm about ready to doze off. Would you be offended if I said I have about enough energy to make it up the stairs to my apartment and that's it?"

I put a hand on his knee. "Want to just call it a night?"

"Yeah. I'm beat." Then he offered a sleepy smile. "But you're still welcome to join me."

"Don't mind if I do."

On the way up to his apartment, I was glad he'd already thrown the fatigue flag on the field. My legs ached with every step, and the only thing I could think of doing in bed was sleeping. Between Alex and Wilde's, I was ready to cry *uncle*.

Alex unlocked the front door and let us in. He tossed his keys on the table. Turning to me, he said, "You're sure you don't mind staying over like this?"

"Not in the least." I put my hands on his waist and kissed him. "Besides, if I changed my mind, you'd have to drive me back to my apartment, which—"

He put up a hand. "Looks like you're stuck here, then. I am not going anywhere for the rest of the night."

"Well, actually, yes, you are."

"I am?"

"Mm-hmm." I nodded down the hall. "Bed."

It never took us long to get from the front door to the bedroom, and tonight was no exception, but even as we pulled the covers up and wrapped our arms around each other, fatigue trumped anything else.

Alex kissed me. "I'm dead tired tonight," he whispered, "but I can't promise I'll let you leave in the morning without doing something."

"You'd better not," I said against his lips. "Because I fully intend to make up for this tomorrow."

"Good. I was looking forward to it tonight, but..." He shook his head. "It's just not gonna happen."

"We'll make up for lost time. Come here." I rolled onto my back, and he rested his head on my shoulder.

I absently stroked his hair, just staring into the darkness. It had been eons since I'd slept with someone like this: getting close in bed without first fucking each other into oblivion. I'd forgotten how comfortable it could be, even without the fading tingle of an orgasm or two.

Alex drifted off in minutes, but in spite of my exhaustion, my mind kept me awake awhile longer. I ran through the conversation we'd had at the café.

The thought of the way he'd been treated growing up cooled the blood in my veins. It wasn't that I was unaware of the way many gay kids were treated by their families—I was extremely fortunate, and I knew it—but this one struck home for some reason. The thought of Alex living in fear of anyone, never mind his own father, made my skin crawl.

I held him a little tighter, closing my eyes and breathing him in.

"*Some people might disagree,*" he'd said, "*but I think this is the healthiest thing for me.*"

Maybe it was, maybe it wasn't, but if what we were doing kept him from going through what I had in the past and helped him break away from the bullshit of his youth, then I wasn't going to question it. At least that meant he got to bypass some of the things whose memories left guys like Rhett and me shuddering even years later. He'd learn how good sex could be, and he'd learn it at his whim, not mine or anyone else's.

Sooner or later, Alex would move on to other men. There would be other lovers who damn well better not even consider hurting him. Hopefully he took me at my word when I said he had every right to kick a guy out of bed if the jerk was selfish or reckless. Whether he tried to con Alex into going bareback, or tried to tell him "don't worry, I know what I'm doing" when Alex insisted that, no, actually it hurt, or chastised Alex for liking or disliking something, anyone who even tried to pull such a stunt would be wise to hope I never caught wind of it.

I pulled him a little closer and kissed the top of his head.

Anyone hurts you, Alex, I swear to God I'll break his fucking arms.

Chapter Twelve

Shifting on the uncomfortable wooden bench, I could think of about a hundred places I'd rather have been.

At work. That would have been nice. I liked my job, and even if it was one of the shitty jobs I'd had in the past, it would have been better than this.

Cleaning my apartment. Much as I loathed cleaning—yet another reason I had such a tiny place—I could have been persuaded to pick up a mop right about then.

Or, better yet, I could have been in bed with Alex. Naked, out of breath, hard as hell, and—

Calm down, Frost.

I closed my eyes and took a deep breath. The last thing I needed was to let onto those sitting around me that my mind was...elsewhere. Especially not when my body was parked here on this pew. In a church. In California.

At my father's wedding.

I gritted my teeth. I'd made it through the rehearsal, and now I only had to survive the ceremony and the reception, however long they turned out to be. I could do this. At least the reception would be well-stocked with booze. I wasn't a heavy drinker by nature. Today? Oh, I would be drinking like a fucking fish.

People filed into the church, murmuring among themselves as they took their seats. They were all smiles and Sunday best, and I wondered if any of them knew the truth. If they were genuinely oblivious, or just putting on a happy face because God help anyone who scowled during a wedding.

Why did I agree to come to this thing again?

I exhaled. It didn't matter. I'd agreed to it, and here I fucking was.

My father and the minister emerged from a side door near the front of the church, and my hackles immediately went up.

You're really doing this, Dad. You're actually *going through with this.*

And, oh, didn't he look pleased with himself, standing there in his Armani tux and beaming as he waited for his bride to come down the aisle. Smug son of a bitch. I wondered if he'd already cheated on her, or if he planned to hold out until after the honeymoon. Who knew? Maybe they had a good thing going. Maybe Dad was a changed man. Maybe Lacey was "the one" and gave him a reason to settle down.

And maybe Mount Rainier was full of penis-shaped confetti.

I took a deep breath.

Relax. It'll be over soon.

I caught myself wondering if I meant the wedding or the marriage.

Some sort of respectfully festive music started, and I somewhat respectfully kept myself from groaning aloud. So began the parade of bridesmaids and groomsmen and whoever else was involved. They all lined up at the front of the church with bouquets, tuxes, and boutonnieres, doing whatever it was bridesmaids and groomsmen did.

Then the music changed, and like everyone else, I stood and did an about-face.

The double doors opened, and in walked Lacey and her father.

So this was my stepmother. All of eight years older than me, in a dress that likely cost more than my car, smiling like she was actually in love with my dad.

I'd met her a few times before, but still couldn't believe they were getting married. It wasn't just because she was younger than him. In fact, I wasn't opposed to age differences at all. If I'd ever met a single guy like Ethan or Rhett, and could get over my aversion to relationships in general, I wouldn't have batted an eye at a twenty-plus-year age gap.

These two, though, were ridiculous. Monogamy—or at least fidelity—and my father were total strangers, and I still had yet to figure out what he and Lacey had in common. Last I'd heard, she was still after him about wanting more kids, and Dad had steadfastly refused to even consider it. He already had three adult children, at least one of which could have gone to high school with the woman. She liked to travel. He was a homebody. She was a professional dancing instructor. He couldn't be blackmailed into dancing. Dad was adamant about buying American, while Lacey drove a BMW and drank imported wine.

She also had a reputation for making eyes at any man with a wedding band, and he was a cheating whore.

Huh. Maybe they were made for each other after all.

Lacey's father handed her off to my dad, then went to the front pew to take his seat beside his own wife. Beaming like they had no idea what a dick the groom was, they watched the minister call the wedding to order.

"Dearly beloved," he began. "We are gathered here today..."

Yeah, yeah, yeah. Heard it all before.

Dearly beloved, we are gathered here today to witness the union of two people who probably don't even like each other all that much, but he has money and she puts out, so they'll try to make it look like they've put in some effort before they call it quits. 'Til death or five years do us part and all of that.

My own thought almost brought a chuckle to my lips, but when they started on the vows, my stomach turned. I clenched my jaw as the son of a bitch repeated the same words he'd said to my mother three decades ago. I wondered if he meant them now any more than he did back then. Maybe he meant them the first time around. I didn't know. Maybe he really had stayed faithful for the first seventeen or eighteen years like he swore he had. He might have actually meant the vows when he said them, even if he'd changed his mind later.

I supposed it was possible. He might have started cheating around the time he was teaching my sister to drive, keeping after my brother to practice his trumpet, or struggling to get his head around the fact that his middle son was gay. It might have happened earlier, back when Jackie's soccer, my baseball, and David's horseback riding lessons ran my parents ragged and sucked their bank account dry. For all I knew, he'd cheated on her from day one, wandering off with some girl in between posing with his new bride for all those now-faded photographs that were still on the walls of my childhood home.

The only thing of which I was certain was that, at some point while we were busy being kids and Mom was busy being Mom, Dad was off banging other women. How many? I didn't want to know. The three I knew about were more than enough. Rumor had it, there were more. Plenty more.

And now he expected everyone here, particularly the woman in the white dress, to believe he actually intended to have and to hold, to love and to cherish, and all that other shit he'd already lied about once.

"I do," my father said to his almost-wife.

Yeah, I'm sure you do, asshole.

I sniffed sharply and wiped my eyes. No way in hell was I breaking down here. Not where someone might think I was just that fucking happy, being all moved to tears at a wedding. Not a chance.

As I struggled to get my composure as close to collected as it was going to get, I tore my gaze away from the happy couple and glanced down the pew toward my sister. Her eyes flicked in my general direction, but then she looked forward. Her expression was stoic, and when her cheek rippled, I imagined her jaw was as tightly clenched as my own.

Beyond her, my younger brother had the same posture, staring straight ahead, not a hint of happiness on his face. His girlfriend put her hand on his leg and whispered something to him. He responded by squeezing her hand, but his expression didn't change.

I turned my attention back the front of the church. Thank God the three of us were all well past twenty-one, because there *would* be drinking at today's reception.

"By the power vested in me by the State of California," the minister said, drawing me back to the farce of a wedding, "I now pronounce you husband and wife."

Funny. I didn't recall the man asking for objections. Wouldn't that have been tempting? But I'd forever hold my peace for the same reason I'd come to the damned wedding in the first place: to keep the family drama to a minimum.

Once the ceremony ended, the photographer herded family members out to the garden beside the church for some family portraits. My stepmother would probably be less than thrilled when the photos came back with Jackie, David, and me looking like we'd rather be having root canals. I could fake a lot of things. Pretending to be happy about this was not on that list.

With mug shots taken, everyone piled into cars to head off to the reception and its bottles and cases and *truckloads* of booze. I was riding with my brother and his girlfriend, and since she hadn't been in the picture long enough to need the bottled anesthesia like we did, she'd volunteered to be designated driver. God bless her.

The reception was across town at a country club. David pulled up in front of the stairs, and the three of us stepped out into the sweltering heat. Northern California was brutal during the summer, and my time in Seattle hadn't done much for my heat tolerance. Especially not when I was wearing a shirt, a tie, and a festering grudge.

David handed off the keys to a valet. Then the three of us trudged up the stairs to the front door. There, we stopped. He and I both took deep breaths and exchanged tired glances. Air-conditioning and booze waited inside, but I debated staying out here anyway.

"Ready for this?" David asked.

"Do we have a choice?"

"If we did," he muttered, reaching for the door, "we wouldn't be here."

He opened the door, and we stepped into the air-conditioned hellhole. Most of the family was already here, along friends and neighbors I hadn't seen in some time. I was happy to see all of them, and as I scanned the crowd, I promised myself I'd have a good time in spite of my issues with the wedding itself.

After the bride and groom made their grand entrance, I went to the bar for a bottle of beer, and just the first sip was enough to relax me so I could mingle a little. I caught up with my sister Jackie and her husband, who were being civil to each other for a change. He must have started drinking already, then. He was a mellow drunk, but she'd have her hands full in the morning when he was hung over. Liquored up, he was pretty easygoing. Sober, he was insufferable. Most marriages involving drunks deteriorated as the alcohol consumption increased. Theirs had gotten progressively worse since he'd cut back on the booze.

Why she hadn't divorced his sorry ass, I didn't have a clue.

"I still love him," she'd sobbed on my shoulder last Christmas when he hadn't yet dipped into the eggnog and was still being an utter dick.

"Look how he treats you, though," I'd said, and Jesus, how many times had we had this conversation? "You deserve better than that."

Months later, here she was, still glaring at him and wearing his ring.

That was being in love? Oh yeah, sign me up.

No, wait, not love. Beer. That was what I wanted. Another fucking beer.

I went back to the bar, and I tipped the bartender five bucks before he'd even handed me the bottle. That beer unraveled some more of my nerves. My hackles settled down, and some of the knots in my neck and shoulders relaxed. I distracted myself by catching up with friends and family, and for a little while, managed to forget why I was here in the first place.

Until the groom caught up with me, anyway.

"Hey, son." My dad put his arm around my shoulders. "Glad you came. Didn't have trouble getting time off work or anything?"

"No, the boss owed me a weekend off." I casually removed myself from under his arm. "It was no problem."

"Well, I wish you could've come down sooner so we could've spent more time together." He gestured at his wife. "But, we're leaving first thing tomorrow for our honeymoon."

"Oh?" I said through gritted teeth. "Where are you going?"

"She insisted on Cancun." He rolled his eyes. "What the princess wants..."

"Isn't it your honeymoon as well as hers?"

He laughed and clapped my shoulder. "Son, it's a good thing you don't need to understand women." Before I could comment, he said, "How's your mother doing?"

I tightened my jaw. "Dad—"

He put up a hand. "I'm just asking, Kieran. I worry about her."

Sure you do. "She's fine."

"Is she?" He inclined his head and gave me that raised I-see-right-through-you eyebrow that had pulled countless confessions out of me as a kid.

Not going to work this time. "She's *fine*, Dad."

He narrowed his eyes slightly, but must have decided I wasn't going to offer any more than that. "Well, glad to hear it. I guess I'd better go see to my other guests."

And probably a bridesmaid or two, knowing you.

He went off to mingle, and I realized my beer was entirely too close to being empty. On my way back to the bar, Jackie caught up with me.

"Old man cornered you up?" she asked.

"Eh, I figured I couldn't make it through his wedding without talking to him for a minute or two."

"I'm surprised you're here at all, to be honest."

"Can you imagine if I'd flaked out?" I shook my head. "No way, I'd never hear the end of it."

"You could've said you couldn't afford it or couldn't get the time off work," she said. "At least you had some excuses at your disposal."

I sighed. "It would come back and bite me somehow. Showing my face at the wedding was the lesser of two evils."

"Hmm, true." She looked around. "So, did you bring anyone with you?"

"No, not this time."

"Are you seeing anyone?"

"Not at the moment." *Nothing serious, anyway.*

She sighed. "Kieran, when are you going to settle down?"

"Settle down?" I gave her a horrified look. "I'm twenty-seven. What's the hurry?"

"Well, I mean, haven't you found anyone?"

"I haven't been looking."

"You don't get lonely?"

I grinned. "Hasn't been a problem, no."

Jackie wrinkled her nose and shuddered. "Oh God, I don't want to know."

I shrugged, chuckling. "You asked."

"Not for details!"

"I can provide them if you—"

"Shut up, Kieran."

We laughed and went to the bar together.

The reception went on. And on. And on. I stopped drinking after four beers, though. I wasn't nearly drunk enough, and I had a designated driver, but my mood wasn't improving. The higher my blood alcohol content rose, the harder it was to hold my tongue when I was within earshot of my dad. I'd come to the wedding to keep drama to a minimum; getting drunk and instigating my own would sort of defeat that purpose.

After dinner, while everyone partied and danced, I lingered at my deserted table, enjoying what was left of my fading buzz. From my seat, I scanned the crowd of people who'd come to celebrate my dad's marriage.

A couple of parents bickered as they tried to keep their young kids away from the cake. A husband scowled at his wife as she swung her cocktail around. A *very* married friend of my father's—whose wife had been ill and unable to attend—chatted up the bride's sister. A bridesmaid made eyes at a waiter, evidently as oblivious to her fiancé's hand on her leg as the waiter was oblivious to the ring on her left hand.

And tomorrow, I'd go visit my depressed mother who, after three years, still wasn't over finding out her thirty-year marriage had been a lie.

Sighing, I reached for my water glass. At least my father had had the good graces not to marry one of his mistresses. I doubted he'd dumped any of them, but his new wife was, to my knowledge, added to the roster after the divorce.

My parents' marriage had been like the gold standard of happiness. No two people were as adoring and devoted to each other as my mom and dad. Not until my mom found out about my dad's long string of affairs, anyway. Thirty years of "this is how a marriage should be" went down the shitter in the space of a week.

Mom got depressed. I got depressed. My boyfriend at the time got tired of it. I told people we broke up because we'd drifted apart and wanted different things out of life, but that was just because I didn't want to tell them the truth. It was too hard to explain that the man I'd loved had walked away from me because getting over my parents' divorce took longer than he was willing to wait.

My sister's marriage was on the rocks. Most of my friends' parents were divorced. Of my co-workers at Wilde's, four had been in long-term relationships when I'd started two years ago, and only one of those relationships was still intact.

Even Ethan and Rhett had nearly fallen apart. When I came into their world, renting a room in their house after I'd moved to Seattle to escape all this madness, they were as good as done. In fact, they were done. The only thing tying them together was a mortgage, and they'd rented the room to me as a way of speeding up the process of paying down that mortgage so they could sell the place and move on.

They were back together now and stronger than ever. I envied the deep, genuine love between them now, but I could never forget what they were like when I met them. They'd been done, over with, and searching for the quickest escape from each other. I wanted the kind of love they had now, but not if the price was going through something that painful. What they had, and the fact that it had recovered like it had, was the exception, not the rule.

All around me, marriages imploded. Long-term relationships crumbled. People got hurt. And my friends and family wondered why I was so damned cynical about love.

I wasn't commitment-phobic or any of that nonsense; I'd just watched what happened when these things fell apart. Marriage was a joke. Falling in love was just asking to get hurt, and I'd seen very little evidence to the contrary. If love wasn't such a brutally risky gamble, I'd let myself go down that road again, but no. Not after everything I'd witnessed. The fact was, I was afraid to get so close to someone that it hurt to let them go.

Casual lovers came and went, usually leaving me with little more than a pang of disappointment if the sex had been good. I'd stayed friends with a lot of them—Seb, Rhett, Ethan, plenty of others—because there were no feelings involved. Sine there was nothing to get hurt over, no one got hurt. Life was so much simpler that way.

I drained my drink and set the empty glass on the table, all the while staring at the people on the dance floor.

A waiter appeared with a pitcher of water. "Refill?"

"Yeah, sure." I gestured dismissively. "Thanks."

He leaned past me to pick up my drink, and a shiver went down my spine so suddenly, I jumped. The waiter shot me a puzzled look, but I just pretended nothing had happened. Like I hadn't just reacted as if something had shocked me.

And it certainly wasn't the waiter's faint, familiar cologne that had done it.

After he'd gone, I closed my eyes and drew a breath through my nose, searching the air for one last taste. I found it, savored it and relaxed against the back of my chair as I exhaled. Rolling my shoulders, I smiled to myself. My mind wandered back to Seattle and into Alex's rumpled bedsheets. A pleasant tingle worked its way from the base of my spine up to my neck.

All I had to do was make it through the rest of the reception, then tomorrow at my mom's, and I'd fly back to Seattle the following day. Less than forty-eight hours, and I could put all this behind me and get into bed with Alex. Ah, the world was suddenly a much more tolerable place, knowing what waited for me when I got home. I wondered if he was itching for a night together like I was. I wondered if he did anything about it while I was gone, and if he thought of me while he did. I'd certainly thought of—

"Kieran?"

I opened my eyes.

My brother cocked his head. "You all right?"

"Yeah." I forced a smile. "What's up?"

He gestured over his shoulder. "Dad wants a few more pics with us and Jackie."

"Great." I got up and followed him.

So much for my good mood.

Chapter Thirteen

I pushed the guest bedroom door shut with my back. Leaning against the door, I closed my eyes and let my head fall back as I released a long, exasperated breath. One afternoon with my mom, and I was exhausted.

I came back to Sacramento every six months or so to visit family and friends, and I swore my mother aged a decade between every one of my visits. Throughout my life, she'd always looked ten or fifteen years younger than her actual age.

Since the divorce, she'd lost more weight than she could afford to lose, and though she didn't look as emaciated now as she had that first year, she was still gaunt. She'd abandoned all her painstaking efforts to hide the gray in her dark hair, and it was more gray than brown now. In a few months, she'd be fifty-two, but she looked like she was creeping up on seventy.

I understood her depression and her need to grieve for her marriage. My own depression over their breakup had darkened six solid months of my life, and managed to kill my relationship. I'd tried to be sympathetic for the first year or so, but she refused to be anything but miserable. Now I was just frustrated. What could I do if she was going to let the bitterness and sadness consume her? She still had their wedding portrait on the wall, for God's sake.

"Have you given any more thought to selling the place?" I'd asked for the millionth time.

She'd released a breath, her slumped shoulders dropping a little more. "I have, but...I don't know."

"A change of scenery might do you some good," I said. "There's a lot of good memories here, but sometimes those can be the worst, you know?"

She nodded but said nothing.

"You could always come up to Seattle," I said. "You'd like it up there. The weather's not nearly as bad as people say, and you've said yourself you're tired of the heat."

"But, this is *home.*"

Around and around and around.

I exhaled and rubbed my eyes with the heels of my hands. There was nothing I could do, and damn, it was exhausting. It was one of many reasons I'd ditched Sacramento for Seattle a year after the divorce. There was only so much of this I could take.

I pushed myself off the door and shuffled across the room. Blowing out a breath, I dropped onto the bed and pulled my phone off my belt. Without looking, I dialed.

As the call rang on the other end, I leaned back, reclining across the bed and resting my head on one hand.

"Hey," Alex said.

Closing my eyes, I smiled. Just the sound of his voice let me breathe out. Ah, something to look forward to when I got home. The best thing for me right then would've been to get tangled up in limbs and bedsheets. Let a few hard-earned orgasms carry me away. My mouth watered at the thought of tasting his cock.

But for now, I was here, he was there, and talking to him was the next best thing.

"Hey," I said.

"How was the wedding?"

I groaned.

"That bad?" His tone was sympathetic but not without with a hint of amusement.

"It could have been worse," I said. "And Mom's still having a tough time with it, so that hasn't been pleasant, but what can you do?"

"Sorry to hear it."

"I'll live. So, what have you been doing?"

"Working, mostly," he said. "Store's been busy the last few days."

"That's good. More hours, more commission."

"Commission?" He laughed. "Please. I'm lucky I can buy a cup of coffee with the commission that place pays. I'm just in it for the hours and the discount."

"That's all most jobs are good for."

"Yeah, but at least yours has interesting scenery."

"True, it does have that perk," I said.

"So, what are you up to tonight?" he asked.

"Dinner with my mom and sister." I rubbed my forehead. "Can't fucking wait. How about you?"

"I'm going out with Sabrina and some friends in a little while."

"You're actually going out?" I scoffed. "My God, did they blackmail you or something?"

He cleared his throat. "Yeah, something like that."

I smiled at the mental picture of his cheeks coloring.

"Actually," he said. "I had fun last time. Granted, I spent the whole time with you."

"Can't help you tonight, I'm afraid."

"It's okay, I'll manage." He paused. "By the way..."

"Hmm?"

"I, um, took some of your advice."

I opened my eyes. "Advice?"

"Yeah. I went back to that shop you took me to. The...what was it called again?"

"The Oh Zone?"

"That's it, yes."

My heart beat faster. "Oh really?"

"Yeah." He gave a quiet laugh, letting some shyness come through. "Amazing how much money you can drop in a place like that."

I swallowed. "What did you buy?"

"I...um..." He paused. "Something not *quite* cock-sized."

My mouth went dry. "And? How do you like it?"

He hesitated. "It was a little weird at first, but I like it." He paused. "Starting to wonder why I ever second-guessed that I'd like it."

I shuddered, closing my eyes and imagining the look on his face and the way he must have moaned the first time he felt that kind of orgasm. He probably had to just lie there and tremble for a few minutes afterward, trying to comprehend the magnitude of the sensations he'd just experienced.

"You still there?"

"Yeah. Yeah." I coughed. "So does this mean I get to say I told you so?"

He laughed. "Yes, yes, you were right. Absolutely right. In fact..." He took a breath. "I want to take things further when you get back."

My pulse ratcheted up. "How...much further?"

He was quiet for a moment. I didn't say anything, mostly because I couldn't get the air in my lungs to move. My heart pounded as I waited for him to answer. I shifted a little and adjusted the front of my jeans, which were tight as hell all of a sudden. Getting comfortable was impossible as fuck when I was this hard.

Alex cleared his throat. "I'm still not totally sure about, um, receiving, but I'd..." He paused again. "Let's just say I bought some condoms and lube, and I'd really like to use them."

Oh, Jesus, I'm dreaming.

I moistened my lips. "Are you saying you want to fuck me when I get home?"

When he replied, I expected more shyness and uncertainty, more stumbling over his words.

"Yes." Nothing but pure, unflinching boldness. "I want to fuck you."

I. Almost. Came.

It took another quiet cough to get my breath moving again. "I think I might have to arrange for an earlier flight home, then."

"What time does your flight get in?"

"Four thirty."

"I have to work until six anyway." He paused. "Your place or mine?"

"Wherever we can get to a flat surface and some condoms in short order." The words came out as a growl. I closed my eyes, letting my imagination run wild with anticipation.

"How about my place?" he said.

"Sounds good to me." *Oh my God. We're going to do this. Finally.* My cock strained the front of my jeans, and the bed creaked as I fidgeted. My mind's eye couldn't even focus on a single fantasy. I wanted him so—

"Kieran?"

"What? Sorry." My cheeks burned, and I was thankful he couldn't see me. I coughed. "Distracted."

The way he chuckled made me wonder if he'd caught on to what I was thinking.

"I'd better let you go," he said. "Sabrina should be here soon. I suppose I should make myself presentable."

I licked my parched lips. "Okay, have fun tonight."

"But not too much fun, right?"

"Have all the fun you want," I said, "just save some energy for tomorrow night."

"Oh, don't worry. I will."

"See you tomorrow."

"Looking forward to it, believe me."

"You and me both."

After we'd hung up, my phone had barely landed on the bed beside me before I started scrambling to unfasten my belt and zipper.

Sex with Alex. *Oh God. He wants me. He wants me. I fucking* need *him.*

I wrapped my fingers around my cock. Tonight, I couldn't even be bothered to hunt down some lube or a reasonable substitute. How many times I'd fantasized about sex with him—being on the giving or receiving end—I couldn't count, and tomorrow, I'd get to live that out, and my hand couldn't move fast enough to relieve this insanely unbearable ache.

Sex with Alex. Fuck. Behind me, fucking me good and hard. Him on top. Or on his back, letting me do all the work while he enjoyed the ride, oh, fuck, I was so desperate for his cock. He had no idea. No idea at all.

I stroked even faster, until my eyes teared up and my back lifted off the bed. I screwed my eyes shut, tried to breathe, then didn't care if I could breathe or not because all that mattered was being this damned turned on and needing that release, oh God, I couldn't wait, I couldn't wait, if I didn't come soon, I'd…I was…this…

"*Fuck.*" The word escaped my clenched teeth, and a split second later, I came so hard, my eyes welled up.

Then I was still. Not breathing, not moving. My heart still thundered in my chest, but I couldn't move while the last ripples ran their course.

When they had, I slowly relaxed my hand and released a breath. Then I fumbled around for the tissue box on the bedside table. Once I'd cleaned up, I lay back again and stared up at the ceiling, letting out a long breath and listening to my pounding heart as it slowed.

Twenty-four hours. Less than that, in fact, and I'd be with him again. I hoped he wouldn't get cold feet or have second thoughts, that he really wanted to cross this line with me. Even if he backed off, I didn't care. I just wanted to be with him. After two solid days around my family and all of their drama, two solid days *away* from Alex, I needed to get away from the craziness and back between the sheets with him. Hell, just being in the same room with him, though ending up in bed was inevitable.

I squirmed, trying to get comfortable. Damn it, I was horny, and my hand was just not going to be enough tonight. The itch was scratched for now, but how long would that last? Knowing me, not long.

I glanced at the clock. It was only four thirty. Dinner with Mom would probably be done by seven, leaving me free for the evening. Plenty of time to myself.

I still had a few friends—*that* kind of friends—in this area. It wouldn't take much to find someone who was able-bodied and willing.

It wouldn't take much, but what it *would* take, I just couldn't muster. Digging up numbers. Calling around. Working up the energy to go someplace else and the desire to be with anyone who wasn't Alex.

I sighed and stared up at the ceiling again.

Twenty-four hours. Less than that.

I could wait.

Chapter Fourteen

When I got to Alex's apartment the next day, I took the stairs two at a time. I knocked on the door, tapping three times with my knuckle, and the sound continued in the form of my pounding heart. And the footsteps on the other side of the door. *Oh God...*

Alex opened the door, and as soon as it was out of the way, we grabbed on to each other. From zero to a deep, passionate kiss in mere heartbeats, and we didn't let go. We stumbled against the door frame. Into the apartment. My shoulder hit the wall. His hip hit something.

He kicked the door shut, and I slammed him up against it. Kissing, panting, clawing at each other, we just couldn't get close enough fast enough. I inhaled deeply, saturating my senses with his cologne, and growled into his kiss as a shiver raised goose bumps under my shirt.

I wasn't the only aggressive one, either. Alex forced my shirt up and off. Then he kissed me again, shoving his hands into my back pockets and pulling me against him. Jesus, he was hard. I wanted him to fuck me now. Hard. Fast. Violent. *Now.*

But no, not yet. I had other plans first.

I unbuckled his belt, and before I went for his zipper, I slid my hand over the front of his pants. As I cupped his erection, I couldn't tell who shuddered more violently.

Oh God, I'm going to have this cock inside me tonight.

I somehow remembered how to work his zipper, and we both gasped when I closed my fingers around him. I stroked him slowly, every inch of my body aching and tingling as if *his* hand were on *my* cock.

"Wait," he said, panting. "Kieran, I...if you... Fuck, you'll make me come."

"I know." I kissed him. "That's the idea."

"But I—"

"Trust me on this."

Before he could protest, I dropped to my knees, and the moan he released when I ran my tongue around the head of his cock made my own erection almost unbearable. God damn it, I wanted him.

I groaned and stroked him faster, taking him deeper into my mouth, my cock aching and my hands trembling at the very thought of having *this* cock inside me.

Alex's back arched off the door, and his hips moved in time with my strokes, and the more he fucked my mouth, the more he turned me on. I squeezed harder with my hand and swirled my tongue around the head of his cock again and again and again.

"Oh...God..." One hand smacked against the wall. Then the other. His hips jerked, his knees buckled, and with a helpless whimper, he surrendered and came on my waiting tongue.

When I stood, resting a hand against the wall to counter my shaking legs, Alex grabbed the sides of my neck and kissed me hard.

"I thought you wanted me to fuck you," he said, panting between kisses.

"Oh, I do." I guided his hand to the front of my jeans and over my very hard cock. "I want you so bad I can't see straight."

"But you—"

I cut him off with another kiss. "If there's one thing most people say about their first time, it's that it was over too quickly." I bent and kissed his neck. "I want you to enjoy it." I trailed light kisses along the side of his throat and onto his collarbone. "Savor it." Another kiss, lingering for a second. "Remember it."

He shivered. "I don't think that last part will be a problem."

I nipped the side of his neck. "Good." I raised my head, and just before our lips met, I whispered, "We have all night. Let's use it."

In a tangle of clothing and kissing, we made it down the hall and into his bedroom, and there we sank into his bed. Clothes came off between long kisses, revealing hot skin to wandering hands. In spite of our mutual, undeniable desperation, everything was slow and sensual. Hot skin, cool sweat, sharp breaths; if I was this overwhelmed, I could only imagine how this was for him. My head spun and my hands shook, and my breath caught every time his hip or his hand or his lips brushed over my erection. I found just enough control, just enough restraint, not to lose my ever-loving mind, and more than once I wanted to beg him to let me fuck him. If he'd enjoyed a toy, he'd love a cock, but not yet. That had to be his move, even if the wait drove me insane.

His kiss gradually moved back into the territory of feverish, just like it had been up against the door earlier. Beyond that. Way beyond that. It was a hungry, breathless, *frantic* kiss, demanding and unrelenting, and I swore if I got any harder, I'd go insane.

Alex pinned me to the bed and pressed his hips against mine, and I moaned into his kiss. The touch of another man's hard-on had never aroused me this much. I couldn't wait another damned minute.

"Condoms?" I murmured between kisses.

"Drawer." He kissed me once more, then pushed himself up. "I'll get one."

As he opened the box of condoms, his hand shook.

I touched his shoulder. "You sure you're ready for this?"

Condom in hand, he set the box down and turned back to me. His free hand went around the back of my neck, and he kissed me. "I've been thinking about this constantly since before you left for California." He dragged his lower lip across mine. "This is the worst my tennis elbow has been in years." We both laughed softly before he covered my lips with his. Fingers tangled in hair, limbs tangled in limbs, and he finally broke the kiss just enough to whisper, "You're damn right I'm ready for this."

"Tell me," I whispered.

"Tell you?"

"What you want." I tightened my fingers in his hair and forced him to look me in the eye. "Tell me."

He moistened his lips and held my gaze with the most spine-tingling intensity. "I want you." He swallowed. "I want to fuck you."

My cock twitched between us. "Please do."

With trembling fingers, he struggled with the condom wrapper.

"Here." I held out my hand. "Let me."

Our eyes met. Then he set the condom on my palm. I tore the wrapper with my teeth. As I rolled the condom on him, Alex bit his lip, and I couldn't tell if it was nerves, excitement, or the fact that I was touching his cock. Maybe all three. The same three reasons *my* hands were unsteady as all hell.

Alex picked up the lube, and as he put it on, he met my eyes. "I'm, um." He raised his eyebrows. "Position?"

"From behind usually requires the least amount of contortion," I said. "And you'll be in complete control. Fast, slow, hard, gentle. However you want it."

He kissed me this time. "How do *you* want it?"

"Doesn't matter." *Fuck, how am I already out of breath?* "I just want you inside me."

Alex shuddered against me.

"It's easier..." I struggled to form coherent words to articulate semi-coherent thoughts. "It'll be easier...from behind, I mean. On my hands and knees." I licked my lips. "Less awkward for you."

He swallowed hard. Then he moistened his lips and whispered, "Turn around."

I kissed him lightly before doing as he'd asked.

An uncertain hand rested on my hip. The mattress shifted ever so slightly as he leaned closer to me. The room was silent, everything still, and I thought nerves might have gotten the best of him, but then he drew a long, ragged breath and pressed against me.

Groaning softly, he pushed in. I closed my eyes, exhaling at the same speed—slow, *so* slow—he slid into me. An inch, no more, and he pulled out. Pushed in again. Slow, progressively deeper strokes, and I fought the urge to rock back against him and force him all the way in; this had to be at his pace, no matter how much I needed every last inch of him.

All the way in, he stopped. We both exhaled, and I moaned as he withdrew so damned slowly. Even slower now, he slid back in. As he got the hang of it, he still didn't fall into any kind of rhythm. First it was a few long, smooth strokes. Then he'd pull all the way out and slide back in again. His fingers trailed up and down my spine, and I imagined him staring in disbelief at every place we made contact. I wondered if he saw the goose bumps on my back, or if he was aware of them beneath his wandering fingertips, or if he couldn't stop watching his cock moving in and out of me.

Part of me wanted to beg him to fuck me as hard and fast as he could, or at least pick up some sort of steady rhythm to take me from painfully horny to a much-needed orgasm, but I bit my tongue. This was new to him. I could be patient while he found his sea legs. Just his cock moving inside me, especially when I was this insanely turned on, was enough to make my breath catch, so if he wanted to keep doing this for a while, he was welcome to it.

As long as he didn't *stop*.

He stopped. All the way inside me, he fucking stopped. My fingers curled around the sheets, and I closed my eyes. I gritted my teeth, silently begging him to do...to...to do *something*.

He moved. Adjusted his position somehow. His center of gravity shifted, and I instinctively adjusted my own position to accommodate the change. Grasping my hips, he withdrew, and I exhaled, relieved he was no longer still, and when he pushed back in I—

"Holy...oh, my God..." All the air rushed out of my lungs, and I clutched the sheets for dear life. Whatever he'd done, whatever he'd changed, it was breathtaking. With every stroke—

every slow, rhythmic stroke—he hit just the right spot to make me dizzy.

Hello, male G-spot. Meet Alex's amazing cock.

"You all right?" he asked.

"Yeah. Yeah. I'm…fuck, don't stop doing that."

"This?"

I nodded, biting my lip as he slid across that perfect spot again and again and again.

"Oh, my God, this is…" His fingers twitched on my hips. "I don't know if seeing or feeling it is hotter. This is…" He groaned, thrusting just a little harder. "Do you like that?"

"Jesus, yes," I moaned.

"Fuck, I just want…" He gasped, his rhythm faltering slightly. "I want to…do it harder…and fucking lose it."

"Do it," I whispered.

"I don't want…" He paused, struggling to catch his breath. "I don't want to hurt you."

"You won't. I promise, you won't. Just…God, fuck me hard, Alex. *Please.*"

He did. Holy fucking hell, he did. My eyes watered as much from pain as pleasure, and he felt so goddamned good I could barely breathe, let alone tell him how amazing he was. My balls tightened with an impending climax that wasn't going to back down, and I bit my lip. This was going to be one hell of an orgasm, I knew it was, and…fuck…

He said something I couldn't understand. A question, maybe? I wasn't sure. All I knew was he'd spoken.

I licked my lips. Again. Tried to speak. Failed. Screwing my eyes shut, I rocked back against him, but I couldn't find the words, my voice, anything.

One hand left my hip and slid up my back, following a shiver from the base of my spine to my neck. A split second's worth of awareness made my heart skip as I realized what he was about to do, but I still gasped when he grabbed my hair and jerked my head back, sending deliciously violent tremors right through me.

"I asked if you like that," he growled.

"Yes," I managed to choke out. "God...yes..."

He let go of my hair, grabbed my hip again and thrust as hard as he could.

Had I trusted one arm to hold me up now, I'd have stroked my own cock, but as it was, I could barely keep myself up on both arms. Not that it mattered; every thrust he took hit just right to send sparks crackling up my spine.

"Fuck, Alex," I moaned. "Don't...stop..." My hands clawed at the sheets. My mind clawed at consciousness. Alex's fingers dug into my hips, and he fucked me harder and better and more violently than any virgin had any business being capable of fucking me, and oh my God, I hadn't expected this tonight. There was no way...this wasn't...it couldn't...not with someone this inexperienced. How? Oh, Jesus, how did he know just the right angle, just the right speed, fuck, *how*?

I rocked back against him, and with a moan of surrender, I shuddered and came.

Through the blur of delirium, I was vaguely aware of Alex releasing a helpless whimper. Then he pulled my hips against him, forcing his cock as deep as he could. I moved my hips as much as I could to draw out his orgasm, but his grip didn't allow for much motion.

He slumped over me, resting his forehead between my shoulders, and wrapped his arm around me. Sharp, uneven breaths cooled the sweat on my back, and somehow, God only knew how, my trembling arms kept us both up.

We were still. Panting, shaking, but otherwise unmoving.

Alex wasn't a virgin anymore, but in that moment, for the life of me, I couldn't have said who was more overwhelmed.

Chapter Fifteen

Alex withdrew, but we both stayed still for a long time, just catching our breath and reeling. After a while, when the dust had apparently settled enough for him to move, he pushed himself up. We barely kept ourselves from collapsing before we'd cleaned up, but once that was done, we both dropped onto the bed on our backs.

"That…" I closed my eyes, licking my dry lips. "That was amazing."

"You sound surprised," he said, his tone soft and shy.

"I am." I lazily laced our fingers together. "Nothing personal, you know that."

He chuckled. "No offense taken."

"Good." I turned onto my side and ran my fingers through his sweaty hair. "I knew you'd last awhile after coming once, but *damn*. Most guys don't last anywhere near that long their first time."

He smiled sheepishly as he trailed the backs of his fingers down my cheek. "To be fair, I'd already come twice today."

"Twice?"

"Well, okay, the first time was a few hours ago…" He grinned, inching closer to devilish than shy. "Had to find some way to stop thinking about this."

"Did it work?"

"For about five minutes."

We laughed. Then I kissed his forehead. "I'm not kidding. Seriously, that was incredible."

He gave me another sheepish look. "I did have a little help."

"Help?"

He gestured toward the nightstand. "Second drawer."

I furrowed my brow, then rolled over and reached down to open the second drawer. Inside, there must have been a dozen books. I picked up the first one off the stack and rolled onto my back again.

"*The Man's Guide to Men*," I read off the cover. Then I flipped through a few pages. "Been doing some reading, have we?"

"Just a little." He draped his arm over me and kissed my neck. "I told you before, I'm a bookworm. Used studying to explain away my lack of a girlfriend." He let his stubble brush the side of my neck as he nipped my earlobe. "Kind of a hard habit to break, don't you think?"

The warmth of his breath on my skin made me shiver.

"It served you well," I murmured. "You read all of these?"

"Hey, being an obsessive student has its advantages. I read pretty fast."

"You ain't kidding. Good God."

"Well, I didn't read all of them cover to cover. There was one that was like two hundred pages of 'talk to your partner and see what he wants'." Alex rolled his eyes. "Yeah, thanks, got it. Now how about some suggestions and ideas?"

I chuckled and slid the book onto the nightstand. Alex rested his head on my chest, and I wrapped my arms around him, clasping my fingers together on his shoulder.

"So, what else have you been studying since I've been gone?"

He shifted a little, so I released him. He pushed himself up onto his forearms. "Oh, I've just been...experimenting. Like you told me to. And you were definitely right about the toy." He closed his eyes and didn't quite suppress a shiver.

"You are an apt pupil, aren't you?"

"When the subject interests me, yes."

"Well," I said, "keep experimenting, and you just let me know when you're ready for the real thing."

He kissed me lightly. "Will do."

He rolled onto his back beside me, and we lay in silence for a while. I thought he might have dozed off, but a surreptitious glance at him revealed he was still awake. He stared at the ceiling with distant eyes and an unreadable expression.

I turned on my side and ran my fingers through his hair. "You okay?"

My voice startled him, but he tried not to let it show. "Yeah, I'm fine. Just thinking."

"Something wrong?"

He pursed his lips and took a breath. Then he shook his head. "Never mind."

"You sure?" I lifted his chin so he'd look me in the eye. "If something's wrong..."

Again he drew a breath, and he shifted his gaze from mine. "I was just thinking. You remember when we went into your ex's tattoo shop?"

I cocked my head. "Yeah, of course."

Chewing his lip, he met my eyes. "It was...weird..."

"The tattoo shop?" Guilt twisted in my gut. "Or being around my ex?"

"Your ex didn't bother me." He put his hand on my arm and traced little arcs with the pad of his thumb. "He's a nice guy. And hot." Alex winked. "I can see why you were into him."

I laughed. "You know, I got the feeling you were uncomfortable or something that day, and all this time I thought it was Sebastian that bugged you. Like I shouldn't have thrown my ex in your face."

Alex shrugged. "Nah, it didn't bother me. I didn't even think about it, honestly."

I ran the backs of my fingers down his cheek. "So, what was it?"

He took a breath. "I want a tattoo. Have for a long time. I don't know, maybe it's an act of rebellion, but I kind of want something to emphasize that my life is *mine* now. But..."

"But...?"

He exhaled. "When I looked through the book at all the designs, I couldn't find anything. Not even an idea. There was just...nothing that said 'me'. A million options, and absolutely *nothing* clicked on any level." He paused. "It's like, I realized just how much I didn't know who I was. I'm sure it sounds completely corny, but my entire life since I was a teenager has been this smokescreen. Trying to convince people I wasn't something. And ever since I came to Seattle, I've finally been able to at least try to be myself, whoever that is." He shifted his weight onto one arm. "And that's just it. The tattoo, everything." He put his hand over mine on my chest. "*This* is the only part of me I get. What we're doing. It's just sex, but it makes sense, and the more sense it makes, the more I realize how little everything *else* makes sense."

"Like, what else?" I asked. "What else doesn't make sense?"

"School and a career, for one thing."

"I thought you had a pretty solid path there."

"Oh, I do," he said. "Heading straight for a lucrative, respectable profession with job security and all of that bullshit."

I furrowed my brow. "But...?"

He sighed. "I'm busting my ass in pre-med because that's what I've been working toward since junior high. After this, med school. Then a residency. And..." He made a sharp, frustrated gesture. "A career as an MD." He ran a hand through his hair and sighed again. "And now I can't help wondering if that's really the path for me, or if it's just a continuation of Operation Get the Fuck Out of Rayesville."

"What *do* you want to do?"

"That's the thing," he whispered. "I don't know."

"Ever thought about it?"

"I never really thought further ahead than leaving my hometown," he said. "Everything I've done, everything I've planned, everything I've studied for, it hasn't been because I wanted a career in medicine. I just wanted to get out. Following in my dad's footsteps was the perfect cover. He never questioned it. But...now what?"

"It's not too late to change directions, you know."

"Yeah, but change to what?"

"Maybe you need to take some time off." I ran my fingers through his hair. "Work a shit retail job, do some soul-searching, and figure out what you really do want out of life."

"That might not be a bad idea. Can't imagine trying to explain that one to my folks, but..." He shrugged. "Fuck 'em."

"That's the spirit."

He managed a halfhearted chuckle. Then he asked, "What made you move up here?"

"Honestly? I just needed to start over after my parents' marriage fell apart and my own relationship imploded." I paused. "I guess I was trying to get away from something too."

"Isn't everyone?"

"Yeah, probably."

He was quiet for a moment. "Can I ask something personal?"

I smiled. "I think we know each other well enough to ask personal stuff, don't you?"

"True, I guess we do." He bit his lip. "The whole thing with your folks, and the relationship you had at the time..." He hesitated. "Is that why...you know, why you're..."

"Why I'm a total manwhore?"

"I was going to say promiscuous, but okay."

Chuckling, I shook my head. "No, I was like this long before all of that shit went down. I settled down with my ex for a while, but that's about the only time I've been monogamous for any length of time."

"How long were you with him?"

"Three years."

Alex blinked. "You? Monogamous for three years?"

Cheeks burning, I nodded. "Yeah, hard to imagine, isn't it? We actually had an open relationship for a while. A year, year and a half maybe. But it was just us after that."

"You must have been really into him."

I sighed. "Yeah. I was."

"Sorry," he whispered. "Didn't mean to—"

"It's okay." I met his eyes and stroked his hair. "It was a long time ago. I'm over it. Love's just a bitch."

Chapter Sixteen

That night was the first time we'd had sex, but it was far from the last. I couldn't get enough of him, especially the more he found his stride. He was a willing lover, a fast learner, the type who adapted his technique to benefit the man he was with, not just himself. I ached to top him just once, if only to show him how it felt, but until he was ready for that, was more than happy to let him top me.

For two solid weeks, between our jobs and the time we spent in bed, we barely saw the light of day. Whenever I was off while he was at work, though, I did manage to drag myself to go work out at Ethan and Rhett's. High-intensity weight training and cardio were more than a little challenging when my body was in a constant state of blissful exhaustion. The guys, of course, found this endlessly amusing.

"Damn, Kieran, what's that kid doing to you?" Rhett had asked the other night.

"You tell him not to break one of our favorite playthings," Ethan had said with sternness that was almost convincing.

"Yeah," Rhett said. "Twenty-something sex junkies aren't easy to find, you know."

Ethan gave it a moment's contemplation, then said, "On second thought, maybe you should bring him over."

He gave a quiet laugh. “I can only imagine.” He rested his head on my shoulder again and draped his arm over me. “I suppose we should get up and take a shower eventually.”

“Probably.”

“But I don’t feel like moving.”

I kissed the top of his head. “We’ll get there. I’m not going anywhere until you do.”

“You might be here awhile.”

“Fine by me.”

At least they understood why I kept bowing out of any three-way action. Too tired, too sore. Something like that, anyway. They were good sports and never took it personally, though they did keep exchanging these odd looks that they refused to explain. Some inside joke between the two of them, no doubt.

Today, I'd gone over early to get my workout done and out of the way before my shift started. Standing behind the bar now, every inch of my body ached, and I couldn't tell where my workout ended and last night—and this morning—began. No complaints, though. My God, I had met my match. It had been a long time since I'd been with someone who could leave me so exhausted and satisfied.

And after work tonight? Aching muscles or no, it was *on.*

The crowd at Wilde's was unusually "meh" this evening. Sure, there were some lookers, and it was a safe bet a lot of men in this room would be getting laid before the night was over, but the turnout just didn't turn my head. There was no one in the crowd who'd make me drop a bottle or forget how to mix a drink, and with the guys who frequented this place, that was saying a lot.

"I am *so* glad I'm not closing tonight," Chad, one of the other bartenders, said.

"Why's that?" I asked as we both dried glasses. "Got a hot date tonight?"

Grinning, he looked around the club. "I'll have one before I leave, that's for sure."

I raised an eyebrow, then followed his gaze around the room. We had very similar taste in men—turning our noses up at the burly body-builder types while drooling over pretty boys with tattoos—but tonight? Nothing caught my eye. Like I always did, I sized up every man in the room according to whether or not I'd sleep with him, and only a handful warranted a second look, let alone a tepid "oh, I suppose I could."

Maybe I just wasn't in the mood tonight.

"What can I get you?" I asked a customer.

"Long Island Iced Tea, please."

I put some ice in a glass and set it on the bar. Then, with two bottles in each hand, started pouring it.

I'd barely upended the bottles when Wes appeared beside me and whispered, "Hey, isn't that your new man over there?"

I looked up. The bottles in my left hand slipped, and had Wes not reached out in time, the Triple Sec would have crashed into the ice bin.

"Thanks," I said, righting all four bottles and pretending I didn't feel like a complete ass. I cleared my throat and looked at the glass on the bar. It was still only about half full, which meant there was...something. Another step. Another ingredient.

"You okay?" my customer asked.

"Yeah," I said. "Just...got distracted." Alex's presence hummed along my nerve endings as he approached the bar. I didn't have to look at him for his brown eyes and shy smile to drive me to distraction. My fingers tingled just thinking about running through his dark hair, and for the life of me, I still couldn't remember what the hell was supposed to go in that half-full glass in front of me. Clearing my throat, I offered an apologetic look to my customer.

"What...what did you order again?"

He chuckled. "Long Island."

"Thanks." I put the half-mixed first attempt aside and dropped some ice into a fresh glass.

"That must happen to you guys a lot," he said. "Being distracted when something hot walks in."

"Yeah." I laughed, pretending my hands were steadier than they were. "Happens all the time. Occupational hazard." My second attempt at a Long Island Iced Tea—what the fuck? I could mix these sons of bitches in my sleep—was successful, and I slid it across the bar to my amused customer. Fortunately, he had a sense of humor, and he left me a healthy tip in spite of my clumsiness.

Once he was gone, I moved to the end of the bar where Alex had taken a seat.

"Hey, you," I said.

"Hey," he said. "I'm a little early. Hope that's okay."

"Of course it is." I leaned across the bar for a light kiss. "I still have a few minutes left on the clock, though. Want a drink while you wait?"

"No, I'm good." He shifted a little. He seemed nervous. Unusually so. He was comfortable with me these days, and God knew he'd gotten over a lot of his uncertainty, but tonight, that skittishness from day one was back. Not to the same degree but definitely there.

"You all right?" I asked.

"Yeah." He smiled with exaggerated ease. *See? I'm fine. Perfectly fine. Nothing wrong here.*

Something twisted in the pit of my stomach. "Let me see if the boss will cut me loose a little early."

"No rush."

Since it was a slow night, my boss did cut me loose, and in minutes, I'd changed clothes, and Alex and I were on our way out into the parking lot. He was still quiet, jittery, and the unsettledness in my stomach wasn't going to let up until I found out why.

I'd walked to work, so we got into his car.

He put the key in the ignition but hesitated.

"Something wrong?" I asked. My heart pounded.

"No, I..." He trailed off, swallowing hard.

"Alex?"

"Before we go, I..." He bit his lip, staring out the windshield. Then, instead of speaking, he turned to me, reached across the console, slid his hand around the back of my neck, and drew me into a kiss. Heart still pounding and stomach still knotted, I put my arms around him and sank against him. I could never get enough of the way Alex kissed, and even my concern about his jitteriness didn't override that.

I inhaled deeply through my nose and shivered. His cologne had long ago become an aphrodisiac for me. One breath of it turned my mind into a collage of fantasies and memories alike. Fantasies and memories that were almost indistinguishable from each other, dozens of mouthwatering images of my hands and lips and skin on Alex. I wanted him too damned bad to be sitting here in a parking lot when there was a bed not far away.

"Let's get out of here." I closed my eyes and exhaled when his fingers drifted over my cock.

"We will."

"Alex..." I breathed. "We...we're only a few minutes from—"

He cut me off with a kiss. A deep, aggressive kiss that could have made me his goddamned slave if he'd asked.

After a moment, his lips released mine, and he descended on my neck. "You've said from the beginning," he murmured, pausing to nibble my earlobe, "the whole point of sex is being intimate enough to push boundaries." His hand drifted higher up my leg. "Doing things you wouldn't do with just anyone off the street." He squeezed my erection, and when my breath caught, he whispered, "Challenging your comfort zone." He kissed me, and when his fingers brushed my cock through my pants, I shivered but didn't break that kiss. Not until he drew my zipper down.

"What are..." I sucked in a breath. "Home...we're..."

"I just can't wait," he whispered, stroking me slowly. "I'm too damned turned on thinking about what I want you to do when we get home."

My breath caught. "And that is?"

He kissed below my ear, and in the same moment he tightened his grasp, he whispered, "I want you to fuck me."

He didn't even let the words sink in before his mouth was around my cock, and my back arched off the seat. I dug my teeth into my lower lip and screwed my eyes shut. There was no possible way I could be any more aroused than I was right then. His mouth on my cock. His boldness, his confidence. The anticipation of being inside him tonight. Tonight. Fucking *tonight.*

I reached back to grab the headrest. "Oh God..."

Anyone who cared to look would have known exactly what was going on in this car, but I didn't give a shit. Alex's lips and tongue worked their magic on my cock, up and down and up again, and his whisper still echoed in my ears:

I want you to fuck me.

"Don't stop," I moaned, my eyes rolling back and my balls tightening with every flick of his tongue and stroke of his hand. "Please, don't stop."

I want you to fuck me.

Tonight. I'd finally be inside him tonight.

"Oh God..."

I want you to fuck me.

The world went white. A cry of pure, unrestrained ecstasy escaped my throat, and I didn't care who heard it. The only thing I cared about was that Alex heard the two words I finally managed to articulate:

"Home. Now."

Chapter Seventeen

The click of his bedroom door stiffened Alex's spine. The unshakable confidence—no, aggression—he'd had in the car, withered. He looked at me with wide eyes, his Adam's apple bobbing.

I put a hand on his waist. "You sure about this?"

The tip of his tongue swept across his lower lip. "I...was."

"You're not committed," I whispered, touching his face. "And even if we start, you don't have to finish."

He looked anywhere but at me.

"Do you want to try?" I asked. "It won't hurt my feelings if you say no." *But please, say yes. Say yes. Oh God, Alex, if you only knew how bad I—*

"We can try," he said with a subtle nod. He managed a quiet laugh as color bloomed in his face. "I've been thinking about this for days, and I want it, but now that we're here..."

"It's okay." I stroked his flushed cheek with my fingertips. "You said you've been using a toy, right?"

He nodded.

"Why don't we start with that, then?"

He made a choked sound, like he'd tried and failed to clear his throat. "Seriously?"

"Why not? You're already comfortable with it. The only difference is, it'll be me holding it instead of you." I kissed him gently. "It's something familiar that'll help you relax."

He hesitated, then whispered, "Yeah. We can...we can do that." He gestured past me. "It's in the top drawer. Beside the bed."

"We'll get there. First things first, though." I slid my hands under the back of his shirt and kissed him.

Piece by piece, we shed our clothes. Step by step, we neared the bed and the drawer. And kiss by kiss, he relaxed, inching closer and closer to that mouthwatering aggression he'd let me taste in the car.

Then he released me and, with a not-quite-steady hand, reached for the drawer.

To my surprise, he'd opted for a plastic vibrator, though judging by the lack of weight when he handed it to me, there were no batteries in it. I'd told him I was pretty sure the vibration function did more for women than men anyway, and apparently he'd either taken me at my word or simply wasn't interested in it. It was smooth plastic and tapered, starting fairly thin before thickening to something a bit more challenging. I hadn't thought of suggesting a piece like this for a beginner, but I could see why he'd chosen it.

"That one looked like it would be more comfortable." His cheeks colored. "It's...smoother."

"Good idea."

He took a breath. "So, how do we, uh, do this?"

"Start with you on your side. With your back to me." I picked up the bottle of lube, and we both got into bed. His body was tense against mine, his spine stiff and his shoulders taut. I kissed the back of his neck. "You okay?"

"Yeah." He took a deep breath. "Just...nervous."

I ran my fingers through his hair. "We'll take things slow." I kissed his neck again. "If you want to stop, all you have to do is say the word."

He didn't speak, just nodded.

I covered the toy in lube, then moved as close to him as I could, touching as much of his skin with mine as possible while still leaving enough room for my hand and the toy to move.

"Comfortable?" I asked.

He swallowed. "Yeah."

"Relax, Alex." I kissed his neck. "We can stop any time, I promise." My lips still touching his neck, I said, "Do you want to keep going?"

"Yeah." He cleared his throat, and spoke again with more confidence. "Yeah, I do."

"Just say stop if you want to." I pressed the toy against him. He held his breath, but when I exhaled against his shoulder, he exhaled too.

Just a little more pressure. I breathed out. He breathed out. More pressure, and the toy slowly slid into him. Alex tensed, so I drew it back and let him relax before pushing it in again. As I inched the toy into him, I kissed the back of his shoulder.

"I've been fantasizing about this since day one," I murmured. "I've wanted you to feel me like you feel this now." I slid the toy a little deeper, then withdrew it slowly. "Just the thought of fucking you tonight has me so. Damned. Turned. On."

He whimpered softly.

"You okay?" I asked.

"Yeah."

"I'm not hurting you?"

"No." He took a deep breath, shivering.

"You know," I murmured, letting my lips brush his neck. Moving my hand a little faster, I went on, "The first time I ever jerked off while I thought about being inside you, I came so hard I thought I'd pass out."

He sucked in a sharp breath. As I withdrew the toy again, his hips moved back against me, so I pushed it back in. He rewarded me with another whimper, and this time it was unmistakably pleasure.

I grinned against his neck. "Like that?"

"Mm-hmm."

I kept teasing him with the toy. Long, deep strokes. Then shallower. Faster. Slower. Whatever resistance he'd offered in the beginning had long since melted away, and the motion of his hips encouraged me to do it faster, harder. My head spun with arousal and anticipation, my rock-hard cock aching with the need to be inside him, and it was all I could do—

"*Kieran.*"

He said my name with just enough force to stop both my hand and breath.

"What's wrong?"

"I can't wait." He turned his head toward me. "I…*fuck me.*"

The words sent an electric shiver all the way down to my toes. I kissed behind his ear and whispered, "Let me get a condom. Why don't you get up on your knees?"

In the time it took us to change position and for me to get a condom on, some of the tension returned to his shoulders. Stroking lube onto my cock with one hand, I ran the other up and down his back.

"Doing okay?"

"Yeah." He looked over his shoulder. "Nervous."

I leaned on one arm and came down to kiss him over his shoulder. "It's okay. Everyone is their first time. But here's what I'm going to do." I kissed him again, then whispered, "You're going to be completely in control. Once I've given you a little, I'm going to let you take over. You decide how fast we move, how deep I am. And we can always stop. Anytime."

He moistened his lips and swallowed hard. "Okay."

I sat up again. "Ready?"

"As much as I'll ever be."

I pressed just enough for the head of my cock to start to slide into him.

Alex grunted, his shoulders rippling with tension. I withdrew, then pushed in again, maybe a half inch deeper this time, and he shivered.

"What's wrong?" I ran my hand up and down his back. "Talk to me, Alex."

"Nothing." The word came out as a choked moan. He drew, held, and released a breath. "It's just...intense."

"In a good way or a bad way?"

"Good." He rocked back against me, drawing me deeper inside him. "*Really* good."

"So you don't want me to stop, then?"

"Please don't."

I took a few more slow, shallow strokes. Then, steadying his hips in my hands, I whispered, "You're in control."

I stayed as still as I could, which was nearly impossible when my body wanted nothing more than to drive my cock into him until we both collapsed. I kept my hands on his hips to guide and steady, never hinder or control, and held my breath. I couldn't remember the last time I'd gone so slowly, letting my cock inch into my lover like we had—and intended to use—all the time in the world. And to do it so passively like this, letting him decide how deep and how fast, was a new sensation entirely.

He faltered. Then again, his elbow almost buckling beneath him.

I leaned forward and put my arm around him. "You okay?"

"My arms, I..." He shivered. "Can't hold myself up."

"Then don't." I kissed his shoulder. With my body weight, I nudged him down, down, down, until he was on his stomach on the bed.

"This comfortable?" I asked against the back of his neck.

"Mm-hmm."

I withdrew, pushed back in, and he moaned. When I exhaled, goose bumps rose on his skin. Then on my arms.

I slid my hands under him and hooked them over his shoulders for leverage. Alex tucked his arm beneath him and clasped my hand. I separated my fingers so he could slip his between them, and I held his shoulder tighter, and he held my hand tighter, and I tried—fucking *tried*—to keep it together.

Using his shoulders for leverage, I pushed all the way inside him, and my vision blurred. Just being this close to him overwhelmed me.

My lips brushed his ear as I whispered, "How does this feel?"

"It's...awesome." The word came out as little more than a sob. "Oh God, Kieran..."

"Can you handle it a little harder?" I asked, wondering if I could handle it myself.

He nodded.

I thrust harder, and he whimpered as his back tried to arch against my chest.

"You okay?" I asked.

Another nod.

"Tell me how you want it," I whispered. "Fast, slow..." I swallowed hard. "Tell me how to fuck you, Alex."

He shuddered, then slurred, "Slower."

I slowed down. "Like that?"

"Just a little..." He exhaled. "Fuck, just like that. That's perfect."

Digging my teeth into my lip and my fingers into his shoulders, I forced myself to maintain that deliciously, agonizingly slow pace. "Oh my God, Alex. I've...I've fantasized about this...but you're...this..." I kissed the back of his neck and shuddered. "My fantasies had nothing on the real thing."

"Neither did mine," he moaned.

As much as they could when pinned between my body and the bed, his hips moved with mine, and the world blurred around me. I closed my eyes and struggled to stay in control. My skin moving over his, even my nipples brushing his back with every slow, smooth stroke, was nearly as overwhelming as my cock moving deep inside him. Kissing the back of his neck, breathing in his cologne and the hint of sweat and him, oh God, *him...*

"Oh fuck, I'm gonna..." He shuddered. "Oh God, Kieran, keep...just like that..."

"Like this?"

He whimpered an affirmative.

Holy fuck, if he came now, if I felt and heard him come like this, I'd lose it. I couldn't imagine anything hotter than Alex unraveling beneath me, falling to pieces with every stroke I took—*oh God, I can't believe I'm inside him*—and it was happening now, right now. I dug my teeth into my lip, fighting to keep my rhythm steady without letting myself come. He had me well past the point of turned on, but there was no way in hell I'd come before he did.

"Oh...my...God..." His voice dropped to a growl, and he suddenly pushed back against me, driving me deep inside him as he released a delirious cry and came. Holding my breath, I kept thrusting, my eyes rolling back and my head spinning as I fought the orgasm his body tried to bring out of me. When Alex shuddered again, then relaxed, I nearly lost control, almost lost control, *finally* lost control.

Groaning into his hair, I thrust one last time, as deep as I could, and fell apart. Some sort of choked sound, half-sob, half-moan, escaped my lips. There wasn't an inch of my skin that didn't tingle with the orgasm that electrified my body, from the hair standing on the back of my neck to my toes digging into the bed for just a little more leverage.

When it was over, I had just enough coherent thought to keep myself up on my forearms so he could still breathe. Not that I had any desire to move my arms anyway; our hands were still clasped tightly together against his shoulder, and I didn't want to let go.

"You okay?" I asked.

He replied with a murmured affirmative.

I kissed his neck, pausing to breathe in the sweat and cologne I was so fucking addicted to. "That was absolutely amazing."

"Yeah, it was." He exhaled. "God damn, it was."

When we could finally move without collapsing, we cleaned up and grabbed a shower together, then got under the covers.

Holding each other's gazes, we traced featherlight lines down each other's faces, necks, and arms with our fingertips.

"Guess you're really not a virgin anymore," I said.

Alex laughed. "I don't think I've qualified as much of one since the night we met."

I huffed. "Why does everyone keep *saying* that?"

"What do you mean?"

"I asked Ethan and Rhett for some advice about this...situation," I said. "And they've been teasing me ever since that you lost your virginity the first time we stood in the same room together."

Alex snorted.

I rolled my eyes. "Great. I have a slutty variation of the Midas touch."

"Well, you do have quite a touch."

"Yeah, but I don't think it's quite enough to negate someone's virginity, you know?"

"You never know," he said. "So, you were asking them for advice?" He raised an eyebrow. "*You?*"

"Not about sex, if that's what you're wondering."

"Then...?"

"Just how to do this without hurting you." I touched his face. "Or giving you something to regret."

Alex ran his fingers through my hair. "You haven't done either, just so you know."

"Good."

We held each other's gazes for a moment. I trailed my fingertips along his jaw, and he stroked my hair.

I broke eye contact this time and cleared my throat. "So, now that you've tried both, do you like topping or being topped?"

"Hmm, might need to do a little more research first." He kissed me. "Try one, then the other. See which one I prefer."

"You want to do both tonight?"

"Depends. You game?"

Caressing his cheek, I laughed. "You're going to be the death of me yet, you know that?"

"No, you can't die. Then you wouldn't be able to fuck me like that again."

I shivered. "In that case, I might have to stay alive. I mean, if there's more sex like that in my future."

"Which there is."

"Just say when."

"Get a condom."

Chapter Eighteen

Once we started switching, Alex and I were lucky we ever left either of our apartments. Now that he was past being afraid that receiving would be painful, he loved it. He even liked it when it *was* painful, when I fucked him hard enough my fingers left marks on his hips or shoulders. Or the other way around, said the bruises beneath my own jeans.

Our neighbors must have hated us.

Some evenings, whether because of our jobs or everything we'd done the previous night, we were too exhausted to do anything. I didn't mind those nights at all. There were worse ways to relax after a long shift than lying in bed with Alex, just kissing lazily in between talking about our days.

But damn, those crazy nights? I sure paid for them sometimes.

Like today, when I wondered why I'd never tried to talk Ethan and Rhett into getting tickets closer to the baseball field instead of the damned nosebleed section. My hips and back bitched all the way up from the ground level, but every twinge just kept me grinning about what Alex and I had done last night and what we would do tonight.

When I made it to our section, Ethan and Rhett were already there, along with Rhett's friend, Dale. Rhett and Ethan sat together but with a few inches between them. Tactile as they were, some people still had issues with men showing affection in public, so the two of them kept it to a minimum in places like this.

On my way up to their row, I realized Dale was drinking soda today instead of beer. He was a scrappy drunk, and after Ethan nearly took a punch on his behalf last season, Dale had reluctantly eased off on the booze at games. Thank God. I loved him to death sober. Drunk? I was more apt to beat him to death.

"Hey, hey, hey," Ethan said as I came up the steps to their row. "Look who finally showed up."

"Whatever," I said. "Just took me a while to find a place to park."

"Excuses, excuses," Rhett said.

"Isn't the late one supposed to buy the beer?" Dale asked.

I eyed him. "What good will that do you?"

"Oh, fuck you," he said with a flippant gesture.

I laughed and sat between Rhett and Dale, hoping none of my friends noticed the way I gingerly lowered myself into the seat.

"Ready to watch your boys get screwed?" I asked Ethan.

Dale snorted.

Ethan glared at us. "Seems to me Toronto is having a better season than Seattle. I think *your* boys are the ones getting screwed today."

"Boys, boys," Dale said, smoothing the air with both hands. "There are plenty of boys and plenty of screwing to go around."

"Dale," Rhett said in a loud whisper. "Behave."

"Whatever." Dale gestured dismissively. He sipped his drink, then nodded toward the game that took place about twelve miles below us. "You know, I'd be more inclined to root for them if they'd just call themselves the Toronto B. Jays."

"Well," I said. "Then they'd have an excuse to suck."

Rhett choked on his beer.

Ethan glared at Dale and me. "You know what? Fuck you both."

"I wish," Dale said under his breath.

Three men in their forties, me in my late twenties, and anyone overhearing us would've thought we were a bunch of fourteen-year-olds. God, I loved baseball games with them.

We settled in to watch the game. During the second inning, my cell phone vibrated—only way I could hear it in a place like this—and I groaned. Damn it, my boss had better not have been calling me into work.

I unclipped it from my belt, and my heart fluttered at "*Alex-work*" on the caller ID. I flipped the phone open.

"Hey, you." I very carefully ignored the three heads that turned in my direction.

"Hey," he said. "Sorry to bug you, I—"

"Don't worry about it. What's up?"

"Just wanted to check, did I leave my cell phone charger at your place?"

I furrowed my brow. "I'm not sure. It was on the kitchen counter this morning, but I don't remember if it was still there when I left."

"Damn," he muttered. "Well, I didn't take it with me. If it was there this morning, it's still there. Any chance you could grab it for me on your way over tonight?"

"Yeah, no problem, I—"

The crowd around me roared.

"Sorry about that," I said over the noise. "They just scored."

"Lucky bastards," Dale muttered.

I laughed.

"What?" Alex asked.

"Nothing," I said, still chuckling.

With a note of amusement, he said, "I'll let you go; I just wanted to make sure I hadn't lost that damned thing. My cell's almost dead."

"Don't worry about it. I'll bring it by."

"Thanks. I'll see you tonight."

Oh, yes, I can't wait. "See you tonight." I snapped my phone shut, and as I clipped it to my belt, I realized there were three sets of eyes staring very intently at me. "What?"

"Nothing." Rhett looked at Ethan. "Were you thinking something?"

"Me?" Ethan put a hand to his chest. "No, no, not me. Dale?"

"Oh, *no*, not me." Dale shook his head. "Not a thing."

"Uh-huh," I said.

"Though that call reminds me," Rhett said, "you still seeing that kid? The virgin?"

I nodded. "Yeah, I—"

"The *what* now?" Dale sputtered. "You?"

"Yes, me."

He sniffed. "Well, if that's not a case of the fox guarding the henhouse."

"Guarding?" Ethan smirked. "Yeah, right. I assume he's not a virgin anymore if he's been around you this long."

Heat rushed into my cheeks as I dropped my gaze. "You could say that."

Rhett leaned forward and eyed me. "Kieran, are you…*blushing*?"

"No way," Ethan scoffed.

"Kieran? Blushing?" Dale said. "Not possible."

"Shut up, all of you," I said, trying and failing to keep a straight face.

"Look at me," Rhett said.

I shot him the dirtiest look I could muster, and all three of them laughed.

"Holy shit," Dale said. "You *are* blushing."

"Isn't that one of the Four Horsemen?" Ethan asked.

I cocked my head. "What?"

"Kieran in love," Rhett said. "Yeah, I think you're right, Ethan."

"Oh, please." I rolled my eyes. "I'm not in love."

Ethan brought his beer to his lips. "Sure about that?"

I glared at him. "Yes, I am sure. It's just a booty call."

"Does he know that?" Rhett asked.

"Yes, I made it very clear from day one."

"Did you copy yourself on that memo?" Dale asked.

I rolled my eyes again. "Whatever. You guys also thought I was in love with Sebastian."

"Only because we didn't see heads or tails of you for three months," Rhett said.

"Especially tails," Dale said, chuckling.

Ethan laughed. "Yeah, what he said."

"Seriously, though," Rhett said. "We just figured you were into him if you of all people decided to give monogamy a go."

"Which I haven't done with Alex." *About the* only *thing I haven't done with Alex.*

"Been with anyone else recently?" Rhett asked.

"No."

"And we haven't seen you in so long," Ethan said, "I barely remember what you look like naked." Rhett threw him a *would you not say stuff like that so loud in public?* glare but said nothing.

"That's just dementia kicking in, Ethan," I said.

"So," Rhett said. "You haven't been with us. You don't have anyone else on the roster. Which leaves you with Kieran."

"One guy," Dale said. "Sounds like monogamy to me."

"That," Ethan said, "and I have never seen you get that ridiculous look on your face about anyone."

"He's right," Dale said. "I think it's kind of cute, actually."

The heat rushing into my cheeks negated any defense I could have given. I wasn't in love with Alex, damn it, but as the three of them laughed and clapped my shoulders, I figured I didn't stand a chance convincing them of that. The more I tried to, the more they'd give me hell, so I just let it go and watched the game.

Sometime during the fifth inning, Rhett turned to Ethan. "Whose turn is it to get beer?"

"Yours," Ethan said. "I got the last one."

"Damn it." Rhett pulled out his wallet. "I'm a little short, do you have another twenty?"

"Yeah, I think so." Ethan took out his own wallet, then handed Rhett a twenty. As the money changed hands, they exchanged one of those fleeting but unmistakable looks. The closest they allowed themselves to affection in a place like this, and I was amazed the entire stadium didn't home in on that crackling instant of chemistry up here in the cheap seats.

Then Rhett stood and moved to the aisle. He paused. "Kieran, you mind coming with me? I could use an extra pair of hands." The subtlest lift of his eyebrow encouraged me to read between the lines.

"Sure. Yeah." I got up and followed him.

We left the stands and went into the vendor area, into the air that was saturated with the fumes of hot dogs, popcorn, grease and peanuts. Ugh, the sooner we got out of here, the better.

But before we even made it to the beer vendor, Rhett stopped me with a hand on my shoulder. "I'm curious, is there something going on with you and Alex? Something serious, I mean?"

Shaking my head, I put up my hands. "No, I'm telling you, it's *just* sex."

His chin dipped slightly and his eyes narrowed, taking on his classic *I see right through you* look.

I blew out a breath. "Seriously, Rhett. It's nothing. Why are you guys so convinced I'm involved with him?"

"Hey, take it easy," he said in a gentle voice. "We were just giving you a hard time, but I was curious. That's all. Though it does seem like you're pretty wrapped up in him."

"Nah, it's nothing like that," I said, shaking my head. "The thing is, he's enjoying this. He's trying new things, and he's got a few years of pent-up sexual frustration to burn off."

"Well, he's definitely in good hands for both of those."

"That's what he says." I shrugged, probably not near as dismissively as I intended. "Anyway, yeah, we're spending a lot of time together. It doesn't mean anything."

"It's not the time you're spending together that's making us wonder," he said. "Okay, Dale's just ribbing you because yes, you were blushing. But Ethan and I have been wondering for a while now."

I inclined my head to bid him to continue.

"You've just been a little, I don't know, spacey. Not yourself."

"That's exhaustion, Rhett. Just because Alex has exhausted me to the point of monogamy doesn't mean it's anything more than physical." I laughed. "Just means any other guy, especially you or Ethan, would probably kill me."

He chuckled. "No, I've seen you exhausted. This is, it's..." His expression turned serious and he made a sharp, frustrated gesture. "Different. It's something we've never seen with you before. It's..." He paused. "It's interesting, what can I say?"

"How so?"

"Well, you know how Ethan is with tequila, right?"

I shivered. "God, yes."

"Me too. All he has to do is suggest doing tequila shots, and I'm horny as fuck. Like flipping a damned switch."

"Right..." I raised an eyebrow, wondering where he was going with this.

"You remember the other night, when we were all shooting the breeze in the kitchen after you worked out?"

I shrugged. "Yeah, why?"

A knowing grin drew up the corner of his mouth. "Because you were talking about Alex at one point, and you didn't even notice the bottle of Patrón or Ethan slicing up a lime."

The hair on the back of my neck stood on end. I retraced a few dozen mental steps back to that night and vaguely remembered Ethan going through the motions. I'd known, on some level, what he was doing, but consciously? It had never even connected in my mind. The Pavlovian response hadn't happened. At all.

My cheeks burned again. "I'm sorry about that, I didn't mean to blow you guys off or—"

"No, no, we're not insulted by any means." He smiled. "It's good to see someone who can keep up with you and drive you to distraction. The tequila thing just tipped us off you were preoccupied. And the way your eyes lit up when he called earlier?" There it was again, that knowing look.

Silently blaming the goose bumps prickling my skin on a cool breeze blowing in from outside, I looked him in the eye. "It's just a casual thing. I mean it. I don't want anything more, neither does he, so..."

Rhett pursed his lips. Then the humor evaporated from his expression again, and he lowered his voice. "If there's more to this than sex, don't try to pretend it's not. Kieran, in all seriousness, you know I know what I'm talking about here." He glanced back toward our seats, where Ethan waited for him to come back, then looked at me again. "Don't do something stupid and let a good thing go like I very, very nearly did."

"It's *nothing,*" I said. "Really. I don't want anything serious, and neither does he."

"Which is usually when it happens."

There was no breeze to blame that time. I put up a hand. "And if it starts heading in that direction, I'll nip it in the bud. We're not... What we're doing, it's not like that, and it's not going to be."

Skepticism raised his eyebrow, but he didn't press the issue. "Okay. Well, I was just curious."

"Suspicious is more like it."

"Something like that." Rhett laughed. "And you do know that if you decide to get serious with this it's-nothing-serious kid, we have to meet him."

I clapped his shoulder. "All the more reason to not let it get serious."

"What? Why?"

"Because you'd be a bad influence on him."

"Oh, and you're not?"

"Well, he's not complaining."

"That doesn't mean a damned thing." He gestured toward the concession area. "Now let's go get some beer before Ethan and Dale send out a search party."

Chapter Nineteen

The Mariners took quite a beating that day. Well, I thought they did, anyway. They were down a few runs when I left during the seventh inning stretch, and though I had the game on in the car on my way home, I never did catch the final score. I was too busy muttering at all the cars that had the audacity to get in front of me. I'd left early to avoid traffic, and apparently about seven million other people had the same idea.

"Come on, come on, *go.*" I smacked the wheel with the heel of my hand and muttered a string of profanity that would've made Ethan and Dale blush. What was wrong with all these people? Didn't they know I had somewhere I needed to be?

I glared at the clock on the dash. It only left me with thirty-five minutes to get across town, grab a shower and haul ass over to Alex's. Perfectly feasible.

I shifted my glare to the traffic in front of me. Okay, thirty-five minutes from here to there was perfectly feasible on most days, but not when I had this line of unmoving cars clogging up the road like a giant paralyzed caterpillar made out of glass and metal. Inch by inch, we crept along the arterial. Whoever put up that thirty-five mile-per-hour sign must have had a twisted sense of humor; it was in my line of sight for a full ten minutes. Thirty-five miles-per-hour, my ass.

Eventually, I made it past the freeway, which was where most of the congestion was. It always struck me as ironic that people would sit in traffic for the better part of an hour just to get stuck on the freeway. Supposedly that would get them where they were going faster. Whatever. I wasn't in the mood for irony today.

Shortly after I broke out of the gridlock, I made it home.

Finally. I threw the car into park, got out and barely kept myself from sprinting across the parking lot. I took the stairs two at a time up to my apartment, ignoring the ache in my legs. They could complain later. Tired muscles were just not a priority right now.

At my door, my house key couldn't seem to remember how to work the dead bolt, but after a couple of tries and a lot of swearing, I persuaded it to turn and let me into my damned apartment. At least I'd finally made it home. Now I just needed a few minutes to—

Fuck, I'm supposed to be there in ten minutes?

I groaned and quickly thumbed a text to Alex while I kicked off my shoes and tried not to trip over them.

Running late. Probably be there in fifteen or twenty.

With the message sent, I tossed the phone on the bed, stripped out of my clothes and went into get a shower. After I got out, I shaved as quickly as I could without missing a spot or slicing open an artery. Then I dressed, grabbed my keys and Alex's charger, and I made it halfway down the stairs before I realized I'd forgotten my wallet.

Most of the collective occupants of Seattle wisely stayed off the streets between my apartment and Alex's, and even that one light that was *always* red surrendered me a green for once. In minutes, I turned into the parking lot below his apartment, and for the first time since I'd left the game, I relaxed.

Sort of.

Hands unsteady now for entirely different reasons, I managed to lock the car and get my keys into my pocket without dropping them more than once. Okay, twice, but the second time, I caught them before they hit the pavement. Isn't a fumble unless the ball hits the field.

Keys in pocket, feet under me and heart thundering in my chest, I made it to his apartment and knocked.

As soon as he opened the door, I exhaled. *Ahh, there you are.*

I reached for his waist. "Sorry I'm late."

"I won't hold it against you." He put his arms around me.

It started as a light kiss hello, one that was only meant to go on for a second or two, but neither of us pulled away. Right there in the open doorway of his apartment, we held each other a little tighter and indulged in a longer kiss than we'd intended. Not a deep, feverish, "get a room, you two" kiss that would lead us to the nearest flat surface, just some gentle, unhurried affect—

Restraint.

It was restraint. That was all it was. We'd get to the passionate, sweaty embraces later. Anything more than this, and we'd never get out of here to find something to eat. And Alex had just gotten off work, so he was probably starving.

He broke the kiss and met my eyes, nearly knocking my knees out from under me when he quickly swept the tip of his tongue along the inside of his lip.

"I guess if we're going to go," he said. "We should get going?"

"Right." I cleared my throat. "Any place in mind?"

"Hadn't gotten that far yet." He kissed me, lightly and quickly this time, and gestured into his apartment. "Let me get my wallet and keys. We can figure it out on the way."

I followed him inside, nudging the door shut with my foot. "Here's your charger, by the way."

"Great, thanks." He set it on the kitchen counter beside his wallet and keys, and as he put those in his pockets, I slid my arms around his waist from behind. Nuzzling his neck, I murmured, "So, you just want to get something quick? Or a decent sit-down place?"

He put his hands over mine and tilted his head so I could kiss more of his neck. "I could go either way."

"But what do you want to do?" I let my lip brush just behind his ear.

"Whatever you..." He shivered, sucking in a breath. "Whatever you want to do."

"I asked you first." I kissed my way down to his collar, then started back up again. "It's up to you."

"So if I suggest that Indian restaurant down—"

"Anywhere besides that."

"Anywhere such as...?"

I flicked his earlobe with the tip of my tongue. "Wherever you want to go that's not that Indian restaurant."

Alex turned around. Wrapping his arms around me, he said, "You're being indecisive."

"So are you."

"No, I'm just asking what you want to do."

"And I'm asking what you want to do." I leaned in to kiss him. "Which I guess puts us at an impasse."

“Hmm.” He broke the kiss just enough to speak, and at the same time, nudged me back a step toward the kitchen doorway. “Maybe we can”—another kiss—“figure it out in the car” —another step—“on the way.”

“But if we do that”—I pulled him toward me, and with one more step, we were out in the hallway—“we have to know which way we’re going.”

“True.” He kissed me. “But then we can always”—a deep kiss, a stumbling step—“turn around if”—we stumbled again, this time into a wall—“if we’re going the wrong way.”

“Good point.”

He started to turn us one way, but I pulled him the other direction, and we continued our clumsy shuffling pace down the hall.

“Speaking of going the wrong way,” he said, pausing to kiss me again before gesturing over his shoulder. “The front door’s that way.”

“Is it?”

“Mm-hmm.”

I opened the top button of his shirt. “Well, you said yourself...” I kissed him, then opened another button. “We can always turn around.”

“That’s true. We can.” Grasping my wrists, he pulled my hands away before I could undo another button. He clasped our hands together at our sides, but keeping our hands occupied did nothing to stop our mouths. If anything, the physical restraint just made us kiss more hungrily, more desperately. If I couldn’t touch him, then damn it, I was going to taste him, and his mouth didn’t even try to make mine slow down, tone down, calm down.

“We’re not making much progress,” he said against my lips.

Barely breaking the kiss, I said, “No, we’re not.”

“At least not if we want to get out of here.” He nudged me a step farther down the hall.

“Getting out of here is getting progressively lower on my to-do list.” I pulled him back another step.

“Is it?” Step.

“Mm-hmm.” Step.

“Mine too.” Step.

The end of the couch stopped me. Our eyes met. I pulled one hand free. Then the other. Sliding both up his chest, watching him draw in a ragged breath as my fingers neared the button he hadn’t let me finish undoing. His hands found my hips, and even through a thick layer of denim, I didn’t miss the slight tremor.

Not long ago, I might have believed he was nervous, but not this time. *Oh*, no. Not when he sucked his lower lip into his mouth for one more taste of my kiss while his hands followed my belt around to my ass.

“Well, we made it this far,” he said, narrowing his eyes slightly and grinning. “Guess we can’t go any farther.”

“Not in this direction, anyway.”

“Probably not, no.” His hands slid into my back pockets and, rather than drawing me to him, held me in place while he leaned in a little closer. Our lips nearly touched when he said, “And we’re not closer to figuring out where we’re going.”

“You have any ideas?”

“Not yet. You?”

“Nope.”

His eyes darted past me, toward the couch, then met mine again. “No ideas at all?”

"You know," I whispered. "I've never been good at thinking on my feet." Grasping his shirt, I leaned back and dragged him down onto the couch with me.

Alex didn't miss a beat. We'd barely landed on the cushions before his mouth was over mine, and nothing about his kiss said we were going anywhere. Clawing at the back of his shirt, I returned his kiss with just as much fervor.

Then Alex raised his head, and both panting, we locked eyes. He licked his lips, and a second later, without thinking about it, I did the same.

"Okay, fine," he said. "I'll make a decision." He pinned one of my wrists to the couch above my head. "We'll stay here." Then the other wrist. "And we'll order takeout." He bent to kiss my neck.

Biting my lip, I closed my eyes. "Pizza or Chinese?"

"Don't care." He worked his way up to the underside of my jaw. "Whatever takes..." Another kiss, and I swore he damn near sank his teeth in. "Whatever takes the longest to get here." His stubble brushed the side of my throat, and I squirmed beneath him.

"Doesn't matter which is faster," I breathed, closing my eyes as his lips teased my earlobe. "We'd have to call and place an order." I trailed my fingers down his back until he shivered. "Which means stopping."

"Hmm. Good point." He raised his head to kiss me. There was no witty remark, no comment, just a passionate, unrelenting kiss that said the conversation was over and we weren't going anywhere.

My, my, you have *come out of your shell, haven't you?*

I slid my hand up the back of his neck and into his hair. When I tightened my fingers around his hair and pulled his head back, he broke the kiss and sucked in a hiss of breath.

“Maybe we should take this somewhere else,” I growled, lifting my head to kiss his neck.

“Maybe we—” A low groan cut him off. He tilted his head to one side, letting me take advantage of even more bared flesh, and he pressed his hard-on against mine. Finally, he managed a slurred, “Maybe we should.”

He pushed himself up and stood. He offered me a hand, which I took, and even after I was on my feet, neither of us let go. This time, though, there was no stumbling and shuffling and tripping over each other’s feet. Nothing but a straight, decisive path from the couch to his bedroom, where he dragged me down into bed.

Kisses were desperate and frantic. Clothes came off. The comforter tangled around us until we finally kicked the damned thing out of the way. Lube and a condom came out of the drawer, but in the heat of a breathless kiss, landed forgotten on the bed beside us. I just wanted him. Needed him. Needed to be as close to him as I could get, except when getting that close meant separating for even a few seconds.

I rolled onto my back, and Alex got on top. Pinning my wrists to the bed, he met me kiss for violent, desperate kiss.

The underside of his cock pressed against the underside of mine, sending shivers through both of us. He moved his hips just enough to create a spine-tingling friction, and when he did it again, I couldn’t even tell who’d moaned.

“Like that?” he growled.

The only response I could manage was a complementary motion with my own hips, and he got the message. Our bodies fell into a steady rhythm, moving fluidly together in some dance my brain couldn’t follow. With every brush of skin on skin, every breath, every shudder, my vision blurred and my mind fogged.

I cradled his head in both trembling hands. Our foreheads, hot and slick with sweat, touched, but we both panted too hard to kiss. Probably wouldn't have remembered how to anyway.

Then Alex closed his eyes tight. "Fuck, Kieran..." He groaned, shuddering against me. "I want..." He gasped. His whole body shook, and his voice inched closer to a sob than a groan. "I want you to fuck me. Please. Please, Kieran, I...oh, God..."

"You want me to fuck you?" I whispered.

"Yes," he moaned. "Yes, I...oh...fuck..." His lips pulled back over his teeth, his eyes screwed shut, and he moved his hips just a little faster.

"I will," I said, struggling to keep it together as his cock rubbed against mine, as he fell apart above me. He was on the edge, right there on the edge, and I knew just how to drive him over it. "If you want me to fuck you, I will."

With that, he whimpered, shuddered, and came, and I *almost* came with him.

He let his head fall beside mine and panted against my shoulder.

"Still want me to fuck you?" I asked, stroking his hair.

"Yes. *Now.*"

I bit my lip as a shiver went through me. "Then you'd better let me get a condom, shouldn't you?"

On shaking arms, he pushed himself up. After we'd cleaned up, I picked up the condom we'd dropped on the bed earlier and tore the wrapper.

"I don't know if I can hold myself up," he said.

"Wasn't planning on having you hold yourself up." I nodded toward the pillows. "Get on your back and put one under your hips. Behind you." Once the pillow was in place, putting him at a more comfortable angle, I positioned myself against him.

Holding my breath, I slid into him, every nerve ending in my body tingling with the awareness of *him*. Not just being inside him, but being over him. Against him. This close to him. Even as my strokes quickened and my body ached with the need for release, I was acutely aware of his hands on my arms, his legs around my waist, every way we touched

Overwhelmed, I closed my eyes and let my head fall forward, but it took only a heartbeat or two before I had to look at him again.

You have the most beautiful eyes. And I can't stop...can't stop looking at them. At you. God, Alex, I want you so bad. I need you so damned bad. I—

"Oh, fuck, you feel good," I murmured, thrusting a little harder.

He gripped my arms. "So do you."

My hips ached, my abs burned, but I didn't stop or slow down because being inside him like this was *perfect*.

Stroke after stroke, I moved inside him, and all the while, we held each other's gazes.

Somewhere in my mind, I was aware this was the kid who'd stared at me with a mix of fear and lust from where he'd stood against a brick wall one night. Back when we'd never touched like this. When he'd never been touched at all. When I didn't know if he was more afraid I'd encourage him to move forward or if I'd stop altogether.

But he wasn't afraid now. His eyes didn't plead for guidance, for me to show him what to do. He knew what he wanted, and he wanted more. He wanted me. And, Jesus, I wanted him. Like I'd never wanted another man, I wanted him.

Not just the novelty of someone who'd never gone this far with anyone else, *Alex.*

"I'm not in love," I'd insisted to the skeptical three at the baseball game.

"Sure about that?" Ethan had asked.

Banishing the thought, I leaned down to kiss Alex. He rolled his hips back, drawing me a little deeper, and I thrust harder. A tremor forced me up onto my arms, and I forced myself deeper, harder, damn it, I couldn't get enough of him.

Alex moaned, digging his fingers into my shoulders.

Oh God...

He bit his lip and closed his eyes, his back arching beneath us.

"Look at me, Alex," I said, panting. "Look at me, please."

He opened his eyes.

Oh God...

Aching. Shuddering. Teetering. Almost...almost there...

"Oh God, Alex, I—" *Love you.* My orgasm lodged the breath and the words in my throat, but my pounding heart thundered an undeniable Morse code in my ears: *I love you. I love you, Alex. I fucking love you.*

I buried my face against his neck, breathing in his sweat and cologne as the aftershocks coursed through me and his fingers trailed up and down my back. How could I have been so stupid? How did I *not* see this?

And what the hell did I do now?

Alex was too young. I wasn't much older, but he was both young and inexperienced. He hadn't had a chance to be stupid and reckless. He hadn't had a chance to have his heart broken, and I didn't want to be the first one to break it.

I also didn't want him to be the one to break mine.

Chapter Twenty

A week passed. Alex left me a voice message after two days. Another after three. On the fifth day, he called but didn't bother leaving a message.

Between the guilt and the lack of sleep, I barely functioned. I mixed drinks mechanically, not even trying to add any of my usual flair and flirtation, and my tips reflected my lack of enthusiasm. Not that I cared. Just making it from one end of the day to the other was like dragging my feet through wet cement. As long as a glass or bottle didn't end up shattered in the ice bin, I was happy enough.

No matter how much I told myself time would make the distance easier, I was only kidding myself. The longer I stayed away from him, the more it hurt, which just drove home the reason I'd walked away in the first place. And, of course, the guilt worsened by the day, especially because I hadn't spoken to him. I spent every night, wide awake, staring into the darkness and trying to come up with a solution, but with every day that passed without me contacting him, the more I cringed at the thought of breaking this silence. The less I could justify this silence's existence at all.

I felt like a jerk, but I was scared to talk to him.

As I wiped down the bar, a hand on my shoulder startled me.

Wes pulled his hand back and furrowed his brow. "You all right, man?"

I blew out a breath and rubbed the back of my neck. "Yeah. Just..."

"Church mouse giving you trouble?"

"Something like that," I muttered.

"What's going on? I've never seen you this out of it, especially over—"

"I'm *fine*," I said with just enough force to hint that if I had to say it again, it would be much less polite.

"Okay, okay." He put up his hands, but his eyes spoke of nothing but skepticism. "Just checking on you."

I forced a smile. "Thanks. I'll be all right."

And for the most part, I was. I had hundreds, if not thousands, of drinks committed to memory, and if I couldn't recall the ingredients of Liquid Cocaine or a Dancing Queen, the computer or card file were there as a backup. Muscle memory got me through pouring, mixing, shaking, blending, garnishing, and *not* dropping anything.

My customers were a monochrome mix of "meh" and "whatever." Every time I tried to distract myself with some people-watching during downtime, I ended up searching the gaps in the crowd for the one person who was distinctly and unavoidably *not* here. I never could decide if I hoped to find him in those shadows, or if I hoped he didn't show his face.

Whatever the case, he didn't.

Movement from the corner of my eye signaled the approach of another patron to the bar, but when I looked up to take his order, I almost jumped out of my skin.

It wasn't a guy.

Nor was it a stranger.

"Sabrina," I said.

"Hey," she said.

I cleared my throat. "This is a surprise."

"Yeah, I know." She looked around at the sparse crowd. "Any chance we can talk privately for a few minutes?"

"About?"

She looked me in the eye, and the upward flick of her eyebrow said I'd damn well better know why she was here. And with a sinking feeling in my gut, I realized I did know.

Dropping my gaze, I said, "Let me check with the boss. See if I can take my break."

I didn't wait for a response before I stepped away from the bar and went into the back. I was an hour early for my scheduled break, but my boss was a cool guy and let me clock out now. Knowing him, he'd caught on that I wasn't my usual self. And why wouldn't he? Wasn't like I'd done a stellar job of hiding it.

I returned to the front of the bar. "I've got some time. You want a beer or anything?"

"No, it's okay," Sabrina said. "I drove here. Thanks, though."

"No problem."

We looked at each other for a moment, each waiting for the other to do or say something. Then I realized I was the one who needed to take the initiative. I knew the club better than she did, so I'd be the authority on where we could find someplace quiet.

"This way," I said, and she followed me through the thin crowd to an unoccupied booth at the quieter end of the club. I sat on one side; she slid into the other.

Wringing my hands, I said, "So, what's up?"

"You tell me. You doing okay?"

"Yeah. Sure."

Of course she knew I was lying. She had her father's *I see right through you* look, and I avoided her eyes. I swallowed hard. God, where do I start? I didn't even know how to talk to Sabrina about it. How the fuck was I supposed to talk to Alex?

All around us, people chatted and danced while music erupted from dozens of speakers. Here I was with a lump in my throat, and an arm's length away, people flirted and touched and talked and made out. It was like being at a funeral with a party going on in the next room.

"I saw Alex last night," she said.

And we're off. "Oh?"

"Did, um, did something happen between you two?"

Guilt tugged at my gut. "What do you mean?"

"I mean, did guys have a fight or something?"

I chewed my thumbnail and stared at the table. "No, we didn't."

"Then, what happened?"

"Nothing happened, things just got..." I made a frustrated gesture. "Complicated."

"How so?" She leaned closer to me. "Look, he's my friend, and so are you. I don't want to pry, but I don't want to see you get hurt. Either of you."

Too late for that. I said nothing.

Sabrina's expression hardened. "Tell me you didn't just fuck him and run." Her tone was half-pleading, half-accusing.

"No. No, we had an agreement, this was just sex and nothing more."

"So, what?" she asked. "He feels something more?"

"No." I closed my eyes and released a breath. "I do."

"You…you do?"

I ran my fingers through my hair and nodded. "Yeah."

"He put on the brakes, then?"

"No, I just don't want this going any further than it already has. I didn't want it getting to this point at all, but…"

"But it did."

"It did." I sat back and exhaled. "I didn't set out to just disappear on him. I just don't know how to face him. I don't…" Dropping my gaze, I said, "I don't know how to tell him I can't do this."

"Is it possible that's because 'not doing this' is the wrong solution?"

"No. I'm not going down that road again."

"Jesus, Kieran," she said with a sharp edge to her voice. "Please tell me this isn't just some fear of commitment, or I swear I will put my foot in your ass."

Any other day, her threat would have included a grin and brought one to my own lips, but not this time.

"No. It's not." I swallowed. "Look, I love him." I flinched. It was the first time I'd said the words out loud, and my God, it hurt. "I love him, and that isn't going to change. But I'm not going to set myself up for something that won't last. I'm not afraid of commitment or having to give up the bachelor lifestyle. I'd give that up and commit to someone in a heartbeat if I had any faith at all that these things ever *last.*"

"Why don't you?"

"Because just about every marriage or long-term relationship I've seen has eventually fallen apart. My folks split after almost thirty years, and it's still killing my mom. I don't think I could go through that."

Her voice softened. "So you're just cutting it off now? Preemptively hurting both of you and saving him the trouble?"

"Something like that." I blew out a breath. "I can get over a few weeks or a few months with him. If it hurts this much now, it'll just be worse if we split after a year, or two years, or five years. Why drag it out?"

"Kieran, they say pain is a sign something's wrong," she said. "If it hurts this much now, maybe that means you're making a huge mistake." She paused. "Look at what Dad and Ethan went through. When they split, it was killing both of them. You saw it."

"Yeah, I did," I said. "And I can't imagine going through that with anyone." Especially not Alex. God, that would be too much.

"It was killing them because it was *wrong*," she said, thumping her knuckle on the table to emphasize the last word. "I think they both knew it too."

I avoided her eyes. Hadn't I even called them out on that? After things had hit the fan between them, and I'd been caught in the middle, I'd snarled, "You two act like you don't want each other, even though it's so painfully obvious to anyone else that you do."

"Kieran, that's ridiculous," Rhett had replied.

"Is it? So I'm just imagining all of it?"

"Ethan and I are done," he'd said, his voice shaking. "Whatever it is you think you're seeing—"

I'd laughed. God, were they both deliberately being obtuse? "Listen to yourself, Rhett. You don't even believe what you're saying."

"Kieran, what—"

"I have never seen two people so hell-bent on pretending they can't stand each other. Any idiot can see that you guys are anything but over each other."

Back in the present, Sabrina went on. "They figured it out, though, and they worked it out. I think they'd both tell you in a heartbeat it was worth it. Sometimes you have to go through lows. It makes the highs that much better."

"And I haven't seen many relationships survive the lows. It's the highs that make *that* part that much less bearable." I rubbed the back of my neck and sighed. "You know me, Sabrina. I'm not usually this negative or pessimistic about things, but I just don't..." My voice cracked. "I don't want to get hurt, and I don't want to hurt Alex."

"Kieran, you need to talk to him. Whatever you guys decide to do, I promise you, you *will* regret it if you let it end like this. He deserves to hear this from you." She inclined her head and gave me a pointed look. "You owe him that much."

I nodded. "You're right; I will."

"Okay." She reached across the table and put a hand over mine. "And one more thing."

I raised my eyebrows.

"I watched what Dad and Ethan went through," she said softly. "I still remember my parents divorcing when I was four. My mom's second marriage ended worse than Dad and Ethan almost did." She squeezed my hand. "But I *still* think people can make it work."

"I wish I was as optimistic about it as you are."

"Me too," she said, almost whispering.

I held her gaze for a moment. Then I said, "Thanks for the pep talk. I'll give him a call."

She smiled. "Good. I guess I'd better go. Let you get back to work."

After Sabrina had gone, I still had a few minutes before I needed to be back on the clock, and I desperately needed some air. I went out behind the club and took my cell phone off my belt. I leaned against the wall, then sank down until I could rest my elbows on my knees. Rubbing my forehead with one hand, I stared at the phone in my other.

Call him. Talk to him. Tell him.

How?

"You know what you're doing now, so maybe you're ready to see other guys."

"This is...I mean, what we're...it's..."

"We can't do this. I love you too much."

I blinked a few times and sniffed sharply. Damn it, how the hell had I gotten myself into this? For that matter, how had it gone this far without me realizing it? The signs were there all along. Ignoring them didn't change them any more than ignoring the graffiti on the wall behind me would restore it to plain, unblemished brick. Deep down, I knew all along this was different. Gradually, minute by minute, things between us had shifted from a sex-only arrangement to something...different.

Oh, but denial is a powerful thing. Those long talks were just to help him trust me and be more comfortable with me. My inability to mix a simple drink while he was in the room was a result of nothing more than anticipation. I'd have been this protective—hackles going up and fists clenching at the mere thought of someone hurting him—of anyone who'd been through what he had.

How long did I think I could convince myself of *any* of that? The worst part was, the longer I stayed in denial, the deeper this whole thing went, and the more I was going to hurt him when I finally admitted the truth to both of us. So much for nipping it in the bud.

"Don't do something stupid," Rhett had said, *"and let a good thing go like I very, very nearly did."*

I exhaled, still staring at my phone. Maybe it was stupid. Maybe letting Alex go would be the biggest mistake of my life. Maybe so, but I couldn't do this. I couldn't let myself get in any deeper, only to watch him walk away six months, a year, two years down the road.

"Kieran, just talk to him," Sabrina's voice echoed in my head. *"Whatever you guys decide to do, I promise you, you* will *regret it if you let it end like this."*

Well, that much was true. I owed him the truth, and I would always regret just walking away without a word.

Finally, I took a deep breath and dialed.

The call went straight to voicemail. *"You've reached Alex Corbin. Leave a message, and I'll call you back."*

An automated voice came through and took its sweet time running me through a few dozen options. *Come on, come on, beep already before I lose my damned nerve and hang up.*

About the time I was ready to grind my phone into the pavement under my heel, the tone finally sounded.

"Hey, Alex, it's Kieran," I said, my voice shaking. "Listen, um, sorry I haven't been in touch the last few days. I'd..." I hesitated, biting my lip. "I'd like to talk. Could you give me a call when you get a chance?"

Chapter Twenty-One

After a few hours of phone tag and voice messages, we finally resorted to texts. We were both at work, and the occasional surreptitious text was easier than trying to get us both on the line at the same time. I couldn't decide if this was better than talking, at least for now. Brief, noncommittal texts weren't as emotionally charged as a conversation could be. On the other hand, that made it impossible to gauge if he was angry, hurt, or what.

But after closing tonight, I'd find out, because our messages about needing to talk and preferring to do it face-to-face eventually culminated in one stomach-knotting conclusion:

I'm off @ 12. My place?

Gulping, I stared at his message. Then I wrote back: *Can be there @ 12:30.*

Send.

Sending.

Sent.

I exhaled and put my phone back on my belt. It was a little after ten thirty. Two hours, then we could get this whole thing over with.

I spent those two hours rehearsing everything I needed to say. Articulating it so I didn't make myself look like a commitment-phobic jackass was tricky to say the least, and I caught myself wondering a time or two if that was exactly what I was. No, no, it wasn't commitment I was afraid of. Not in the least. It was the aftermath when the person I'd committed to decided he didn't want to stick around. Been there, done that, watched too many other people do it too.

My shift ended. I didn't bother changing out of my work clothes, instead taking off the bowtie and cummerbund and zipping a light jacket over my tux shirt. The night wasn't particularly cold, but I was.

Pulling into the all too familiar parking space at the foot of that all too familiar apartment building, I was even colder. I parked, got out of the car, and stuffed my hands in my coat pockets as I took the stairs, one at a time, up to his floor. At the door, I paused. I stared at the black plastic twenty-two above the peephole, searching the twin numbers for the nerve to just knock and be done with this whole thing.

The twos didn't offer anything, though, After a long moment, I finally just took a deep breath and knocked.

I couldn't hear Alex's approach over my own heartbeat, so when the chain rattled on the other side of the door, I jumped. The deadbolt clicked, and he opened the door.

For a moment, we faced each other across the threshold. Minimal light came from the apartment behind him, and the overhead lights in the hallway barely illuminated his face, but he looked as exhausted as I felt. Dark circles underscored his heavy-lidded eyes, and his shoulders slumped under an unseen weight.

He stepped back and gestured for me to come in. Without a word, I did. He shut the door behind us, and the click of the dead bolt made the hairs on the back of my neck stand on end.

Of course I could leave any time, but the sound had a note of finality to it. This was it. I was here. This was happening.

"You, um, want something to drink?" he asked.

My mouth was dry, but I shook my head. "No, I'm okay. Thanks."

We moved into the living room. I was too restless to sit, and apparently so was he. With a few feet of floor between us, we both shifted our weight and avoided each other's gazes.

I made a futile attempt to moisten my lips and finally broke the silence. "Listen, I'm sorry I disappeared on you."

"Yeah, you mentioned that," he said quietly. "So...what's going on?"

Tiny icicles prickled beneath my skin along the length of my spine. I took a deep breath. "I, um..." Fuck, where was everything I'd rehearsed and memorized and thought out while I was at work? "I'm...not very good at this."

"Well, chances are, I'm not either," he said. "So why don't we just jump in, stumble through it together, and get it over with?"

Together. Right. The words, the words, where are the goddamned words?

Alex shifted his weight. "Kieran?"

I exhaled. Apparently I'd be improvising this one. "I guess I needed a little time to sort some things out."

"And did you?"

"Yeah." My shoulders dropped. "Alex, I don't know if I can keep doing this."

His eyes narrowed. "So you got what you wanted, and now you're done?"

"No, not at all."

"Then…?"

I couldn't find the words. I thought I knew what I wanted to say, but now I wasn't so sure.

"Is this because of what we agreed on?" he asked quietly. "Just sex, nothing more?"

Closing my eyes, I nodded slowly, and my heart sank into my feet. *Here we go.*

Alex released a breath. "I didn't think you knew."

It took a second for the words to connect in my brain, and when they did, my eyes flew open. I stared at him. "Wait, what?"

His cheeks colored, and he looked down. "I thought I'd kept it pretty well hidden. Kind of had a feeling this would happen if…um, if you know."

"I…" I furrowed my brow. "You mean…you're…"

He looked at me. "In love with you?"

My heart jumped back up into my throat. "Yeah. That."

"Isn't that why we're having this conversation?"

"Not quite, no."

"But you just said this was about—" His eyes widened. "*Oh.*"

We stared at each other. I hadn't expected this. Neither, apparently, had he.

"That means…" He gulped. "You…?"

I nodded.

"Oh." Alex fidgeted, hooking his thumbs in his pockets as if he just needed to give his hands something to do. "So, now what?"

I dropped my gaze. "We can't do this." I paused. "I can't do this."

"Kieran, if we both feel the same way, then—"

"No." I shook my head. "We can't. There's just, there's no way."

"Why not?"

I exhaled. "Because I'm jaded as hell and you're completely new to this. You don't even know who *you* are yet, Alex."

"Well, maybe this is part of figuring that out." He paused. "For both of us."

I released a sharp breath. "That's easy to say now, but I'm your first lover, Alex. How do you know I'm the one you really want?" I paused, willing my voice to stay even. "How do *I* know that?"

"Only one way to find out."

"Try it?" I asked, my voice shaking in spite of my best efforts. "Find out how much it hurt when this shit falls apart? No, Alex. I'll introduce you to a lot of things, but not that."

He laughed humorlessly. "A bit late for that, isn't it?"

I flinched. "Yes, and I'm sorry. Which is why I think it's better we don't get any deeper into this. So neither of us gets hurt any more than we already have."

"That doesn't make sense," he said through gritted teeth.

"You still need to find yourself," I said. "Live a little. Play the field and figure out what you want in a man."

"Except since I've been with you, I'm not interested in playing the field anymore," he said. "And it's not just because of the sex."

"How do you know that?" I could barely force the whispered words out.

Alex swallowed hard. "My guess is, if I wasn't in love with you, I'd lie awake at night thinking about having sex with you. As opposed to just...you."

I winced and dropped my gaze.

"Whatever this is," he said. "It's something. It has to be. And I don't want to give it up. I don't want to lose it." He took a breath. "I don't want to lose you."

I flinched. "I don't want to lose you either, but..."

"So, what's the problem?"

I forced myself to look at him. "What happens when it all goes south?"

"Who says it will?"

I laughed bitterly. "Who says it won't?"

"Why would it?"

"You get bored," I said with a shrug. "You realize I'm not the only man who's willing to do the things I do to you."

"Do you really think this is just about sex?"

I sighed. "No. It was supposed to be, but..." I rubbed my eyes with my thumb and forefinger, struggling to gather my thoughts. "The thing is, all I've ever seen are good relationships meeting bad ends, and bad relationships continuing while everyone in them is miserable." I tightened my jaw against the emotions rising in my throat. "This, it scares me, because I..." I exhaled, then swallowed hard to force back the lump rising in my throat. "Because I'm afraid if this goes any further, and I lose you..."

Alex inclined his head. "So you'd rather walk away?"

"I don't *want* to walk away," I said. "The last thing I want to do is walk away, but..." I swallowed again, fighting to keep myself together. "I'm just afraid to fall any harder for you than I already have."

Alex winced this time, and he said nothing for a long moment. He didn't speak, didn't look at me. Finally, he took a breath. "There's something I want you to know."

"Okay, go ahead."

"My mom got married when she was seventeen," he said. "Her first love. First guy she ever even dated."

"And they're still married?"

He shook his head. "No. He was killed in an accident two years after they got married."

I blinked but said nothing.

Alex went on. "Took her a long time to get over that, and she was almost thirty when she met and married my dad. But, I asked her about her first husband a few years ago. She said if she'd known how things would have turned out, she might not have married him. Going through that was hell, and she'll be the first to tell you that. But she *didn't* know, and to this day, she'll also be the first to tell you she doesn't regret it, because those were some of the happiest years of her life." He paused. "My point is, anything could happen with us. It might work, it might not. It could fall apart in six months. For that matter, it could get me disowned from my family." He gave a slow, one-shouldered shrug. "I just can't help thinking wherever this could go is worth the risk of it falling apart before it gets there."

I avoided his eyes.

He stepped closer, and I couldn't decide between letting him narrow the distance or backing away. My legs decided for me. I didn't move.

An arm's length from me, he stopped. His eyes had always been so shy and uncertain, but not this time. Nervous, yes, but he held eye contact with me even when it took everything I had not to avoid his gaze.

"You've gone out of your way to make sure everything about this was enjoyable for me," he said. "You've taken the time to be exactly what I needed, and you never treated me like a stupid, naïve kid. I knew when you wanted things to go further, and I knew when you held back for my benefit even though you could have been spending the night with someone who didn't hyperventilate at the sight of a condom. Kieran, you've been everything I could ever ask for in a guy." He reached for and gently raised my chin. "You tell me why I should walk away from all of that on the off chance I *might* find something else as good as this."

"This is your first time, Alex," I whispered. "Everyone thinks their first time is the last, but..." I shook my head. "It isn't."

He shifted his weight. "And if it is?"

I had no answer.

"Yeah, it's my first time with sex, love, everything." He touched my face with an unsteady hand, trailing his fingertips along my jaw. "Hell, this is the first time in my life I can actually say the words 'I'm gay' out loud, never mind actually say it to someone. But what if we got it right? Maybe that's why fate made me wait so long. So my first could be my only."

"You believe in fate?"

"Didn't used to, but I'm starting to wonder." He paused. "What about you?"

I shook my head. "I really don't know. All I know is what I've seen, and that's people falling hard and crashing harder when it's over."

Alex took his hand from my face and rested it on my waist. His soft touch didn't make this any easier, but I couldn't make myself pull away. Not from him.

He took a breath. "Look, I probably wasn't supposed to spend my formative years being afraid to be gay, but I did. And maybe I'm not supposed to get it right the first time, but I can't help thinking the only way I could have avoided that was to meet someone before you. That didn't happen. I can't change it. I don't want to."

Damn it, this would have been so much easier if he didn't feel the same way. I sank onto the sofa and rested my elbows on my knees. Pressing my thumbs against the bridge of my nose, I exhaled. "Look, I know everyone jokes about guys being afraid of commitment or feelings or whatever. That's not it. That's not me. Relationships freak me out, I'll admit it." I swallowed. "But this...this situation freaks me out twice as much."

The cushion shifted slightly, and Alex's hand materialized between my shoulder blades. "Why's that?"

"Because I've been avoiding falling love with anyone for a long time." I raised my head and looked at him. "And I never even thought it was possible to fall this hard for someone. With the way I've watched everyone else's relationships turn out, feeling this much for someone terrifies me."

Alex's posture stiffened and his fingers twitched on my back. Then he said, "Being alone doesn't scare you?"

"Sure it does. Being with someone and then *left* alone scares me more."

He lifted his hand off my back and put it over mine. "This scares me as much as it does you. Nothing quite like the fear of the unknown, right?"

"Yeah," I whispered with a slow nod. "Exactly. That, or the fear of repeating everyone else's history."

"So, that's it, then?" he asked, a note of frustration creeping into his voice and mingling with an undercurrent of uncertainty. "You'll just keep walking away any time you feel this way about someone? For the rest of your life?"

I chewed my lip. Maybe that was exactly what I would do. I hadn't thought that far ahead because I'd never expected to feel this way about anyone anyway. I didn't think it was possible to feel this way.

He squeezed my hand. "Kieran, I'm not asking you to commit to the rest of your life, and I'm not promising to commit for the rest of mine," he whispered. "Six months from now, we might realize we're not right for each other, but today? I'm not ready to let this go. And I don't think you are either."

I looked at him, eyebrows up slightly.

A cautious smile pulled at his lips, and he nodded past me, toward the door. "If you were, I don't think you'd have stayed this long."

I took a breath. "I wasn't going to leave until we were on the same page. At least until I'd explained myself."

"Which you have." He nodded toward the door again. "You can go."

My heart skipped, and I stared at him. "Are you, are you kicking me out?"

"No." He swallowed. "I want you to stay. But if the only reason you're staying is to make sure I understand where you stand, then..." And for a third time, he inclined his head to indicate the door. His voice was steady and solid, but there was the faintest hint of fear in his eyes.

I looked down at my wringing hands. My escape was there if I wanted it. He'd all but opened it and shown me out. All I had to do was get up and leave. Walk away now and get back to life as a perpetually single, blissfully happy slut. Back to life without Alex.

And I didn't.

I couldn't.

Closing my eyes, I drew a long, deep breath. All the way up until this moment, I was sure nothing could hurt more than someday watching Alex leave after I let myself fall for him. I was wrong.

Getting up off this couch. Walking out that door. Leaving him behind. Pretending that would ever change the way I felt for him. Even going through the motions in my mind was too damned painful.

I released my breath in one heavy, surrendered exhalation. "Alex, I..." The words caught on the lump in my throat, and I swallowed hard. Finally, I forced myself to look at him.

His eyebrows knitted together, the unspoken question written in his eyes and the three grooves on his forehead. I couldn't even tell if he was breathing. I sure as hell wasn't. I couldn't remember how.

With an unsteady hand, I reached for his face, hoping he wouldn't draw away, wondering when I had become the shy one who had a hell of a time holding his unflinching gaze. My fingertips brushed his cheek, and though we didn't break eye contact, we both jumped like we'd shocked each other.

"I'm..." I cleared my throat. Drawing a gentle arc across his cheekbone with my thumb, I whispered, "I'm sorry, Alex."

Relief flickered across his face, followed immediately by a hint of panic. Furrowing his brow, he said, "For...leaving before?" He gulped. "Or because you're about to leave now?"

I slid my hand into his hair and drew him closer. "For even thinking I could leave. At all." Our lips met, and when he didn't resist, when he melted against me like I melted against him, cool relief flooded my veins.

"Whatever you guys decide to do, I promise you, you will *regret it if you let it end like this."*

Sabrina, you don't know just how right you are.

After a moment, I broke the kiss and met his eyes. "This scares me to death," I whispered. "But I do love you."

"I love you too. And it scares me too, but..." He shrugged with one shoulder. "I don't know what we can do about that."

"Probably not much we can do." I ran the backs of my fingers down the side of his face.

"Probably not, no." He kissed me lightly. "I'm glad you came back, though."

"Me too."

Alex pulled me closer and kissed me again. One breath at a time, the kiss intensified, easing from light and gentle to desperate and passionate. We were somewhere between relieved and aroused, every kiss and touch stemming from my need to feel him and some deep sense of gratitude that he'd held on long enough for me to realize I couldn't leave if I wanted to. He'd only opened the door, hadn't shoved me through it even if that was what I'd richly deserved.

After God only knew how long, I broke the kiss and looked at him. I caressed his face, still disbelieving we were still here. That I wasn't resisting this anymore. That I'd ever resisted this.

I released a breath. "Not really sure where we go from here."

"I guess we just jump in, stumble through it together, and see what happens." Our eyes met, and we both smiled.

"Sounds like the best approach." I kissed his forehead.

"Well, we have plenty of time to figure things out, I guess." A sly expression narrowed his eyes. "In the meantime..."

I raised an eyebrow and cocked my head.

He gestured toward the bedroom. "There's still a few things we haven't tried."

"Such as?"

The grin broadened and completely negated the attempted innocence of his shrug. “Oh, I don’t know. I did a little, um, shopping in the last week.”

“Did you, now?”

He rose and extended his hand. “Come on, I’ll show you.”

Taking his hand, I stood. On the way down the hall, I said, “Just what kind of mischief have you been getting into?”

He glanced over his shoulder. “You’ll see.”

And he kicked the bedroom door shut behind us.

Epilogue

About a year later

Victoria, British Columbia

Midsummer in the Pacific Northwest is always more comfortable than the same time in Northern California, and while it was certainly warm in the garden behind the elegant hotel, it wasn't oppressively so. It would have been perfect had I been in a T-shirt and shorts, but even in a shirt and tie, it was fine, especially with the breeze blowing in off Victoria Harbor.

Alex put his hand on the small of my back. "Any sign of the grooms yet?"

I nodded toward the hotel's lounge, where the reception would be held later. "Rhett was out here a minute ago. I think Ethan's still getting ready." I put my arm around Alex's waist. "You look great, by the way."

The shy smile appeared, just like I'd hoped it would. That smile never got old, nor did the flush of color in his cheeks.

"Thanks," he said. "So do you."

I tugged at my tie. "I feel like I'm underdressed."

"That's only because it's not a tux." He clicked his tongue and shook his head with mock exasperation. "Jesus, Kieran, you can slum it for one day, can't you?"

I gave a dramatic sigh. “Oh, just this once, I suppose.”

“Hey, Kieran.” Sabrina’s voice turned both our heads, and she came down the steps from the lobby. “Can I borrow you for a minute?”

I raised an eyebrow. “Last time you asked me that, I ended up meeting him.” I gestured at Alex.

“So it’s in your best interest to listen to me, isn’t it?”

Alex chuckled. “As long as she’s not introducing you to another guy.”

She rolled her eyes. “No, Ethan just needs help with his bowtie.”

“What?” I snorted. “How can a man in his forties not know how to tie a bowtie?”

“I think he does, actually.” She laughed, gesturing in the direction of Ethan’s room. “But he’s a little nervous.”

“Guess I should help him before he strangles himself with it.” I kissed Alex’s cheek. “I’ll be right back. This shouldn’t take long.”

“It better not.” He put a hand on my waist. With a stern look that threatened to become a grin, he said to Sabrina, “No introducing him to other guys.”

We exchanged looks, laughed, and I followed Sabrina. Alex had nothing to worry about, and we both knew it. Promiscuous though I may have been in a past life, I’d never been a cheater, and besides, no other man had turned my head in ages.

Ethan and Rhett’s room was on the third floor. Sabrina showed me to the door, then gestured down the hall. “I have to go finish getting ready. Thanks for giving him a hand.”

“Any time,” I said. As she walked away, I knocked on the door.

When he opened the door, Ethan exhaled. "Oh, thank God." He gestured at the untied bowtie hanging around his collar. "I was about five minutes away from going and finding a clip-on."

I gave an indignant sniff as I followed him into the room. "A clip-on? You'll do no such thing."

He glared at me. "Then give me a hand."

"Hold still." I reached for the ends of the tie, and arranged them the way they were supposed to go. Well, tried to. Wait...how did... "Damn it."

"What? What's wrong?"

I shook my head. "Just not used to tying it on someone else."

"You're a big help."

"Hey, I'm still one up on you."

"Okay, true," he said. "Have you seen Rhett today?"

"Yeah, he was outside earlier."

"How does he look?"

I grinned. "Like his tux will be in a rumpled heap on a hotel room floor tonight."

"Oh, it will be." Then he exhaled. "I can't believe we're doing this."

"It's about fucking time, don't you think?"

"Yeah." He took a deep breath.

"Nervous?"

"Very."

"Relax," I said. "What do you have to be nervous about?"

"I don't know. If I figure it out, I'll just get more nervous, so I'm trying not to think about it."

I laughed. "You'll be fine. Not getting cold feet, are you?"

"After almost fifteen years?" he chuckled. "Little late for that, don't you think?"

"Well," I said, adjusting the bowtie now that it was properly tied, "since this is long overdue, I wouldn't think you'd be so nervous, but you are."

"If I said it was because I was getting up in front of people and speaking, would you believe me?"

"No." I let go of the bowtie. "There. You're good to go."

He looked in the mirror, scrutinizing my handiwork. "Great. You're a lifesaver." He faced me, taking a deep breath. "Do I look okay?"

I touched his arm. "You look fine, Ethan."

He released his breath and managed a slightly more relaxed smile.

"Oh," I said, reaching into my pocket. "Almost forgot. I have a little gift for you."

His eyebrows jumped. "What? You didn't have to do that."

"I wanted to." I chuckled and withdrew my hand. "Just a little something for your wedding night." I held up a tiny bottle of Patrón.

Ethan smirked. "You think this is enough to get me horny?"

"No, I figure Rhett in a tux will take care of that."

With a fond smile, Ethan nodded and set the bottle on the dresser. "Yeah, that should do it."

"I imagine it will."

He took one last glance in the mirror, then turned to me again. "Thanks for coming, by the way." He hugged me.

"Are you kidding?" I whispered, returning his embrace. "I wouldn't have missed it."

"Well, I certainly hope not," he said. "You helped us get back together; you'd damn well better be here when we put on the ball and chain." We both laughed, and when he let me go, he pulled back his sleeve and looked at his watch. "Guess we should get going."

"Yeah," I said, fighting to keep a straight face. "You're not getting any younger, after all."

"Oh, shut up."

The ceremony was a simple affair. Their closest friends and family gathered in two dozen or so folding chairs on the hotel lawn, and while the grooms wore tuxes, the rest of us weren't quite so formal.

Alex and I sat in the second row beside Dale, and the nervous grooms took their places at the front.

While the minister started the ceremony, Alex put his arm around my shoulders. I rested my hand on his knee, and we exchanged glances. A year ago, I'd never have imagined we'd be here now. The fact that Rhett and Ethan had finally decided to tie the knot was shocking enough, but Alex and me? Still together and going strong? I should have known, really.

Throughout the past year, I'd wondered a few times if we could make this work, but day by day, it did. We settled into the comfortable routine of being in love and occasionally bickering over stupid shit like every couple does from time to time, and I was less and less afraid that he—or I—would walk away. My phobia of love was a distant memory, and I could still work myself into a chilly panic just thinking of how close I'd come to leaving this behind.

Like our relationship, life hadn't been all sunshine and roses. Alex's parents had, as he'd predicted, all but disowned him. That was devastating for him. Not a surprise but painful as hell when it actually happened. In the back of my mind, in the weeks leading up to the fateful phone call, I'd worried he would resent me after everything went down. After all, he'd said himself the reason he wanted to come out to them was because we were together. Through his grief, he could have easily blamed me, but he never did. He cried on my shoulder and never once gave me the cold shoulder.

At my suggestion, Alex had taken a year off from school to figure out what he really wanted to do. Since his parents had cut him off, the year gave him a chance to save some money for tuition, not to mention coping with the crap they'd put him through. This coming September, he was starting classes again, this time pursuing a degree in psychology. His plan was to become a therapist, most likely specializing in helping kids who'd been through similar upbringings as his own.

Me, I was still happily pouring drinks and people-watching at Wilde's, and to this day, Alex could still make me fumble a bottle just by showing up. I'd long ago learned not to look at the door or crowd while I was mixing a drink, just in case he walked in at an inopportune moment.

And one of these days, I swore, we'd figure out where to go for dinner without twenty minutes of "I don't know, where do you want to go?"

Then again, we just wouldn't be us without that. Maybe we'd keep it going for a few more years.

Rhett cleared his throat, drawing me back into the present. He slipped a note card into his inside pocket as Ethan withdrew one from his own. They'd written their own vows, and in my momentary reverie, I'd missed Rhett's. I'd read the note card a few times while he was trying to get it right, though, so at least I knew what he'd said.

Ethan took a breath and alternately looked at the card in his hand and the man he was finally marrying. The first part was typical of wedding vows: love and cherish, sickness and health, better or worse, richer or poorer. But he wasn't finished.

"Because of you," he said so softly I could barely hear him, "I've had the privilege of being stepfather to a little girl who's turned into an amazing young woman. You and I have had our difficult years, but I wouldn't even trade those for the world, because the years I've spent with you have been the best years of my life. And..." He paused, pressing his lips together.

Rhett sniffed, then cleared his throat.

"You're not helping," Ethan said, wiping his eyes. They looked at each other and both smiled. Ethan muffled a cough and finally managed to continue. "Those have been the best years of my life, and I know the future will be even better. We've had plenty of ups and downs, but—" He couldn't hide the way his voice cracked this time. They shared a glance, squeezing each other's hands, and when Ethan continued, he said, "My only regret is waiting this long to do this."

If he'd said one more word, everyone within earshot, myself included, probably would have lost it. Instead, he slipped the note card back into his pocket and took Rhett's other hand. Closing his eyes, Ethan let go of a relieved breath, and Rhett just smiled.

They exchanged rings, and at the minister's cue, the grooms shared the tenderest kiss I'd ever witnessed between them. Between almost anyone.

Alex and I looked at each other for a moment. Then we returned our attention to the front.

Rhett pulled back and met Ethan's eyes. Speaking so softly no one in the world except Ethan could have heard, his lips formed the words, "I love you."

It had been three long years since the day I met them, back when they'd glared at each other across their kitchen like they'd rather have been around anyone but the other. Their relationship was as dead and gone as my faith in love.

Amazing what can change in three years.

After the ceremony, Ethan grinned at Rhett. "This is the part where we get to drink and party, right?"

Rhett laughed. "Yes, we get to drink and party now."

Their small group of guests cheered, and everyone followed the grooms into the lounge. Alex and I hung back for a moment, though. There'd be a line for drinks, so why rush?

Alex slipped his hand into mine. "Think you'll ever want to do this?"

Grinning at him, I shrugged. "Maybe in ten or fifteen years."

"Don't want to rush these things, right?"

"Exactly."

We both laughed. He kissed my cheek, and hand in hand, we went in to join everyone in the lounge.

The truth was, I had no intention of stumbling through wedding vows and getting choked up in front of our friends and family in ten or fifteen years. If I did, I'd have waited ten or fifteen years to buy the gold band that was in my pocket.

I hadn't decided when and where I'd ask. Tonight, if I could work up the nerve. Maybe we'd walk down by the water after the reception, or I'd wait until we were alone in our room. Or in the morning, when we'd probably be lazing around in bed. Soon, though. That much was certain.

I hoped he'd say yes.

Deep down, I knew he would.

About the Author

L.A. Witt is a M/M erotica writer who, after three years in Okinawa, Japan, has recently relocated to Omaha, Nebraska, with her husband, two cats, and a three-headed clairvoyant parakeet named Fred. There is some speculation that this move was not actually because of her husband's military orders but to help L.A. close in on her arch nemesis, erotica author Lauren Gallagher, who has also recently transferred to Omaha. So, don't anyone tell Lauren. She's not getting away this time...

Website: www.loriawitt.com

Contact: thethinker42@gmail.com

He'll bend for them. But they may break over him...

Out of Focus

© 2011 L.A. Witt

For twelve years, Dom lovers Ryan "Angel" Morgan and Dante James have run a successful photography business, and satisfied their need for a submissive with the occasional sizzling three-way. On a wedding job, they both zero in on the bride's beautiful brother, but as professionals, they keep their attraction on the down-low—for now.

Jordan Steele has no trouble establishing mastery over his stallions. When he hires Angel and Dante to shoot promotional photos for his stable, though, there's something about them that calls to his inner submissive. After a little flirtation and a photo session that gets almost too hot to handle, Angel and Dante are happy to show him the ropes. And the whip.

Once they break the ice, their sexual chemistry burns hotter than a macro flash. Everyone gets what they need...until emotions come into play. Their power could develop into something permanent, throw everything off balance—leaving one of them the odd man out.

Warning: Contains lots of sarcasm, a double helping of steamy erotic photography, and two dominants having their way with one very enthusiastic submissive.

CPSIA information can be obtained at www.ICGtesting.com
Printed in the USA
LVOW051510240912

300098LV00002B/87/P